DROP

MAT JOHNSON

BLOOMSBURY

Published by Bloomsbury USA, New York and London.
Distributed to the trade by St. Martin's Press.

ISBN 1–58234–104–4

Typeset by Hewer Text Ltd, Edinburgh, Scotland
Printed in the United States of America by
R.R. Donnelley & Sons Company, Harrisonburg, Virginia

For Pauline K. Johnson and the people who've helped me up when I've fallen.

I

A Hungry Man

Me: poor and broke, alone, thirty-one-years-old and only just finishing as an undergrad at a third-rate Pennsylvania state college, no work experience except comforting my mom before she passed. A man with no connections, and even if I did have contacts they'd be back in Philly, and I'd be stuck going up and down Lincoln Drive to I76 for the remainder of my life, East River Drive or West, cursed to pass the same buildings (windows, façades, steps), the same people (skin, breath, voices), the same damn trees (spruce, poplar, pine) and streets to match (Spruce, Poplar, fucking Pine) over and again and more, stuck in a city that was a tidal pool, never swimming down the Schuylkill past that net by the Art Museum or floating serenely along the Delaware into oceans beyond. And this meant pain and anger and fear because me was also: ambition and the desperation dreams create.

So there, within despair, six months from graduation and my impending fall back into the Delaware Valley, I was walking under the dusty fluorescent lights of the marketing department of the university that had promised, but was not providing, my career in advertising. I listened to the slow methodical thump of my soles on the gray linoleum, and that sound as it died against the cinder block walls. I was going to see my advisor, to plead with the small balding man who chewed the backs of ten-cent pens with such ferocity that while you tried to pump him for information on internships, job opportunities, or recommendations, your voice was given a background of spittle, slurp, and crunch. So I was walking down a public school hall knowing: this is not a place that provides futures. I was walking towards nothing really at all. It was there where I happened to glance at the cheerily colored Job Board, giving myself a moment's reprieve from frustration by looking at the sea of glossy ads for military enrollment, ghetto schoolteaching, up to $400 a week envelope stuffing, federally auctioned used cars (starting at just $1) and bulk-rate spring break vacations. I was just about to pull away a brochure for the chance to win a new motorcycle when, at the bottom of the scarred corkboard, I saw it. Below the multitude of glossy false hopes, a strikingly plain white sheet of paper was flapping around in the wind provided by the correctional facility fan blowing down the hall, dancing for me at the bottom of an otherwise still wall. A white sprite of light into my ever darkening abyss.

I got on my knees to see it, pulling it straight from its folded, envelope-fitting form to see what secret it was trying to conceal. There was a picture on it, black and white, blurred. It could have been me: the back of an upturned head, of a shirt collar showing as a white band above a gray suit and beyond, in the gaze of its unseen face, towers of skyscraper glass. It looked as if he could reach out to them, palm their tops like pre-dunked balls. Over his shoulder, hanging like an urban palm tree, was a street sign. The way it was turned, one of the streets was indiscernible, but the other shined back at me in big letters that said it all: Madison Ave. *Can you make it here?* read the caption. *Create a new and invigorating advertising campaign for an existing product, and you could find yourself working at one of the nation's top advertising firms.*

The contest, where pauper and prince were on equal footing. The only way that the pauper got to be king. And I knew, as I ripped the notice from the wall, staple included, that I could be Arthur in this story. So clearly sent to me, this challenge, my trumpeted escape. I wasn't even discouraged when I saw that the postmark due date was the following day, because I understood that miracles worked that way.

I spent nearly four hours in the CostSaver behind campus, breathing too loud, staring at shelves on top of shelves on top of shelves as if I had lost something there (on the packaging, on the labels, between the words), dodging prime Middle American consumers as they awkwardly pushed their gluttonous carts. A security guard, female, caucasian, approximately 5′4″, followed me for a while, stared down from the top of the aisle as I tried to ignore her blue form in my vision's periphery, making me nervous the way cops can. But then she got bored, approached me slowly, and asked me what I was up to, then left me alone with all those products and the realization that I didn't know what I should be doing and that staring at poorly packaged detergents and cosmetic aids, bland potato chips and inedible jerky treats, wasn't helping. I had gained nothing and lost time.

I retreated to the fruit and vegetable section, away from the barrage of packaging and merchandise. Trying to slow my breath and concentrate on something besides failure, I watched artificial rainforest showers cover the produce with transparent beads every twelve minutes, knowing that I didn't have time to flounder. It was already night, going on late night, and then it would be morning, and then the day would be gone and so would my life, my chance at an exit from the empire of mediocrity. Or maybe my destiny was never to break free at all. But I knew that was wrong, that I could do this, because it was the only thing I could do. For all the assets I lacked (work experience, money, a family, decent clothes, athletic skills, charm, self-confidence, a background that was middle class), I knew that I had been given one great power: the ability to see things the way others couldn't, or more specifically, as others did but were unable to articulate, identify. I had the power to infect others with my own desire. Nostalgia for outdated fantasies, bottled guest-passes to oblivion or the idea of Pure Fun, I could sell it to you and make you like it, make you think you'd been begging for it all the time. All I had to do to make you want something was fall in love with it first. Then, surrounded by the purity of the products of nature, love came to me. I saw the essence of perfection. And I realized, in a blur of Philly logic, what better to pimp then perfection itself?

It sat before me. A divine gift complete with heavenly packaging: shining Technicolor skin porous like an old drunk's nose and perfectly formed around a product that you could rip apart with your hands to reveal the bite-size pouches of flavor within, the entire structure forming into one graceful orb. And I knew I could take this creation from the most accomplished product designer in the universe, God, and make even perfection greater than it was before. I, the vegetative alchemist, was to bear life (mine) from the common orange. A simple orange. A fucking orange.

That was the pitch, the vision: an ad campaign for the orange, presenting it in a light which the public would cry for, broadening its target consumer base beyond health freaks and concerned moms. This was the challenge. Despite all the orange's attributes, the product was still neglected at the back of supermarkets, a forgotten hopeful of the impulse buy. It was not glorious fruit that the late-night drunks and insomniacs entering convenience stores reached for, but the imperfect creations of man. The fried, salted vulgarities, bubbled from oil and thick with its fat. The glucose-encrusted chocolate kibble treats, leaving fecal-like smudges across their mouths and brown caloric mud in the unbrushed crevices of their rotting teeth. I understood (giddy and grabbing at the pile of oranges in a search of a perfectly round orb rich in the color that named it) what was missing as well: the calculated feeling of transgression modern products imply. The illicit excitement of biting something naughty, a prepackaged revolutionary freedom.

Four P.M. the next day. Sweating, disheveled and sour, I held the finished product in my hands: a portfolio filled with the print ads, packaging design, and market analysis that would start a dietary revolution. I couldn't stop looking at the photos of my creation. Didn't my orange look so utterly marketable in its clear plastic wrapper? Didn't you know that if you reached for it on a store shelf it would crinkle in your hand, calling to you in treble whispers, *Take me with you, devour me, there is no greater pleasure than the life inside*?

In one photo I caught an image that showed that this creation was living, on fire, urgent. Two female hands (thank God for undergrads who sit in libraries eager for any odd excuse to walk away from books too big to be carried with them), fingers long and brown ripping through the fleshes: peel, encasing, pulp. Oh the mist, nearly invisible in real time and noticed more in the snapping away of her head as eyes squint, sweet acid like sun-borne pepper spray. The frozen image revealed an orange ball exploding away from itself, shaped like an orchid beginning its bloom, with skinny hands as orgasmic midwives bearing witness to the wet scream of citric love.

When I took the final work, my images, my impromptu creations, to the post office (4:50 P.M., please let me in the door), I was thinking, This is it; I won. This was the product. They would make me the Prince of Florida; even my offspring would be destined to reign.

Slapping it with the spit side of the stamps, I was already planning the first prize, five thousand bucks and a guaranteed position at one of three Madison Avenue firms. All I wondered was, Which one? Because it had to happen. Broad Street and Market could no longer stand as my east-west, north-south. I was going somewhere, my game was starting. I included my picture in the package as well, as the application had asked for. It was me smiling into the digital camera at five A.M., Friday morning. Yes, slightly disheveled, naps ablaze, but staring into the camera with that kill-stink of victory. At the postal box I pulled the door open and let my message be swallowed into its benevolent blue gut. And then it was patience time. Glory be to me for I am the creator.

Contact

Sure, it was nearly three months later and my original elation had slowly evaporated like water in a dead cat's bowl, been replaced by flashes of despair (I might as well have sent in nothing, what ignorance, pathetic futility, just a punk-ass Philly boy trying to pretend he could be something of worth in this world) that stumbled into pockets of certainty (wouldn't New York be nice, it looks nice on TV, and in Spike Lee movies, how could any controlled attempt at product enhancement put together by someone nearly six years my junior hope to reach the blessed brilliance of my vision), but damn, how could they give me fourth place? How can anyone who could recognize the validity of the work at all not bear witness to the divine inspiration? Or maybe it was crap and I was a fraud, but shit, I needed it so bad. A letter that says 'Congratulations, you have been selected as the Fourth-Place Winner' is a smug thief.

On page fifty-six of the magazine enclosed in my 'victory' packet there was a picture of me, my face looking smiley and hopeful and honest among four other faces doing the same. My shot last, the only one in the bunch not melanin-deficient, my image looking as out of place as Bill Russell on the 1963 Celtics. So is that it? Is that what it's all about? And did it matter? Regardless of origin, wasn't there still going to be a big-ass number four on my chest? Four, all lanky and dumb, staring over its shoulder like Sankofa but without the wings. The mythic number of losers, where no one even knows you played the game. I recognized then that fourth was not simply a statement about my entry in this competition, it was a message from the universe about my place within it. Fourth-rate me, with my pathetic hopes and aspirations, my hunger for greatness when I couldn't even find success in third-rate Philly town.

Or maybe it was the oranges. Maybe that's where I failed. They could have been tasteless, cottonmouth dry. Maybe that was it. Something went wrong, must have, because even though I got my picture and the photos of my proposal in the magazine, all I had on my kitchen table was a seventy-five-dollar check from a bank I never heard of and a thick piece of cotton paper with words forming a message I didn't care to hear.

The letter went into the trash, and then was pulled out and ripped into small pieces and taken to the upstairs the toilet. My advisor called with a congratulations and that message was erased. The check sat on the dresser alone, dejected, until the light bill came and I had no choice but to cash the insult.

In the months that followed, I got other responses from the world as well. From the sixty-seven blind mailings I sent out to advertising agencies nationwide, each complete with a résumé, mini portfolio, and personalized cover letter, I received: nine form-letter rejections, four equally impersonal brochures for summer internships showing pictures of smiling kids nearly half my age, and one actual request for an interview. The letter, from an agriculturally focused firm in Dallas, said that the successful candidate must to be willing to locate to Philadelphia, Mississippi, which, from my research, seemed an even scarier place than the real Philly itself. I got one nice letter from a man in Portland, sent on his own stationery, saying that he liked my work and thought I had 'promise,' but that they didn't recruit unproven talent straight from college, particularly from out of state, something he advised would probably be the norm at other agencies as well. His last line was, 'But don't worry, you're young so there's no rush.' The date of my thirty-second birthday was now closer than my thirty-first was.

Of the seven graduate schools whose advertising programs I applied to the previous fall, I was accepted to five, two of which were both very good and very expensive. Neither one offered me enough cash to make accepting realistic or wise since I'd already blown the money from my mom's policy trying to become middle class (undergraduate tuition and fees). Two of the other schools I was accepted to offered me partial tuition reimbursement, and one program in Ohio even offered me tuition and a stipend, but all three of the schools were just like the one I was already at. Those paths were not inclines, they were plains; at the end of each I would be no higher, just further along.

So, with fantasies extinguished, I walked down that same hall, listening to the sound of my feet beating a track on something that was already dead, moving towards the opportunity to prostrate myself before an advisor in the slight chance that he could help me compensate for the time I didn't have. Staggering and injured, I stopped in the mailroom to check my box and clean out whatever memos had accumulated.

I saw it before I even got close. It barely fit into my slender slot, this envelope, grocery bag brown, so tightly shoved into the cubby hole that I nearly took down the whole structure pulling it out. Its far right corner was covered in odd stamps, different in sizes and colors but all with the profile of the same plain woman, caught watching something dull. The package couldn't be mine. It said my name, but Chris Jones was common; there were two others even on that campus. I wasn't even given that distinction: the sole ownership of my name.

Slipped quickly into my jacket, I held it under my coat by my armpit all the way to the deserted men's room and into a stall. With my teeth, I ripped the envelope's top free, my fingers plucking its contents like a mugger with a pocketbook. What I found: another envelope inside. This one was gray, with 'Chris Jones' typed in large letters on the center. From its corner, a loose string hung, bright orange and as thick as a shoelace, from a small hole. Typed below it was a note that said, 'To Begin, Pull.' I yanked on that thing like it was a parachute cord.

Detonation. Blast. Silence into roar. Fleeting recognition of mortal inevitability as I dropped the package to protect myself, to shield my ears from the pain as noise exploded out from it, hit full speed against the glazed tile walls and then bounced back, making me trip over the toilet and fall back into the urine-stained wall. Even more startling than the sound, on the ground before me the envelope spun around like an insane top. Tangerine smoke rose out of the movement, pouring up into the ceiling in a thick stream and forming an orange cloud there. Everywhere around me the smell of burnt matches, and something like citrus. And then, it began to rain a heavy storm of confetti, gold and white, tiny squares upon me.

I didn't move until most of it had landed. It was everywhere, on my shoulders, hands and hair, stuck to the mirrors over the sinks, in the toilet behind me. It lay on the floor like magic sand, covering something that had broken free of the envelope during the explosion.

It was a card. Plain white, decorated with a golden exclamation point. Careful of further surprise, I opened it. Inside, in bold orange lettering, it said: *'I saw your work in Market Edge. The fruit thing. Stunning. Original. Call me for further conversation.'* Underneath that was stapled a black business card: *David Crombie, Urgent Agency, Brixton, London SW2–4H6, (171)654-782.*

Home I was skipping. Urgent. London. Job. Me.

Conversations

An odd double ring occurred when I dialed the number. *Bring-bring. Bring-bring. Bring-bring* me somewhere lovely where people are so alive you can hear their pulses bump-bumping as they pass you on the street. Take me somewhere like that and let me get going. Save me from Philly town.

'Aw right' was how the male voice answered the phone, very relaxed, hands on his balls, probably. I could hear the muted trebles of a television in the background.

'Hello, I'm calling for David Crombie,' I said. There was a pause. More television: an unintelligible sentence, and then laughter.

'You're American, aren't you?' he said, finally.

'Yes.'

'I know who you are and I know why you're calling.'

'I'm calling for David Crombie?'

'You're calling because you either want a job or I blew your fucking hand off.'

He was doing an American accent, poorly. A ghetto John Wayne. 'Christopher Jones! The tangelo fellow, finally making his appearance onto the scene. Fantastic, man, fantastic work. Bad picture, though, the one they took of you. Pick your afro even next time. You really must mind that. You looked like one of those troll dolls from the sixties, like. One of those little dolls with the big nose and the eyes bugging out and the hair shooting up in the air, cute bastards. Do you know what I'm talking about?'

Yes, I offered. He kept talking. I could almost see him, somewhere on a couch far away in a room I couldn't imagine, staring into that magazine at a picture of me. 'You're a little bit older, aren't you? Than most of the other prizewinners in the magazine, you're a little bit older. Am I right here?'

'Yes, actually I am bit more mature than my peers. I only began my undergraduate degree three years ago. Previously, my mom was suffering from cancer, so I provided home care assistance for her for a while, for my first six years out of high school. I only began my undergraduate studies three years ago and, as of this August, will have managed to finish a year early by taking courses during the summer and Christmas sessions, as well as an increased credit load during the regular terms. A major in marketing and a minor in photography. So, yes, I am mature, and I think I bring that maturity to the work that I do as well.'

'Fuck mature, mate, you're talented. That's what you are. I didn't ask you to call because you're long in the tooth, I called because your work's brilliant.'

We spoke of oranges.

After that, David called me. Usually about once a week, but never at the same time or on the same weekday. I sent him my portfolio, just some clippings of print ads I'd done for groups on campus and a few black-and-white ads in the local paper for some mom-and-pop stores, but he liked it. Every time the phone rang I thought it was David, and due to the state of my social life, it usually was. I feigned illness and stopped going to class so as not to miss a call, but since I'd never been absent or even late before, nobody questioned my claims. I had a sense that school didn't matter anymore. Finally, almost exactly one month after the first contact, David called and asked, 'What's the Grand Canyon like?'

'It's really big, kind of red and orange color, and you can rent donkeys to ride down into it.'

'You've never been there, have you?'

'No.'

'How about Mardi Gras? All that music, the dressing up and the beads. It looks brilliant.' No, it doesn't look smart, but it does look fun, doesn't it? Never been further south than D.C., and then just inside the Smithsonian pushing my mom around, right before she passed. 'Okay then, what about New York? The Big Apple itself. The missus, she's been a couple times for business recently, but I haven't been in years. Usually all I have time for is holidays on the Continent; when I do get a chance to visit, it's down to Jamaica to see my family. I got a job offer in New York once, from Binger-Strauss. How close is that to Philadelphia, then?' Two hours, no more. 'So, do you go there a lot?' I went once, in sixth grade, to the Natural History Museum. I remember the tunnel we drove through. I tried to hold my breath the whole way but couldn't.

'Well, when you weren't in university, what did you do for fun? What did you do to tell yourself you were alive?'

'I don't know. Like I said, I took care of my mom. I read books a lot, got a lot of books from the library. I rented movies. Basically stayed inside and avoided all the craziness.' He was laughing at me now.

'You mean life.'

'That life, the Philly life, yeah, basically.'

'Well, now you're going to start going places.'

'Yeah. I'll be done with school in August.'

'Right. And then you're coming here.' Here?

'London. You're coming to work for me now. Urgent's not much. I broke off from the Patterson Group about nine months past, took some clients with me. But it's just a beginning. I need a real talent by my side, someone I can build something with. And I know you're the one to do it. So, you willing?'

F Philly

Alex was driving, and I didn't notice she was taking Exit 34 off I76 until we were already snaking too fast along the curves of Lincoln Drive into Germantown.

'What the hell are you doing?' Dread, realization that escape was not to be so simple, that I was being forced to confront the beast before passing it.

'Chris, shut up. Your flight isn't for four hours. Why don't you just lean your head back against the window and continue drooling like you been doing since Harrisburg,' Alex said, and kept going. She'd gained a little weight, but she was still that skinny ass, bucktooth, high yellow, crazy thrift-shop-clothes-wearing camera clicker she was when we had gone out years before. My buddy, my confidant, my fellow freak. That's how we understood each other: in this place we were twins of rejection. Alike except she was crazier than I would ever be, because Alex's way of negotiating this city's disregard was to counter with her own blind adoration. Wasting good love on this place.

Kelly Drive: a coiled pathway through a forest where traffic insisted on driving as if the road were straight, a slalom beside a creek within a cave of trees so big, so old that they had been here even before Germantown was a ghetto. Before the blacks, before the Irish, before even the Germans themselves. We drove, under the stone angles of the suicide bridge, into that dip in the road that makes your stomach yo-yo. Together,

15

leaning into curves even before we saw them because our bodies knew this path like that.

'You need to eat something,' Alex told me. 'Get a cheesesteak in you, a hoagie, a couple of Tastykakes, maybe take a goodie bag with you for when you get homesick.' We turned right, along the exit into Washington Lane, up the hill and under the train bridge and another right at the abandoned gas station on Pulaski, turn left and park in front of the Stop 'n' Go, turn the key and listen to the car cough a bit before letting go. Finally motionless, for the first time since we left my campus two hours before, Alex stared at me.

'I'm not eating. They serve food on the plane,' I told her.

'Plane food.'

'That's right, plain old food. That's all I need.' Stop 'n' Go on Chelten Avenue. When I was a kid this was the only place that would sell me beer. Forties of Red Bull I could barely pull down.

'You coming in?' Alex asked me, but she knew I wasn't. She just didn't comprehend why. She didn't understand that if I put a foot down on the sidewalk it would turn the rubber of my sneakers to concrete as well, fuse me to the ground and force me to live the life I was originally destined. The city wanted to keep me here even though it had no use for me.

'Fine. You sit there.'

'Please hurry. I need to check in. It's an international flight, you know? You're supposed to check in early for those,' I reminded her. Al slammed the door on me.

The car stunk like forgotten garbage. She'd parked in the sun, probably on purpose, and it was getting hotter, like Philly could. Outside was home, and I wasn't going to open the door. Home was too many niggers. Too many guts, too many sweaty brows. Too many hand towels held on shoulders as if it was a symbol of elegance. Too many radios on different stations, each one blaring songs about boning or blasting someone away, every noise fighting to take control of the air. Too many *pop-pop* gun shots peppering the night, divulging neither location nor story, only the knowledge that eventually it would come for you. Too many damn kids yelling for their moms, yelling at one another, some just crying to themselves as they walked alone down the sidewalk. Why are poor people so fucking loud? Why can't they all just shut up and go home? Why are the same guys who were here when I left three years ago still standing in front of Stop 'n' Go like anti-security guards, drinking septic beer and speaking some language that sounds as if their mouths are half closed? What is the point of home if this is the way it makes you feel?

'Dukey-head.' I turned around, and Al, crouching, with her Canon 35mm in hand, clicked at me until I put my face down.

'Stop with the pictures. You ready?' I asked. Alex held up a white paper bag.

'Eats,' she said.

The ticket David sent me was in my hand. I had to get on a plane, go to London, get out while I had my chance, and Alex was taking pictures.

'Come on, smile. Pretend you're selling teeth whitener. I don't have any shots of you.'

'You have tons of pictures of me, you have more than I have.'

'You've hardly been back all year. Get out of the car,' Al said. I looked outside my window at the concrete, the litter glitter of broken bottle glass on cracked beige asphalt. A lump of dog crap harder than life. No step outside for Christopher. Christopher was not stepping outside till he got to the airport. Chris's quitting this place for good.

'I don't want to,' I said. The malt-liquor boys were looking over at us, taking a rest from lying. I recognized the big one from summer camp. He was looking at me, pointing, saying something while laughing to the degenerate who leaned against the wall next to him. Look, there's Christopher. They were both laughing now. Wasn't it funny? I was a joke: I was not a thug, I was not a baller, I was not a mack, I was not paid. I was not a comedian, even though I inspired great mirth. All I was was clever and creative, and unless you had a ball in your hand or your mouth in front of a microphone, this place had no respect for either one of those things. I hated them because they were violent and ignorant–and arrogant about both of those deficiencies. They hated me because I was not.

'When you coming back to Philly?' Alex asked me. So we were going to play our game again. The one where Alex tried to get me to love this place and I tried to get her to hate it. Bring it on.

'I'm not coming back. I hate this place.'

'See, that's wrong. This is the community that helped raise you.'

'And made me have to sneak home, terrified, every day growing up so as not to get my ass kicked. The community that broke in my mom's house, taking everything she had that they didn't, three times. I don't owe these people nothing. I'm gone.'

'See, you've become a sellout.'

'Shit, I would love to sell out, but who the hell would buy any of this crap?'

Alex shrugged me off, deciding it was in jest, and took more pictures, her narrow elbows jutting out on both sides as she aimed.

'Get your camera,' she told me.

'I know what this place looks like. I grew up here.'

'Then what the hell are you so scared of?' she asked, dismissive and annoyed. Beyond us, invisible, *pop-pop-pop* went the niggers. Someone was discovering lead. Alex didn't even notice, didn't even hear this answer to her question. That sound: that was my fear. I was scared of becoming them or becoming their victim. I was scared they were all life would allow me to be. Alex took the roll of film out of her camera and then made me move my knees as she reached to the glove compartment for a fresh one. She'd put two ice packs in there, but it still looked too hot.

'Your film's going to go bad. You should buy a cooler.'

'Buy me one. So what happened? You just quit taking pictures?'

'No, I still shoot. Or at least I'll be art directing some shoots. That's part of what I do, Alex. That's part of my job. I have a job now. I have a career. That's why I have to be at the airport, remember?' Suddenly exhausted that I wouldn't reinforce her Philly delusions, Alex got back in the car.

This was my last time seeing this place, so I looked around. Most of the stores I'd grown up with had closed, or changed names, or gotten tackier, just like the people. But those weren't changes: they were continuations. The laundromat still had video games in the back where grown men dealt drugs while their children shot gigabit punks. The bar across the street from the Superfresh still smelled like a whore's hangover, door always open in hope that its patrons would get off their stools and go. Across Pulaski, pushing a stolen shopping cart filled with junk, that same crazy man: skin orange and hot like the pulp of a sweet-potato yam, hair rust-red and dusty and shaped like the top of a mushroom cloud, muscled body taut with the steam of madness, his smell walking twelve feet before him. He was staring at me, both hands pushing that wreck my way. I felt sorry that Alex had to stay in this place. 'You know, after I get settled, you could move out to London, too.'

'Wouldn't that be sweet? Maybe, if this photography thing ever starts happening for me, maybe I could swing through for a little visit. That would be so nice.'

'When your shit drops, you need to just move out by me for good.'

'Move? Chris, why would I want to move?' Alex looked over her shoulder for traffic. Outside my window the yam-skinned man was getting close, smelling like he wore shit for clothes. Next to the car, he stopped pushing his cart and kept staring. All that fire-flesh focusing its rage on me, angry because I was getting out, that I wouldn't be forced to negotiate his existence. Yam-skinned man staring at me angry because I wasn't letting him climb on my back while I pushed his shopping cart up the road. The yam-skinned man, standing there, eyes wide as if I was the abomination, vibrating like he was going to go Osage on me, end my life because I was smiling back at him, daring to yell out, 'Niggawhat? I'm gone!'

'What the hell is wrong with you? All the years he's been out here, that man's got enough problems without you applying your own.' Alex pulled out into the road. Below us, the heat made the asphalt sluggish, soft, and I could feel the Yam-man behind me, still standing there, stinking up his part of the world. Refusing to accept my rejection, willing the tar to slow our wheels and fuse the rubber to the road.

Philly was me, speeding back down I76, looking at the daytime glamour of the crew clubs at Boathouse Row thinking, yeah, they look nice, but they've still got to get into that nasty water. It was me sitting in Alex's car, so damn happy that this was my last victory run.

'You're going to miss this,' Alex said, watching my face as I stared Center City down, passing the violence of South Philadelphia, moving beyond muscle T-shirts and pidgin English, the narrow street parking space fights. Fuck water ice.

'How long do you really think you'll be gone?' Alex asked. She maneuvered her little car amidst the bigger beasts by bobbing her head around like a Rittenhouse Square pigeon as her callused palms tugged at the wheel.

'This is it.' Outside, the oil refineries we passed made the air smell like hot dog vendor farts. In the car next to us a white woman with a man's haircut, sleeveless T-shirt, and *GO EAGLES* sticker on her passenger side was yelling at a little Barbie doll-chewing girl who ignored her, staring instead at me, at my escape. Sorry, I can't take you with me. Sorry you're going to turn into that beast driving.

'For real, Chris, when do you think? Next year? Two years maybe?' No more Moonies selling exhaust-fume pretzels on exit ramps for Christopher.

'This is my terminal. It's over here.' Alex moved her wreck of a car to the curb and let it die for a second.

'So this is it?' It was me asking, too excited to trust just my eyes.

'I guess so.'

'Watch. I'm gonna make you proud.'

'What the hell are you talking about? I already am proud. You earned this. Be proud of yourself.'

'I will be,' I nodded, hopeful.

'You want me to park, come in with you? I brought extra money, I can cover it. I can't park here.'

'Nah, you don't have to. I'm cool.'

'You gonna miss me?'

'Yeah, you I'm going to miss.'

'You're going to miss Philly.'

'F Philly.'

As Alex bent to get something from the back seat of the car, I kissed her on the side of her big butterscotch forehead. Twins: we recognized each other's wounds, the need for their tending. When Alex turned around she had the white paper bag she'd gotten from Stop 'n' Go.

'Don't forget, I got something for you.' She pulled it out. I didn't have to see its slender torpedo shape to know what it was.

'I told you I wasn't hungry,' I lied.

'A cheesesteak. You can eat it while you wait for the plane.'

'I don't want any Philly food.'

'Then save it for when you get there. I don't know, put it in the freezer for when you get homesick.' Yeah, sick and home, but not in that order. Alex placed it in my palm, and it was heavy. Hot, soft and heavy. Weighing down my hand as I hugged her, wanting to carry her with me, praying that she would come to her senses before this city made her its meal.

At my departure gate, as I waited with the other runaways for my plane to arrive, the sandwich sat on my lap like an anchor, thick with greasy Philly nourishment. There would be hot sliced beef inside, melted pale provolone cheese because Alex didn't like the processed kind. If I unveiled the white wrapping and then the aluminum that held that steak, steam would rise slowly from its salted innards; there would be onions, browned by heat and oil, overflowing from the tan, thick crusted roll that attempted to hold them. When my boarding call finally came I left it on the lobby seat behind me, relieved when they took my ticket and I couldn't go back for it.

Landing

I saw 'Chris Jones' written on a white sheet of cardboard, quick black letters from a thick black pen. The woman who held it was tall and light, made up of a group of curving lines (neck, legs, arms, even hair), staring down at a paperback instead of into the current of arriving faces. When I stopped in front of her, she turned up and started aiming the sign at my face like I might forget who I was.

'Urgent Agency?'

'Right.' She dropped the placard and her novel. 'Is that the whole of your luggage?'

'Yeah. Is David Crombie here?'

'No, he's not here. Couldn't expect him to get dressed before noon, could you?'

'Maybe he wanted to get ready,' I said, already making excuses, and I hadn't even really met the guy.

I had already decided I liked this woman, who was David's wife. Maybe it was because I had lost my own mother but, while in the line (because it wouldn't be a queue yet for me) to buy bottled water at the airport kiosk for the jet lag Margaret was sure I was destined to endure, when she turned back to me, stared at my face for a moment, then licked her thumbs and rubbed my eyebrows straight with her own saliva, I fell in love with her. I knew then that I would love her husband as well. All this slightly older (ten years maybe?) elegant, seemingly sophisticated black woman had to do was rub her spit into my face and my guard, whatever insignificant American perimeter I maintained, was decimated.

In the car, Margaret's hands held wheel and stick, pulling and winding and yanking. Those hands were long and lanky, slightly wrinkled on the back where the thin skin was, every purposeful bone visible, thick river veins bulbous, soft and meandering. On a full speed right turn Margaret's book slid across the dashboard and bounced off the glass, onto my lap. Without looking or slowing down, Margaret snatched it from its resting place and threw it in a high arc over her shoulder. I heard the sounds of a dry avalanche behind me and turned around. One paperback had been lost in a mountain of its brethren. Filling the space meant for legs, asses, torsos, the peak of the many hued heap reached all the way up to the back window. Books. Their spines broken, their covers permanently bursting, outstretched, trying desperately to vomit the pages held within.

'I read mysteries,' Margaret offered, so I stopped staring and turned around.

Zip-zip-zipping down roads in a tiny red car in a new land. Why would anyone buy a car so small? And why build streets to match it? And getting nervous every time we came to an intersection (Jesus, what fucking lane is she turning into?). My body was out of step, one minute awake and the next moment glazed. Outside everything looked familiar, then not. Like seeing someone you think you know on the street and realizing they're a stranger when they get closer. So many black folk. Didn't know I wasn't expecting to see them till I did.

'Welcome to Brixton.' Margaret had been quiet except for her light cursing as she avoided automotive contact on one-lane roads with two-way traffic. So quick, these precise maneuvers, pulling into parking spaces to give room for oncoming cars to pass, pulling out with one hand while lighting her cigarette with the hot metal the auto provided for such purposes.

'Do you work for Urgent?' I asked.

'Used to. Not any more. David and I actually started it together, when he resigned from the Patterson Group, but I've gone back to being a solicitor. I suspect that's why you're here.'

'What's David like?' I asked, looking at the side of Margaret's face as she laughed, having forgotten already what this woman looked like and needing to check again.

'What an odd question. I don't know if I'm the person to ask such a thing. Maybe you should ask someone a bit more impartial. Someone who isn't married to him, for instance.'

David was: belly so big, so generous, soft like peat moss. A devious smile on a pudgy face making him look like a wicked baby. Hairline retreating and leaving flags of gray in its wake. Biceps bulbous with muscle, thighs thick with it. Looking like a French-horn sounds if the player is giddy and excitable. Arms in the air, smiling, like he might fall forth upon me right there, swallowing me with his flesh and consume all but the polished bones.

'You look like a hole' was the first thing he said to me, nodding, finishing the can of beer in his hand and then dropping it so he could squeeze me into him. 'Margaret, that is the face of desire,' David said over my shoulder as my ribs struggled for room to expand.

'Darling you were supposed to be asleep.' Margaret picked up the beer can and walked past us out the living room. These people had money. Everything in the house looked either extremely hard or unrealistically easy to break. The only things cheap in the place (besides me) were the paperbacks that filled the shelves that wrapped around the walls. Short, chubby fiction hugging the room.

'You're here!' he said, releasing me. 'The Sound of Philadelphia has arrived! I knew we could do it! I knew we could get you out of there!' And he kept going on like that, as if he were Harriet Tubman and I had hay in my 'fro.

'You are the secret weapon. Do you know that? How could you come all this way and not know that?' David reached up and seized my neck. I once met Dizzy Gillespie coming out of a hotel off Walnut Street and shook his hand: this is how thick David's palms were. 'You're a crazy bastard, Sir Christopher, my wife has brought home a crazy man. This is our time! Things are going to happen, mate! You can feel it, can't you? Tell me! You can, can't you?! It's right, right?'

When you talk to a drunk man you must stand directly before him and stare straight into his eyes. When you look at him you must believe that yellow is the color that always serves as his pupil's sea, that the smell on his tongue is the saliva of knowledge. You must walk his logic's path beside him, comfort him that your feet are on the same ground and that you too can intuit the turns that lie ahead on this trail. You don't grow up poor and not know this, learn this as a means to comfort or just to avoid a beat down. So this I did, to the best of my ability until, a half hour later, I was sent for more beer. The kitchen had white tile on the floor and a window over the sink where Margaret was leaning, cigarette held near her thigh, an arm around her waist, her eyes staring down at her feet or something near there. When she saw me Margaret said, 'It's over to the left. Pull them from the bottom drawer, those are the coldest,' turning up to watch me move. 'I should have warned you at the airport, sorry about that bit. He's been so excited you were coming, he's been up probably as long as you have.'

'I don't mind,' I told her. Why would I? This was familiar, something I knew I could deal with. The house showed that he was good at what he did, but the drunk thing meant that he needed me. That's why I was smiling. If he needed me, it meant I wouldn't be going anywhere. Job security.

'You know, you did the right thing in coming. Give me those.' Margaret reached for the beer. 'I put your things in the guest room; you can rest here until David shows you to your flat. The door's open upstairs, you'll see it. Get settled. I'll call you for dinner.'

I went back into the living room and straight to the steps.

David was on the couch, lying down with his hand on his head. 'Brother?' he said.

'Yeah?' I stopped. Somehow David's shirt had disappeared off of him. The belly, revealed, was larger than the fabric had hinted, seemingly growing in the room's darkness. His exposed skin was the brown of old, polished wood, his hair black and soft as ash.

'I'll take care of you,' David said to me, and rolled over.

After what seemed only minutes, I woke up and the room was shadows. There was music coming from out the hall. There were smells that followed it, sweet, thick, and salty. There was a big hand rocking my foot.

'Chris, get up. Time to make the hole whole,' David told me. 'Here,' he said, and he held a lit thing out to me. Rumpled paper pushed between my lips, sour smallness.

'I don't smoke weed.'

'Flesh of my flesh, swallow.' His hand pulled away, making me hold the thing myself and, fuck it, pull its breath in. 'Welcome to the land of the green man,' David said, as we walked down the stairs, my head lifting as my body moved down.

Feast, blessed consumption, laid out on the table like a trap. Ackie and saltfish, fried plantain, corned beef, yam, cabbage baked salty with shredded pork, curry goat and jerk chicken with coconut rice, chicken tikka, samosas, Margaret pouring me wine that wasn't Mad Dog or Boone's – it even had a cork instead of a twist top. Music so loud (Curtis sang 'Gimme your love, gimme your love, gimme your love') and all amid verbal silence, a long and wordless prayer. The meal continued in that fashion, the room too intimate for words.

'Thank you,' I smiled, breathing heavy, reaching for more as they smiled with me, grabbing at the finger paints of food.

There came a point when we were not eating, when the dishes floated from the table in their hands. I was pregnant with gluttony. I was giggling.

'I'm not hungry,' I told the man that stood in shadow before me, silently investigating me now that I was slow and bloated, unable to flee and too at peace to protect myself, and feeling for once like I didn't have to. Feeling for the first time like this was where I was supposed to be in the world.

'Then what are you without hunger?' A smiling David teetered in my vision, subject to a separate, rocking gravity. His face looked like a ritual mask, wooden and with an expression of timeless inscrutability.

'Smooth' was my answer.

'Yes,' David said, and we laughed. I knew already that I would always owe him. I didn't mind that.

Grass a little too long, and wet, and us running through it. David was in front of me, flying like a hunter chasing gazelle, and I was bringing up the flank, not even running anymore: letting my weight fly forwards on its own, moving my feet so as not to insult my momentum.

'Faster!' he kept yelling, my head sobering with every pant. Wherever, man, I'm just following you. Over the metal fence even though it said *Park Closed*? No problem. Into a vacant field under orange skies someplace that is still nowhere to me? Fine. It seems to have worked so far.

'There she is. The lido.' And I saw brick walls, tall and thick, surrounding a space twice the size of a basketball court. David kept moving until he was at the structure, leaning on it, breathing hard, laughing. Breathing heavy enough for me to say, 'Don't die on me now, I just got here,' and for him to bend back up and say, 'Never, mate. I'm having too much fun. Here's the entrance.' He was grinning because there were no doors anywhere in sight.

'How?'

'How do you think, then? Right over the fucking top. Not a problem. My friend's the director, so no worries. It'll be okay.' I looked up and all I saw was twelve feet of dark brick, not many grooves, just tall enough to fall and break something.

'He couldn't get you a key?'

'Chris, it's four o'clock in the morning. We could go banging on his door if you like, but his missus would kill me. The ground is the highest on this end, it's the only side we can do this on. Come on, up and over. Be a lad.'

I stood on his shoulders. I was covering his jacket with mud and grass but it was obvious I cared about that more than he did. I hadn't slept properly in two days, I was supposed to be here for a job, what the hell was I doing? Well, I was reaching for the top of a wall, trying to get a hand somewhere it could hold on to, and then I was swinging a leg (shit, did I hit your head?) and boom, I was sitting, looking out at a pool shimmering back light at my eyes, happy like a puppy to see me. And then I was laughing, too. We both were. Even when it was David's turn to climb and he was using my leg like a rope and crushing my balls with his weight as I struggled to stay up there. Laughing when I jumped and could feel the sting in my ankles and had to skip it off like a schoolboy holding his pee, laughing when David came down and tripped his way forwards for a couple of feet before he gained his balance.

'Right, then. Off with your knickers.' David started undressing. It couldn't be more than fifty degrees – how cold did that make the water? And it was August. What kind of people built an outdoor pool in a place that was fifty degrees in August? So why the hell was he taking his clothes off? I could dog paddle, but that had been at the YMCA on Green Street over twenty years ago. What were the boundaries? When could I say no? 'Come on, Chris, I didn't drag you all this way to bugger you.'

'Niggers don't do well in the cold, man. You Jamaica folk should know that. It's not in our blood.'

'Then go be a nigger over there by the wall. Because I plan on splashing.' If I planned on being a nigger, I would have never left my block. If I drowned, at least I would have accomplished that final escape. The only thing more pathetic than a brother living like a nigger was a brother dying as one. I started undressing, real fast, throwing my shit away from me at random so I couldn't change my mind when my bare ass hit the air.

'All at once then, don't do any toe-testing shite,' David told me when I got down to my socks. 'Don't dive, though. It's too shallow, you could break your neck in there.'

A flying cannonball to freedom. I was running, teeth gritting, and then for a moment I was in the air, the whole of my body wrapped in a ball. The ice water swallowed me, stealing my heat as I sunk to the bottom. I tried screaming but I was just making bubbles, so I forced myself to relax. Above me, through a rippled membrane, I could still see the color of the sky, an orange haze of clouds. Then my butt hit the ground and I let the rest of my body follow until I was lying down on the concrete bottom like I was tanning, water coming in my nose and me not caring. I thought I heard whales, but it was the echoes of nothing. I couldn't hear anything because home was gone and I didn't know how to listen to this place yet. I felt that, if I looked, I could see America, Philly, everything that was ever pain floating away, dissipating beyond me. Even my air, all my reserves, breathe out breathe out, so that finally, when I suddenly rose, hands flat and arms outstretched and face smiling stoned but happy, a whole new space was filling my lungs. My body stopped at the surface, but didn't my spirit keep soaring?

Drop

I woke up in my clothes on the white canvas pelt of a bare futon. There was nothing else in the room but wood floors, windows and the sunlight screaming in from outside. When David took me back here the night before, both of us still dripping through our clothes, the place had been furnished by the undefined abundance of darkness. Now it was vacant, waiting to be filled.

I gathered myself and rose, my weight creaking on the boards and adding a more immediate sound than the disinterested swooshes of cars passing outside. There was a bathroom in the next room with no toilet paper, and then a glowing living room that contained only a television staring across the floor at a gaggle of beer cans laying empty by the opposite wall. Motivated by the bare cleanliness of the house, I gathered them up and took them downstairs, hunting for a place to put them. This apartment was weird. Not because of its alien additions, like the freakishly large three-prong electric sockets on every wall, but because of what wasn't here. No pee-like water stain circles on the ceiling with exposed plaster and planks at their epicenter, no dirt shadows or scales of paint chipping off the wall. In the cabinets and drawers, no cockroaches, dead or alive. No half devoured mouse poison behind the refrigerator. No radios vibrating the windows as the cars that chauffeured them tore down the road. Outside, just the park we'd walked through to get here and the wind, blowing in cool and welcoming. Beyond, the small hills looked as if you could crawl out and snuggle into them, pull a fold of that grass over you like a comforter and rest.

I turned on the television. There was something wrong with it: no matter how many times I kept turning the dial, the same five channels kept appearing. Giving up, I took a nap, waking only when I heard the keys in the door. David yelled, 'Oi, it's half-past noon. You're supposed to be earning.'

'Earning what?'

'My money. It's time for work. How does Christopher like his new flat?' David walked out into the hall. He had my luggage with him so he dropped it there.

'This place, this is me?' I asked, not prepared to believe it. Not wanting to look like a fool by investing in such an impossibility.

'It's yours. Or mine, but it's yours to use if you choose. You'll have to get some furniture, as you can see. Open the windows up. You should get some plants, I imagine. Nice place, isn't it? It used to be my flat, you know, back in the bachelor days. Been letting it out for years. The last tenants moved months ago, so I held it for you. Your rent'll be the BT, lights, gas, the taxes. I'll take it out from what I pay you so you won't have to bother. So, do you like?'

I just shrugged. Too scared that if David heard my surprise, he would take it away from me, send me to a hovel more in line with the style with which I was accustomed.

The office was on the third floor of their house, a tall attic room with curved ceilings like the bottom of a boat. Urgent Agency had a separate entrance, a door along side the residential one.

'This is your desk. This is it, where you will be working,' David told me, pointing at a long wooden table with a computer covered in clear plastic like a ghetto couch. On the wall was a picture of Margaret dressed up like a gunslinger, smiling at a party, along with photos of random people I didn't know. Piled next to the desk, in a mound that was nearly twice as tall, were more of Margaret's mysteries, seemingly raked together into a pyre.

'She was supposed to clear out her stuff from here. Especially the damn books. I told her, "Don't bring another book in this house until you throw some away." But we'll take care of that. And I'll be right over here.' David pointed to the only other desk up there. Next to it was a tall glass bookshelf, the bottom stacked with oversized magazines and what I recognized as design texts, assembled in accordance to no particular order or respect for gravity. The top shelves were arranged with equal care, but different contents. Paperweights, some glass, some metal, some seemingly gold, in various designs but with multiple versions of some forms. Awards. There had to be over thirty of them. Piled carelessly on top of one another like a spoiled child's toys. The rest of the office was just space. An acre of thin, gray carpeting, exposed wood rafter beams and freshly painted white walls. I coughed and the room echoed back at me. David's ten-pound palm gripped my shoulder.

'Chris, this is going to be it. This is going to be massive. Something like they haven't seen before. I know there's not much at the moment, but see this, look, and dream. We are at the beginning. Two black boys, in pretty black Brixton town, in a very white and very old city that won't know what hit it. I've been working in advertising twenty years, Chris, nearly half my life, and I know the scene: some of these agencies are a hundred strong, and they are evil. We, on the other hand, are two, but we are good. No secretary, no graphic design staff, no production team, no clerks, no receptionist, but also no infighting between creative teams for a chance at the same bone. No locking your office door when you go to lunch because you're scared someone might steal your ideas, no control-hungry project managers or account executives to impose their mediocre visions, or wondering if you're going to get fired every six months if your client decides to switch agencies. The only people on the payroll are you and me. We are the account managers, we are the account creatives. You will compose the copy, I will produce the design. The layout, the Fiery, the blues, I'll take care of everything. Two people but combined together, and I tell the absolute truth here, we have the connections, the money, the talent, and, most important, the desire that will make this happen. All we have to do is show these bastards that we can sell better than the impotent gits they've got on their dole now, from there we can hire the support to fill this office till we have to put desks on the bloody stairs. Now have a seat.' I did. The chair was leather, soft like old lady skin, my back blended into it.

'Close your eyes. I'm serious.' I closed them. In my darkness, I was sure he was either going to punch or kiss me.

'I'm going to put something in your hands. Don't open your eyes until I say, right?'

'Right.' I heard him open up a drawer, pull out something crinkling, and then felt the thin plastic membrane in my fingers. Inside was some type of tightly wrapped cloth. I could feel the hard edge of the cardboard giving it its form.

'OK. It's some type of clothes, probably. What is it?'

'It's your first customer. Open your eyes and tell me what it is.' The packaging was black and white, utilitarian. You could see the product through the clear parts and it had a cheaply illustrated sample of a guy wearing some.

'Underwear.'

'What kind?'

'White. Cotton blend, probably. A three-pack.'

'Cottonal Y-fronts. What do they make you think of? What type of person would wear them?'

'A dad, probably.'

'Your dad?'

'I don't know. Probably. I didn't know him.'

'He took off?'

'No, he died.'

'What was it, a gang fight? A drug overdose?'

'He choked on a plum.'

'All right. Look, Chris, what you've got to do is see this product. See it like it was just invented, see it like its time has just come. Figure out who this product is perfect for, whose needs it best meets. Think of the client who has to sell these things, who wakes up every morning with images of Y-fronts intertwined with their personal ambitions and anxieties, how do they want to see this product? And then, when you know all of that, I want you to come up with an idea that will grab, make them understand the necessity, almost force them into the stores to buy some. You know what I mean?'

'Yeah. I can do that.' They were a pretty plain sight, these drawers.

'Now, when I was at the Patterson Group we might have put two, maybe even four blokes on something like this, given them maybe three to five days to brainstorm ideas. I want you to do this a bit quicker. You have the time it takes me to go meet the client for lunch in the West End, talk it up a bit, and come home. That gives you about two hours to get sorted. Understand?'

'Yeah,' I said, laughing along with his smile.

'I'm not joking, Chris,' David said with a face that went quickly straight again.

I spent the next three hours trying to think of something, staring at the dull package, and then staring at the room around me thinking about dreams. I could see the place full, people in every available space. The floor matted with cords, phones ringing, people laughing, a small radio playing in a cubicle. Maybe a basketball hoop tied to that big rafter in the middle of the room. Then I checked out David's trophies, picking each one up and inspecting them (the earliest date was damn close to my date of birth, the most recent just six-years-old). I took care to place them back into their previous precarious position without making too much noise. As quiet as this place was now, with just me in the corner of an empty, cavernous room, I knew someday I would hear the sounds of the office that would be alive around me.

Three and a half hours later I heard David thumping up the steps. It had just gotten dark outside, and I felt, in my period of note scratching and false paths, that I had come to something that was a good thing.

'Well, first the news. The Cottonal bastards are interested; they're at least going to let me come in there and pitch them next week, next Thursday. I worked on a campaign for the athletic gear segment of their product line, the junior sports kits they were pushing a few years back, made them some dosh. They knew to listen. The geezers understood what I can do for them,' David nodded to himself, confidently. 'So, what you got for me?' In response, I cleared my throat.

'Well, I don't know if this is any good. I don't know if this is just awful, so I guess I'll just throw this out there and you'll tell me if it's stupid,' I began. David actually started cringeing. 'I'm just saying this because, y'know, I don't want to disappoint you but here it is: I was thinking about what we were talking about, about this being a product that, with the popularity of boxers and designer briefs, has probably seen its best day. And then I was thinking maybe, if the product is in some way stylistically obsolete, could that mean that it could make some kind of revival? That might be a good way to make what may be conceived as a dated, dull product into one that might imply individuality and a minor rebellion. So this is sort of what I was thinking – and if it's bad, y'know, just tell me, but I just thought I'd say it, okay? Okay. Wedgies. Maybe we could do a series of ads, I don't know, print, video, whatever you think is better, where the focus would be seeing these really cool or weird people from all walks of life, like street performers, skaters, musicians, world leaders, and then when you look closer you can see the waist band of their underwear, the client's red and black brand strip, peaking out. And the copy I tried to come up with for the slogan is, "Did you know?" Of course that could be totally changed. Really that's the whole idea, and you can tell me if this is the wrong direction, but I kind of figured that might be good, might make it look like there was a whole "in" crowd who wears these, because no one really knows what anyone else is wearing down there, right?' David sat staring blankly back at me.

'Is that okay?' I asked. David continued staring.

'No. That's shite,' he said.

'Excuse me?'

'It. Is. Shite. Shit. It's no good. Actually, I'm sorry, it is good. Stop looking like I just kicked you in the bollocks. But good isn't enough, y'know what I mean?'

'Yeah, I do. You're right, that was awful. I'm so sorry. I'll try harder, I can do better, I'll stay up on this. I know exactly what you mean.'

'No, you don't. I'm sorry, but I really don't think you do. And we can't have that, can we? Especially right here, in the beginning?'

'David, I can do this, man. Shit, give me twenty minutes, I can do this thing.'

'You got any ID on you?'

'Yeah, I got my passport.'

David grabbed his keys and headed for the stairs. I asked if I should follow and he yelled for me to bring the bags of Cottonals. Next thing we were in his car, driving. Neither one of us talking all those minutes we sat there as the road beneath us evolved from one lane to two lanes to three and we were on a highway, speed increasing steadily until David made a right turn at an exit marked Gatwick Airport.

'This is an airport,' I told David, but he just nodded. I'd failed; I was being returned to Philadelphia. David parked the car. It was quiet for a moment, the both of us sitting there, staring at a concrete wall sprayed with a green number 087. I wasn't surprised. A fraud is never surprised when he is revealed, he is only relieved that the act is over. David pulled himself out of his seat and slammed the door behind him. I didn't want to get out, but I unhooked my seat belt and followed him anyway because he wasn't pausing to wait for me. I was too ashamed to apologize. At an elevator, we got on with others and their bags, their conversations about flights, food, and gates. David stood on the other side of the box, separated from me by a woman holding something large wrapped in white grocery bags. The doors opened and we all walked out, pouring like the twelve tribes into whatever direction pulled us. Finally David faced me, staring with his mouth open for a second. 'Give me your passport.' It was in my back pocket, already bent to the contour of my ass from the flight the days before. David took it from me without looking at my face and then walked away, leaving me standing by a cardboard donation placard for burn victims.

'All right, we're set. Now follow me, quickly. We haven't much time,' David said when he reappeared, and then scuttled off in front of me. We were walking towards a security gate, metal detector and cops in goofy looking sweater uniforms, and then walking faster towards the gates beyond.

'Yo, sir, where we going?' The answer was the back of his head, those beaded black naps bobbing as he hustled that body forward. Out among others, David was so much wider than normal folk. So broad that, walking as fast as he was, they must have felt a breeze when he passed.

'Yo, sir, for real, where we going?' As if to answer me, David turned in at a gate that seemed to be at the end of its boarding: a flight attendant just standing by a door waiting for her chance to close it. David stopped in front of her, turning to me while she took his ticket to hand me mine and say, 'I'll meet you by the baggage return when we get there, right?' Then he was gone down the white tunnel towards the plane, lost in the turn of the hall. It wasn't until the smiling lady took my ticket that I noticed the Amsterdam sign at the center of her podium. At the plane door I thought I saw the back of a black man's head to the left, in first class, but I was ushered to the right towards coach before I could be sure if it was him.

When we landed I tried to get out of my seat quickly, make it to the front of the plane, but there were too many others in my way. He wasn't there when I left the gate, and I started hustling past the herd towards the baggage claim, certain he would leave me or take a flight somewhere else or do something similarly fucking crazy. At the baggage area, he wasn't there, no surprise. I kept searching, rechecking that I was in the right place, searching through the growing crowd around me, looking on to the conveyor belt as if he might appear from the magic hole, rolled into fetal position amid the luggage, between an oversized suitcase and a folded stroller. After a few minutes the crowd began to thin, and it was very clear that there was no David anywhere, and that was simple to discern because a random turn of the room showed there were no negroes anywhere at all.

'Chris!' David's baritone echoed, poking his head through the glass exit doors as if I was late, smiling politely and waving quickly for me to follow. Outside it was even colder than London, wind blowing at my non-coated self. David's steps before me were long, stomping, reaching too far for those little legs. People he passed turned after his wake to see if he was joking. Behind him I could already smell the liquor; in the back of the chauffeured car it was like my nose was in the bottle's mouth.

'Bit of a road trip, this.' David put his head against the window and started humming to the song the driver was playing on the radio. Outside was another place I didn't know. Bright advertisements for products I'd never heard of in a language I couldn't speak. New and shiny things in a place that was as old as Philly pretended to be. Look at this. So much beauty and I was in it, zipping around in an unmarked cab that was a fancier car than I'd ever been in. Going into a city that looked so good I wanted to walk the ride. Beside me David had gone quiet, no sound except for heavy breathing and occasional near snores. He didn't move again until we were way into the city, over canals and amid narrow cobblestone streets bumpier than Germantown Avenue. When the car died he came alive.

'This is it,' David said, smacking his lips and giving some notes to the driver. He opened his car door, so I did the same with mine. David glanced around and then started walking towards a shop without even looking back to see if I was following.

Inside the door was the stank of pot smell. The place was set up like an old tobacco shop, with the product in large containers behind humidor doors. David put both fists down on the glass counter and said to the man behind it, 'Give me a sample of the freshest stuff you've got.'

'Any particular taste or high you're going for?' The clerk was David's age, English also. His hair had been sawed down to an uneven brown turf. Maybe he'd done it himself, without a mirror.

'Only that it is the absolute best, truly best, and freshest bit of spliff in here.' The clerk gave a squinty smile of stained teeth, then reached under the counter, lifted a lid, and stood up with a small silver dish filled with the stuff. 'Hawaiian,' he offered. David looked at it close, bending down to smell it, and then without standing back up said to me, 'Chris, do us a favor. Tell me what marijuana is like, physically.'

'I don't know much about it. I don't really smoke this shit. And I don't plan on changing that.'

'Right, but that said, describe the product for me, the uninitiated.'

'It looks sort of like tobacco, except green.'

'Right. What about its consistency.'

'Dried. A bit brittle, I think.'

'Very good, Chris, very good.' The clerk had found some way to make his silly smile even bigger, watching me.

'Now, Chris, look at this.' David took a pinch at the substance under his nose and lifted it to the air, and then to my nose. It didn't smell like anything you'd smoke if you were afraid to die. Its color was dark green and brown, moist and soft like moss.

'Watch.' David held it about a foot over the countertop, and those big ham hock muscles flexed. There was trembling in his hands, like he was trying to pinch coal into diamond. Then, like a forced birth, it dripped. One perfect drop, heavy, dark and thick, fell down to the glass. I bent down to look at it, this oily emerald swirling on the counter.

'Do you see that, Chris?' David asked in awe.

'I see.' Look at that thing. A kaleidoscope of reflections swimming on its surface.

'That's the stuff, that. That's what you should be doing.

Everything you create, everything you bring to the world, that's how good it needs to be. A drop. I know you're capable, because you've done it before. And I can tell you got more than one drop in you.' David turned his pinching fingers up to me, revealing the pulp that was stuck there. 'That, that's you, that is. Fresh, gifted, brought all the way from America. You have it in you, Chris. You just need to accept that.' I nodded, but didn't. But he did. Thankfully, enough for both of us.

Later that night, after we were in the hotel room, David made me call Margaret and tell her where we were. He sat in the next room with the door open, smoking from the ounce he'd bought at the shop, sitting on the edge of the bed watching French TV. I couldn't figure out if he understood it or if he was too stoned to care. Margaret picked up after the first *bring-bring*.

'Hi, it's Chris. We're okay.'

'About bloody time. Good to hear that, seeing how it's almost two in the morning. Where are you?'

'Amsterdam.' Margaret was silent for a moment. Then she was sucking hard on a cigarette, I could tell. Somewhere a little orange fire was beaming.

'Lovely.'

'David told me to tell you we'll be back tomorrow night, after I finished the project we're working on.'

'Great. Could you put him on?'

'He went to the store.'

'Did he tell you to say that, too?' David, forgetting he wasn't supposed to be nearby, let out a shriek of laughter at something he was watching.

'Uh huh.'

'Is he getting stoned?'

'Uh huh.'

'Let me guess: he's sitting right there smoking, staring at the wall or something.'

'Yup.'

'Oh God. Do try to keep him out of trouble, all right, Chris?

From now on, when I'm not around, he'll be your responsibility. Promise?'

'Yes.'

'I'm being serious. Please, I mean this. I worry that he's getting worse. Promise me that when I'm not around you'll watch out for him.'

'I promise,' I told her.

'At least keep him away from the whores.'

When I hung up David heard the click, turned from his entertainment, and asked me if she sounded mad.

'A bit. Not too bad, but a bit. She heard you laughing; she knew you were here.'

'She'll be all right. You know, it could have been the two of us here, working, but she couldn't trust it, could she? She had to go back to her law work. Said our marriage would be better if we worked apart.'

'She just sounded a little worried, that's all.'

'Right then, to work with you. I got the management to bring up a typewriter, we'll put it on the desk in the back, so before it gets here why don't you go to the bog and put a pair of the Cottonals on your bum. Get a feel for them this time, a real feel, so you can come up with some ideas accordingly.'

'Sounds good,' I said, reaching for the bag.

'Give me your clothes. I'll send them down to the cleaners so you'll have some fresh kit to wear out of here.'

'Cool. But what will I wear till then?'

'The Cottonals,' David said. I didn't ask another question because he was staring into my face, ready to answer it.

It wasn't that bad, really. I wore two pairs at a time and when I got cold he let me wrap them around my feet like slippers, around both shoulders like slings, even on my head as a skullcap. The Cottonals were so soft, their downy glowing whiteness straight from their plastic womb, silently holding me there, hugging me with gentle, unconditional support as I slammed my fingers into the old manual typewriter I'd been given. David sat behind me, smoking something pungent he occasionally offered and I steadily refused. The method insane but the only way I would have come up with the idea, *If Comfort Came First*: a campaign bearing that slogan depicting men in a variety of life's duties wearing only Cottonals as the rest of the room, fully clothed, ignored them. A ballroom dancer performing on the floor with evening-dressed partner in hand. A bus driver who opened the door for the camera/passenger while seated in only his Cottonals and his black cap. One Cottonal-clad man on a subway platform amidst a sea of pinstripe, herringbone, and pleats. the method insane but not so crazy when David walked up the office steps a week later, fresh from his Soho meeting, and said, 'We got the bastards,' screaming it again as he spiked his suitcase to the carpeted floor.

Home

My London begins as the view from my window, the park behind me and the street through the trees in front. Then, as I learn the way, it is the distance between the lock on my front door to the buzzer at David's, and everything on that trail. Then, with time, it grows to the distance from those two places to Brixton High Street and the tube there, linking me to all the other places the city becomes.

Soho was tiny streets of cobblestones and heavy buildings that seemed to lean in against one another to create a cave above you. Record shops with only a few records but good ones and they let you vibrate the store with their sounds. Sex shops selling everything but sex (but you could smell it maybe), signs selling amyl nitrate (poppers!) for flaccid love. East London voices trying to bark punters into red neon doors. Sparse hookers at night (are there any actual female hookers anymore?) and pubs that overflow onto the street with smoke, beer, guffaws and too-loud conversations as people carried their pint glasses from one door to the next.

Ladbroke Grove on Saturdays. Get off at Notting Hill Station and walk down till first you get the antiques (so many little white tags with prices so high) and then after a few blocks you get the food (all eatables should be wrapped in off-white paper), then the clothes, the racks of them, dancing to the silent music of the

43

wind. It doesn't matter if it's cold, there will still be brothers hanging in front of Ground Floor Pub, funky dressed and afros tight, sculpted sideburns and silver hoops in ears, pints in hand talking junk. By Ladbroke Grove Station there will always be crowds regardless of rain, weaving between stalls as vendors sit on lawn chairs listening to radios held together by electric tape. And wasn't it a heaven, where Camden was a place of wealth and joy and not just a place in New Jersey for negroes so poor they couldn't even afford to live in Philly's ghettos?

Oxford Street was narrow but endless, padded with cheap synthetic clothes, hung in store windows and off vendor's stalls snug between behemoth chain stores. The screech of the auction shop man pimping whatever cheap shit someone had shoved into his hand, outdated crap with the fragility total incompetence creates, things without packaging, logo or even proper company name. American fast food joints, both the authentic and replicated ones that look like movie props (the main character would work there). Buses fire engine red and soaked in time. End of the world: cockroaches and London buses, them all driving around, having fun till Armageddon remembers itself and comes back for them. Fun fun buses open in the back so I could jump on or off as they paraded down off into Knightsbridge, or back up Tottenham Court Road, ride one all the way back into Brixton or Clapham if I had the time. Or go to places that didn't even exist yet for me. Looking out the window wondering if I'm in the same city at all, if some neighborhoods have their own decade they choose to live in, some time they're so sweet on they never move forth. Riding, knowing that someday, when I had time, I would do that: just get on, just go, just ride, every dirty red bus it had to offer, letting the network of roads provide more grooves for my mind to take hold. I read a book that said that in this old city of Albion, the roads were here before man, cut by animals long extinct, the ground made solid and permanent by hooves and paws guided only by their feel for the energy of this land. Man just came and paved over the trails that were already there, making these roads as sacred as concrete could muster. I was from a people that saw deities at crossroads; I could understand that.

Home was Brixton, this burgeoning outpost of urban negritude. Africans in London since the Romans arrived but never like this: so many native born, a mass to whom their ancestral land was just a second-hand memory. A myriad of melanin born of multiple hemispheres, small islands to big continents, a populace as worldly as their American counterparts were provincial. A negropolis forming, looking at itself, trying to figure out what it was. And here I am, David's newborn pride: an ambassador from the most successful (hah!) black folks in modernity, the culture to which this new community looked for definition, (mis)guidance. A people, who despite defining the popular culture of the new world, barely knew of this other's existence, who rarely made it across the Atlantic for a visit and almost never came to stay. And me, the traveler from this mythic land. This was a city that smiled when it saw me coming. And I smiled back. I had a purpose here. There were mistakes they hadn't made yet, things I could help them with.

When Lennox Lewis (British-born, North American-raised, London-adopted) returned Stateside to fight Alabama holly-roller Evander Holyfield, it was as if Lewis were personally doing me the favor of going back to kick black America's ignorant ass. I said, This is the sign of the torch passing. I said, Look, my former tormentors, there is a bigger, stronger, more articulate Afro-urban nation on the rise. I said, Behold the warrior of the new tribe. David said, You're mad, that big wanker's going down, and proceeded to drop five hundred quid on 'the American one, whatsit' at the off-off-track betting club he'd dragged me to. And after Lewis had made his appearance, had patted the American around the ring for twelve rounds like a cat playing with his food, and the judges had tried to deny fate by deeming it a draw, I didn't even care that I'd lost the two hundred pounds I had riding on the knockout. The message had been sent: that even their champions were in danger. At this club, 100 per cent loss ratio meant chairs flying, male cursing, and female crying. I remained seated, in the tuxedo David had taken me to buy hours before, laughing. Mouth wide, chest bouncing, hands easily behind my head, legs crossed, staring at the frustrated gamblers rioting before me. David, his soft roundness hiding underneath the square table, started pulling on my leg with his blanket hands.

'Chris, you fucking nutter, get under the table before you get killed.'

But it was just funny, that's all it was. Beige, black, and brown hands swinging to claim maroon blood. So many sounds, everything moving: chairs across the room, pictures off the wall, projectile napkin dispensers, even my chest jumping as I go ha-ha-ha and laugh at all this around me. Play on. My first public brawl outside the States and I didn't care because they didn't have guns, did they? It wasn't like home, they could beat on one another all they wanted, there would be no random shooting. The *pop-pop* wouldn't find me here. This was a new, safer world. What were they going to do, kick my teeth in? I could get caps.

We took the night bus home from Trafalgar after that. That was when Margaret wouldn't let David have the car (note: speed bumps are not to be used as ramps, particularly not at four in the morning, in a quiet suburb like Croydon, in a Fiat hatch back when the driver is drunk and the car is too too fast for such roadways). I made us sit on the second level, in the front, my novelty spot. David sat next to me eating the hot dog he bought for two quid right next to the stop and I looked at the road as we wandered south. We were going through hotel-lined streets and I was staring at the buildings, their smooth white facades going on for blocks like an army of cream cakes, occasional small signs hung before them to offer entry to the temporarily homeless and financially secure. No one was on the streets, not even rats. No light was on. No one was awake because no one knew each other. A neighborhood of strangers probably thinking about someplace else, maybe on their way there, maybe not.

'It's lonely out here, isn't it?' I asked. David's hot dog was gone and he was brushing mustard off his face.

'Sure. It's a lonely world. Why do you think people get married?'

'Why?'

'Love shits on lonely.'

'If we ever have Aphrodite as a client, you got to use that one.'

'My Margaret, she's my world. She's what keeps me weighted.'

'I feel the same way about my account at Barclays.' We were crossing over the Lambeth Bridge and I was checking my watch against Big Ben's yellow face and getting off on that, loving a cliché.

'Oi, you little yardie, I know what's in there, I'm the one that puts it. But I'm telling you, you gotta have someone. My Margaret, she's my roots, man. She's like, if somebody shook the world, y'know, she'd be the thing that keeps me from flying off. A man has to have that, can you understand?'

Twenty minutes later, we were at the Chinese take-away off Effra Road bleaching our brown under bright fluorescents. 'Chris, that's what you need.'

'Whatever boss.' I reached for my bag. How did I live before curry and chips? Fuck cheesesteaks. 'Maybe you're right,' I added, but I wasn't thinking about no woman, not in any sense beyond the normal unceasing mindless fantasies that populated straight men's minds. What I was doing was staring behind the take-away counter at the aluminum trays with their clear plastic tops and thinking, That's the only thing I miss about America: Chinese food in white cardboard boxes with little tin handles and red dragons on the side. Going on eight months over here and wow, look at that, that's the only thing missing for me.

Love

Friday, I opened the door for her. This little woman, too proud to even look up at me past the rib she came to. She stood, beneath layers of white skies and before wet sidewalk, a vision. A face so black it was bold, cheeks a duo of sweeping circles beneath the soft rainbow of a head wrap that contained all the colors that could scream or cry for you.

'Is this the place?'

'Excuse me?'

'Is this the place that's supposed to be taking pictures of me?' she asked. She was so much smaller than I'd been expecting, but she had to be the dancer David hired: she was too pretty not to be getting paid for it.

'Please, please come in,' I managed. I shouldn't even have been answering the door because by this time, besides clients growing and waiting for our attentions, Urgent had a secretary too, a bony, Marlboro Light-smoking Brixton boy named Raz who should have been down here with this woman, saving me from my awkwardness. The shoot was scheduled for a half hour before, but models, David reminded, were always late. Taking in the smell of her: of violet water and hot sauce.

'Fionna Otubanjo?' She just walked by me and started heading upstairs; I couldn't tell if she'd nodded. Tiny, this one. The size of a girl but the shape and proportions of a woman, making the stairwell look cavernous as my eyes struggled to keep perspective.

After I took her coat, introduced her to the photographer, the stylist, and even Margaret, who was taking a rare intermission from her reading to make an appearance on the third floor, I showed Fionna to the bathroom that would be her dressing room for the day. Then I pulled David to a far and relatively secluded section of the floor.

'Cuz, she's gorgeous.' Somebody in the room had to acknowledge this.

'Really? A bit of a head on a stick, I thought. A short stick at that. She looked bigger on her Z card. If you like, maybe later we'll go for a curry or something, you could ask her to tag along.' David reached into the cereal box in his hand and threw a kernel into my mouth.

Golden Crowns, an old-brand cereal owned by one of several companies that realized Urgent knew how to implant hunger in even the most bloated, who understood that our work was the stuff people were starting to whisper about, the kind that would be bringing back industry awards in the year to come. Its box stood in the center of the white cove, ready for its picture to be taken, short and proud and belligerent with caloric prophecies. Golden Crowns, a combination of flour, water, high fructose corn syrup, and yellow dye number 24, but also something so sweet it didn't need milk or morning.

'Alright, luv,' David was bellowing at the emerged Fionna. 'What we need you to do is just run, leap right over the box, right? Spread your legs open like scissors, give it as much as you can. We want to capture you directly above the Golden Crowns, almost as if they gave you the gift of flight.'

'I can do that,' Fionna said, looking at me, and wasn't it immediately clear that she could do much more? That she could hold your head in her lap, rub her little palms over your face and wipe away everything else besides the blackness behind closed eyes? That if there were arranged marriages I would have had David call her family immediately on my behalf, have stood behind him smiling and jumping up and down like a horny Masai?

The photographer's tin can lights sat on the floor, hung from erected scaffolding, rested on the ends of tables and chairs, all pointing in one direction, metallic ravens holding brilliant court. The heat almost solar in intensity, pulsing away from the illumination to the rest of the space beyond, the warm touch linking all those in the room together. And within the fire, one body moving. To watch her run, to see her leap. The determined start with bare feet slamming the floor and then the jump, the seizing of space with a ferocious kick, a smile that flashed gloriously as soon as the pivot foot left the ground. How could one so short fly so high? And all this along with a bowl of glued Golden Crowns in one hand and a spoon in the other. Running and leaping and landing. The toe and ball of one foot touched back down and the rest of the body followed, the flesh moving slightly past the limits of her bones for a moment until it bounced back into structure again. David walked behind me and snapped his fingers by my ear – 'Pay attention to the work' – but how could anyone with her perspiring until the midnight fabric of her leotard became even darker beneath the neck and arms, her form becoming an essay on the possibilities of blackness, a diatribe about refusing the limitations of one word? I sat, leaned against David's desk with my shirt open, my sleeves rolled, watching. Witnessing the sweat drip away from her as she ran and explode around her when she landed, giving a shine to the floor. Steaming the windows to opaque rectangles, forcing me to sweat along with her, to feel my own oily wetness and susceptibility, until, in one particularly triumphant soar (spoon and bowl held by hunger), she landed in the puddle of sweat that she created, broke the spell, and bore a new one in a helpless painful cry.

'Oh, fucking hell!'

The first to reach her, I held Fionna's back as she held her ankle. 'Are you okay?'

'No, it's not okay, I'm hurt!'

'Is it broken?'

'No. I don't know. I don't think so.' Inspired by the urgency

of the moment, I moved around Fionna and gently took her leg
into my lap, touched her ankle with my famished fingertips, bent
the joint slowly in my hands up until 'Ow!' and slowly back
down until 'Oh!' and left 'Ew!' and right 'AY!' until 'No, it's not
broken' but damn, isn't it divine to hear you scream and imagine
that the sound must be the same when pleasure motivates it?

After the food, after the drinks, after it was too late for a limping
girl to ride all the way back to East London, I offered my place to
her for the night. It was the perfect time to ask the question: I
had finally reached that delicate plateau where I was drunk
enough for bravery but not too smashed to pronounce the
words. Fionna agreed that would be good, 'Because I'm very
tired.' When I carried her from the cab into my apartment, the
driver looked at me funny: even he knew she was too pretty for a
wreck like me to be holding. I managed to get out my keys and
open the door without dropping her or her overstuffed duffel
bag that weighed nearly as much as she did. What's in it?

'Just some of my clothes. Lately I've been staying with
girlfriends while I hunt for a new bedsit. This is your place?'
Fionna asked inside.

'Yeah. This is me.'

'You live alone then? No flatmates or anything? How much
do you pay?'

'I don't know. David says he takes it out of my salary.'

'I've been looking for a new flat for months, and I haven't
seen one this nice. Not one that didn't cost a fortune.' She made
me feel unusually lucky.

I turned on every light in the house as I carried her upstairs to
the living room, trying to destroy any shadow that might scare
her. Trying also not to bang her bad ankle against a wall. The
swelling had gone down in the hours since the sprain, assisted by
a variety of towel-wrapped foodstuffs Margaret found for her,
but it was still an ugly thing sitting above her foot.

'Were you robbed recently?' Fionna looked around like
maybe she didn't want me to put her down in this place.

'No, is something wrong?'

'You don't have any furniture,' she said, shocked, staring at my apartment with nothing more than its own dust and possibilities to fill it. 'How long have you been living here?'

'About nine months. I bought a kitchen table and some chairs.' Actually, Margaret had made that donation from her basement, along with some dishes, flatware, and pots and pans after the time she came by the house to offer me leftover spaghetti and had to watch me sit on the floor eating it with my hands.

'Do you like it here?' Fionna's was a new voice echoing around these walls.

'I love it. I'm not going back to America.'

'I meant the flat. There's so much room, isn't there? You should really get some more furniture, right? Some carpets and such. Make a home. It could be really nice, once you get the proper things together. Then you could let a room out or something. It's too big for one person.' Fionna took the seat on the futon I offered to her. I turned on my clock radio hoping for something romantic; it was pathetic, that tinny, cheap, mono-tone sound. I slapped it off again and tried to smile.

'Have you thought of painting any of the rooms something besides white?' Fionna asked.

'I like the white walls, actually. It makes me feel kind of free, for some reason. No stimuli. It's like the color of silence. It's an old place: a bit more than a hundred years, I think. You should see what they used to paint the place. In some rooms, I've actually chipped at the paint a bit, with a knife, all the way down to the wood, to see all the layers the walls were covered in before. You know this room was actually pink once,' I said, motioning around. 'And light blue, too.' What the hell was that? I was making things up and I still sounded like an idiot.

Fionna looked around. Her leg hung out of her dress; you could see the light cut a perfect line down whatever angle of it was closest to you. Her toes, poking out the front of her sandals, were long and beige on the bottom, as if she'd been walking through sweet pancake batter. On one toe was a golden ring, a strip of solid metal seizing a strip of delicate skin. If I took her foot in my hand and pulled that ring off slowly, she would be more naked than the mere lack of clothes could ever provide.

'Do you like it?' Fionna asked. 'It's very expensive. I got it in the town of my father. In Nigeria. I could probably sell it here for enough for a car, if I wanted one.' Keep talking. As long as we're talking I won't try to kiss you, and then things won't go wrong. There won't be that moment when you say 'Please, no,' and then that awkward time after I apologize when we're both sitting here, trying to act out the scene that mirrors this perfect time before anything stupid was done.

'I've always wanted to go to Africa. I actually got David to put some of my money aside, a bit each check, into a savings account, and that's the big thing I was planning. Fly down into Egypt, go into Côte d'Ivoire, then go by land the rest of the way into West Africa. Do you go back there a lot?'

'Sometimes. I go at Christmas sometimes, to see them. Christmas, there's parties, things to do. Our house, where I was born, is very big, very old. You would like it. It was the magistrate's, when it was still a colony. Tall ceilings, and so much wood. My whole family lives there. Maybe you could visit. We could have a good time there. I want to go to America someday.'

'No, you don't.'

Fionna fell asleep on the futon, halfway through an Alec Guinness flick on BBC 2. Awake, I stared at her, petrified that if I fell asleep I would succumb to flatulence, or wake up with a viscous pool of my warm drool coating us both. So I just kept looking, scared she would wake up and catch me and then it would really be over. This wasn't like with Alex; it could not be as simple as reaching out to another sibling of solitude. Fionna was of another caste, the one stories were told about and pictures were taken of, so far above my own I was surprised she found me visible. I kept looking at her closed lids as the balls swam joyously beneath them. My ear resting on the mattress edge, listening to her breath.

Saturday, a lack of blinds combined with an eastern exposure meant that, as usual, I woke up at dawn blinded and sweating. Scared that she would awake and then leave me, I got dressed and went down to the supermarket to get some food, cook a breakfast so big that she couldn't move.

At Sainsbury's I resisted the urge to stand gawking at the incomprehensibly large selection of baked beans and pork products by jogging through the aisles, grabbing at staples. Back at my front door, I became sure Fionna had already vanished, that inside was a goodbye note with a smiley face but no phone number, but upstairs she was still lying there, pulling on her top sheet with the blind gluttony of the sleeping. Back down in the kitchen, I cooked in careful silence: shoes off, movements slow and studied, I even turned down the heat on the potatoes when the grease started popping too loud. When I finished, I could hear her above me. A repetitive, scratching sound. Probably clawing her way out the living room window. But when I climbed the steps, the sound was coming from the bathroom. Fionna was in the tub. Crouched down on her knees, working on something. Her back to me, I saw her bare legs. The right ankle was so bloated it seemed to belong to another, much larger person.

'You don't clean the bath very often, do you? How can you take a bath in this?' Pushing all her weight into the brush in her hand, scratching at the stain I had confused for permanent.

'I take showers,' I offered, pointing at the hose that she'd disconnected from the nozzle.

'Well, I prefer baths,' Fionna said, and kept scrubbing. Taking away not just the dirt but the discoloration that hung beneath it. Elbow jerking frantically, purposeful, as if she never wanted to see it again.

Saturday night turned out to be Fionna's club night. Iceni, below Piccadilly: all jungle, free cocktails for the best dancers,

ladies free before eleven, men a tenner at the door. I'd managed
to keep her around all day (you want some lunch, a nap, have
you seen this video, wow it's time for dinner) so I wasn't about
to lose her to my hatred of nightclubs. Once her ankle was
wrapped, I carried her on my back down to the mini-cab, and
then, in the West End, through the streets and into the club to a
table full of waving, pointedly attractive women the same size as
herself. 'My American' was how I was introduced, to which the
response was 'Oh, right!' with smiles and ungripping hand-
shakes.

Everywhere fags smoldering, fags burnt out, snubbed, fags
crushed and left to die at the bottoms of dark bottles. Bright fags
with wet lipstick stains perpetually kissing their butts. And for all
of the hunting for unspent packs and elaborate lighting rituals
(which usually commenced as soon as a new man stopped by to
pay his respects to their grouping), I seemed to be the only one
who was actually smoking, who was actually pulling the dark
cloud into me and letting it spill back, warming my nostrils and
shielding me from this room. It was the perfect evening because
this was the perfect arena for me to go David-less out into the
world: concealed under an unyielding blanket of sound, ob-
scured by a calculated mix of darkness and random, off-color
lights. Snug within the mist of tobacco, sips of my pint-cured
bursts of self-consciousness. Saved by music so loud that it made
my social deficiencies irrelevant. I was actually succeeding.
Everyone seemed very pleased with my presence, introducing
me to strangers for no apparent reason. The other ladies bent
forward to me with occasional questions or comments. Somehow they'd been given the impression I was from New York, so
I endorsed this misconception with several unprovable lies that
we would both forget the next morning. Fionna held tightly on
to my arm as if we were lovers. And then, just when her hand
was getting warm, an intro to a song came on that made
everybody at the table's eyes inflate as they reached out to clasp
one another's hands.

In the seconds it took for the beat to kick in, Fi's friends were gone, off to dancing. Foreplay was over. Fionna released my arm. Everyone was screaming on the floor, hands in the air, bouncing as it there was cash on the ceiling. I stood up to watch. Look at them, bumping, shaking, jerk, jounce. Fionna pulled herself up from her seat by grabbing my leg. Her head bobbed with them. On the floor, slightly below us, the crowd was spreading. These friends of hers could dance, and everyone in the room knew it. No partners: a flock of individuals, simultaneous soloists performing variations on the same work. The crowd grew still because watching them dance was more enjoyable than doing it themselves. I looked down at Fi to compliment them but her head had stopped nodding.

'Lift me.'

Thank the Lord – time to leave. Riding this mood and with a little drink to blame any embarrassments on, I could make my move in the cab home. I grabbed Fi into my arms and started heading for the exit.

'Where are you going?'

Fionna pointed to a wall. 'Over there,' she said, her finger pointing towards the dance floor, that place everyone else in the room was staring at. I walked. Someone brushing past with two drink-filled hands banged Fionna's out-sticking foot and Fi screamed demonstratively, digging her nails into my arm as the guy cursed his spillage and kept going. 'There. Over there.' I was directed to a high table covered with flyers. 'On top,' I placed her rear at the table's edge. 'No, on top.' I lifted her higher till she had put her good foot down and was standing upon it, where everyone could see her. Immediately, knee bent and bad ankle behind her, arms reaching out to the air for balance, Fionna started dancing. 'Chris, come on, come up and dance with me. No, come on, climb up. Now.'

'I can't.' I offered a grin as I yelled back to her. I really couldn't.

'Why?' Because if I got up there they would boo or laugh or throw rocks at my head. Because I wasn't made for the pedestal, I was unsuitable for display. No crowd would ever accept Chris

Jones held up above them. Philly had already taught me that, and who knew me longer than it? Definitely not the graceful Fionna, who reached out to tug my hand while still doing her one-foot shuffle. I grasped hers just so she wouldn't stumble.

'I'll dance with you down here, so if you fall I can catch you,' I told her, and she accepted that evasion, released me of the obligation of humiliating myself.

Look at the way she moves and imagine what she could do with two feet beneath her. Reluctantly fulfilling my promise, I began bobbing awkwardly below her, forwarding racial harmony by dispelling stereotypes of black grace with every pathetic jerk. But then the crowd took even that responsibility away from me. All around me, bodies stilling as they took her in. Little woman up above them moving like there was nothing you could put on her that she couldn't just shake off, radiating life so bright it might even burn your troubles too. Whatever made us alive, whatever it was that made us more than functionally bags of blood, she had it and she was showing it to the room. A sliver of God vibrating there before us. And I knew everyone could see her the way I did because they were all trying to get a better glimpse, pushing me out of the way to do so. Knowing instinctively that I shouldn't even be there to witness this event, the crowd expelled me, shoved me shoulder by shoulder back to the dance floor, now emptied. Fionna kept going; I could make out from over their heads. I don't know if she knew I wasn't there anymore, but I knew she knew the crowd was. That they were yelling for more and she was feeding them.

I went back to the table we'd been sitting at, picked up a drink I was pretty sure was mine. The other seats were deserted, so I commandeered a dark pocket in the corner, against the wall. For the remaining hours, I sat and played shepherd to the jackets and lighters the dancers left behind. The club made snakebites and the waitress didn't care how many I ordered, as long as she could keep the change from the tenner each time. So by the time the music ended and the only sound was my ears buzzing, I felt prepared for the solitary night bus home. But, as I struggled to get up again, there was Fionna, hopping back from the light to greet me, tugging on my hand once more.

'Why you come back for me?' I managed.

'Because we need each other.' Fionna giggled, hugging my waist tightly (or was she keeping a drunken man from falling down?). Propping me against a pillar and hopping back off again to call us a mini-cab out of there. Having the bouncer help me out to the car. Waking me up in Brixton by giving a pinch to my cheek and delivering the words 'Christopher, we're home.'

Sunday, my day-after embarrassment evaporated when Fionna walked into my bedroom, sheet wrapped around her, and said, 'Chris, I have a bag of clothes already packed at my last bedsit that I've been meaning to retrieve. Maybe you could pick that up for me?' Immediately, fueled by hope, I was on the tube to Hornchurch, riding all the way out to the East London address she'd given me. The trip took as long as my last flight to Amsterdam, regardless of how close it looked on the Underground map. Maybe, if it was a large bag, she might stay the whole week.

The landlord was a big woman and a cop, dressed in a uniform when I got there. Her jacket was off and I could see her bra hugging her fiercely underneath the white shirt, her back looking as if it needed to be scratched. Smiling, I said I was here to pick up a bag for Fionna.

'Well, I'm sure you are, but first, let's see the money. Mind you, I told her that from before.' There was a cashpoint a mile back by the tube station, so it didn't take me long to gather up the £180. When I got back the lady was standing at the door behind six suitcases, big enough to hide bodies and heavy enough to make me believe they did. I took a cab back to Brixton, paying the driver nearly forty quid for the ride. From the car I walked to my door with three cases in each hand, letting the handles try to break my bones as the weight hammered my legs with each step.

At my front door, the odors – fried onions, sausage, hot

pepper, and olive oil – all coming from my property. Inside, I stood at the kitchen door, luggage still in hand, looking at the place settings Fi had laid out on my table. 'Try this.' Grinning, she came towards me, one hand holding a spoon and the other guarding underneath it. She was wearing one of my T-shirts as if it was a dress; she'd even found one of my ties was a good belt for the outfit. My hands still caught inside handles, Fionna put the spoon's tip in my mouth and lifted it up so it could pour in. It was some kind of chili, I could taste the salt and the crushed tomatoes. When she pulled the spoon away, excess sauce dropped onto my bottom lip, sliding down to my chin. 'Sorry,' Fionna told me, and she reached forward and grabbed a dick that was already hard for her, pulling me down to her eye level. Slowly, with the end of her tongue, Fionna retraced the drip's path along my chin up to my bottom lip. When she reached it, Fi surrounded mine with both of her own, catching me in her teeth and sucking my flesh clean again. Oh, to put my hands on her, to hold her to me as hard as she was now biting, but at my sides my swollen hands were now stuck in the luggage handles, which made things even more difficult when Fionna started pulling me down to the linoleum. Her teeth released, and I wasted precious time trying to maintain contact with those lips before I realized that she really wanted my face to drift away.

'Talk to me,' she demanded, and my words began pouring confessions of attraction, instant love and des—

'No. Talk to me black,' African woman said to me, and neither one of us thought she meant Swahili, Yoruba, or Twi. Black. And not the black I coveted, not the one I was walking to. The other one. That was her price, the cost of this fantasy. Lady, do you know what you ask of me? Do you know what this payment says about my desire? Take it. So I gave that to her: released the ownership of my tongue to the sound it had been meant for. Oh, and wasn't that sound happy to be free again, eliminating prepositions and conjunctions with its loose grammar and curving my sentences into its drawl? Reveling in its parole and scheming for permanent freedom? Give ear to me,

Fionna. Hear the voice of the life I want to smother. Listen to what the niggers on the corner have to say to you. Her fingers traced the moving lips that spoke to her until those same hands went to my neck and pushed my face lower, down to a place I wouldn't assume clearance. Lips to lips once more. 'Keep talking,' Fionna demanded as my tongue took on additional duties.

My hands still stuck in suitcase handles, my arms outstretched above me like a gull in flight, I continued to rap my ghetto garble. As Fionna's moaning grew, I spoke louder. Wet words wandered within her. Fionna's fingers slipped to the back of my head and stayed there.

Days

Fionna moving into my life was an easy thing because the space was already there for her. My days became Fi's hand lightly shaking my shoulder hours past dawn, my own name whispered along the slope of my ear from her tongue. I rose, dressed, cut through Brockwell Park and listened to my own feet moving, the clack of brown soles on a black asphalt path amid rolling mint hills, mums with arms and legs crossed on benches smoking Silk Cuts and watching children in primary colored clothes hang from metal bars proportioned to their size. Joggers with pink faces and blank eyes and ears attached by wires to radios. Dogs with and without owners, chasing things that moved, sniffing the ground for objects to bite and chew and then let fall to the earth again where they could look at them. I stuck to the asphalt path, walked towards the lido, past the tennis then football courts, onto Brockwell Road and down to David's.

At his door I pressed the bell. Once to wake him up. Another to get him to rise with purpose. With time came sounds from the window ten feet above my head, the snap of a metal latch and the creak of old hinges, and then I stepped back from the gate to watch him (squinting eyes, the snarl of a confused, belligerent animal, shirtless regardless of the weather, look at the belly on that one). When the glass was open, his keys would come down like a flightless metal butterfly and I caught them with two hands, reaching high and then letting my fists flow low with the momentum so they didn't sting my palms.

Keys in my hand was the best part of the day because there it was, physically, in my hands: David's world, heavy and jagged and multiplicitous, held together by a ring attached to a black plastic duck. Everything he had was contained within its weight and I stood on the street alone with it, unprotected, unguarded.

I would find the brown, round-head key, slide it in the door, then walk up the stairs to the kitchen where I heard him yell, 'Make us a cuppa' which meant pour the old water out of the electric kettle and add cold water for the new. Lay mustard on the white bread and cover that with cheddar and put it in the grill hung above the stove.

While water boiled and cheese melted and brown man spat and farted in the bathroom beyond, I read the newspaper that Margaret would place on the table after she left for work hours before (always *The Guardian* and always placed back in order, section within section, without crease or jam stain, just like new although she had surely read it over breakfast hours before). When the sounds of his shower had ended I went back to the kitchen and poured one inch of milk into a mug that held one gray tea bag, then laid the steaming water on top of it. David would appear, in long pajama bottoms and still no shirt but maybe a towel across his thick shoulders or on his head like a frustrated boxer. He would sit hunched over, a few feet from the table, so that his head was nearly level with it as he held his tea mug close to his mouth with both hands. Sipping was the only treble. For bass, he might moan.

When Red Rose had burnt away the encrusted syllables he might begin with explanations of the night before ('After you left, I really tied one on, got right pissed') or show me a souvenir of his travels ('See this sign? I pulled it off last night. Right off a stone wall with my hands, right? I was mad, pissed out of my head. I used to chat up this girl that lived on Thorncliffe, number seventy-four. Lovely, you should have seen her.') or passionately reveal his latest fascination ('Mushrooms are the fruit of the soil. It's like eating the earth when you eat them. That's what it is.'). Then a walk to the third floor. David would get the messages from Raz, and we'd go down the blackboard in the center of the room, figure out the agenda and schedule whatever in-house or client meetings were needed.

But how long could that last? Particularly when the spritz of lager cans being opened marked the top of the hour better than Margaret's antique grandfather clock (the German one, with the thick oak sides, and the two brass pendulums)? Inevitably there came five-thirty, a time to pick up the downstairs before Margaret came home. A time to pull up empty and half empty cans and the ashes of fags and spliff, for the list of chores to be executed while David hit the shower again, this time destined to arise with more clothes than his pajama bottoms. Was the work done? No, but as long as people were contacted, meetings were kept and deadlines were met, I could do all the work I needed to do that night, downstairs in my study, complete now with the drafting table, lamp and file drawers that Fionna'd gotten me to buy, the only distraction being her calling me from upstairs to tell me when something good was on the telly ('Christopher, you'll like this one, come.'). As long as David was there every morning, guiding me, massaging the clients, creating the designs, Urgent could keep going. David took care of the business, dealt with the people, I birthed the ideas. I was good at my job. I liked working. I liked working for him.

If the pre-Margaret chores were quick (get vitamin C, cod oil, and ginseng from Boots, renew the subscription to the *Voice*, mop kitchen floor) I could make my disappearance before six having taken care of things. If the chores took too long it was just 'Do what you can do, I'll take over when she gets here. Wake me when you hear her keys in the door.'

'Are you going to wipe his arse, too?' Fi asked me. I was late. Only a little, but she had been waiting for me down by the ticket machines in Brixton tube station and that short homeless brother with the busted lip and the lobotomy scar had yelled at her. We had opera tickets for the Royal Albert: I'd never gone and she was excited she was going to show me.

'You know it's not like that. He takes care of me also,' I told her, going down the escalator.

'David takes care of himself.'

'David pays my rent, he pays my bills, everything. He got me here. That's how he takes care of me. He's my boy. Without David I would have nothing.' And without David, I would be nothing. Lady, you don't know it, but without him propping me up, you wouldn't even be standing next to me.

'That man will suck as long as you let him, and then when there's nothing more he will fly off like a bloated bat. By then you will be too weak to even swat him down.' Fionna stared forwards while she said this, as if she were watching this unfold. For a second she wasn't a beautiful woman, someone who looked just the way beauty was supposed to. For a moment Fionna was just a skinny little black girl, hair straightened, lipstick done, trying to look cute in a dress she had no hips to be wearing. She could be from Nicetown maybe, East Mount Airy or Ogontz.

'Fi, really, don't worry. David is cool. Just because he needs me doesn't mean he's using me.'

'Chris, who am I? I'm the one who loves you, the one who will always be here for you. I am the woman holding your hand.' Fionna's hand was a light thing, impossibly soft, even at the palm. The thin veins on top could barely be traced without looking. Later, when we got to the show, I held it during the entire performance, letting my hand explore hers as she led me through the sound.

The opera was a story about an old guy who married a young chick and then she cheated on him, and they all suffered, but that didn't matter; I was a Phillystine and didn't care about that silliness. What mattered was that we sat close enough that you could see the spittle shooting out of the actors' mouths, that the voices of these performers were so strong, their sense of the emotion so complete, that when they sang I could feel their sound upon me, vibrating the hairs in my nose, as loud as when you're waiting for the sub at Fairmont Avenue and the express roars by. What mattered was that here was a plain old Philly boy, costumed in a suit and actually enjoying the sounds of this world. The only one under these ornate ceilings who knew what malt liquor tasted like, what to do when someone starts shooting up a party or how to open a Krimpet without letting the icing stick to its plastic bag.

The Fourth

Chris Jones, the American, for once so proud to play the part of the Philadelphia Negro, the apron on and the coals going, cooking on the Fourth. It wouldn't be like home, no walking down to the Art Museum in the crowd's stream, everybody staring to the sky, the small balls of white fire streaking up until they exploded and fell casually down, paper burnt and still on fire drifting back into the crowd as we'd giggle and push each other out the way. When it was over, the pedestrian mass rushing off the Parkway in the newly established darkness. Me and my moms heading back to Suburban Station to catch the Chestnut Hill West, or if she had a boyfriend at the time, walking towards his car and waiting in the traffic until we escaped the side streets and got on West River Drive, joining the chained slalom to Germantown.

So that's what I wanted: to give a bit of what was me to the people I was now loving. To be like, Check this, instead of always taking. To show David what my life tasted like: lemonade with the seeds floating at the top of the pitcher amidst clouds of pulp, and real burgers, huge ones, with chunks of onion and reeking of garlic, and big beef ribs, and chicken (greasy bumpcovered legs or the smooth pink divinity of cleaned chicken breast). And everything covered in barbecue sauce, layered in it, cream rust that bit you pretty behind the tongue and on the roof of your mouth, the meat painted in its burgundy glory and then cooked hard and repeated until the sauce was a skin in itself, chewy and salty and the red-black of Satan's deck chairs. I couldn't cook, but damn, I could burn some flesh, out on the little deck staring over Brockwell Park.

Fi cooked the rest: greens, potato salad, mashed potato, sweet potato with marshmallow, corn bread, pancakes (I explained they were for breakfast but she said we could have them with jam for dessert), corn, broccoli, carrots steamed and cut, the cauliflower brains of the Green Man. It was a feast Americana, planned for months in post-coital discussion sessions and during Coldharbor Lane pub crawls as David himself made suggestions.

At three the doorbell rang. Margaret stood there, smiling, her hair tucked behind her ears, holding a bag whose weight was shifted from one hand to the other as she leaned forward to hug me.

'David's just gone to park the car,' and then a kiss, on one cheek and then the next. Margaret offered Fionna a hand, but Fi called, 'Hi! No!' pausing briefly at the sink to smile. So much food and nobody had even died. The bloodshot cartoon eyes of deviled eggs, bulbous baked apples pouring over with their own beige pulp and dusted with cinnamon sand, sourdough muffins shaped like volcanic islands.

'David is going to be completely enamored.' Margaret faced the bounty and held out her arms as if she intended to hug it all. Instead she hugged Fionna, who looked so toyish in the older woman's arms.

Margaret lit her cigarette on the stove pilot, the blue turning its white tip a haggard gray. Standing, she took a few drags, then stared at her fag, snug in the crotch of fingers. When she saw me looking at her Margaret laughed, reached into her Marks and Spencer's bag and handed me a large white container. 'A gift.' Within it was my childhood obsession, just the way it used to look behind the glass display case in Melrose Diner.

'Lemon meringue, right?' So right, nearly the size of a hubcap, those full whipped waves frozen in chaotic turbulence, the white valleys and baked brown peaks.

'David found the recipe for me.' I was kissing the taut cheek of a smile. 'Well then, I'm glad David was right; he said you might like it. It's rather sweet, isn't it?' It is what sweetness is, and such a day it was to be.

So rare to see them together, these women, especially with the fat boy not here to pull the attention away. Margaret looked younger when David wasn't in the room; maybe it was just because she wasn't frowning. When Margaret went upstairs, Fi squeezed my hand with her wet, cooling one, leaving me rubbing the soap between my fingers as she squeaked away on rubber sandals. 'So I can serve?' she asked.

'Yeah, in just a second. David should be at the door in just a minute.'

So an hour and a half later I said it, because I knew Margaret was uncomfortably, thinking it and worse, as his wife, claiming it: the absence that was now becoming clear.

'David probably nipped down to the shops. The off-licence is my guess. We could use some more beer. And I forgot to get the ice cream.' No, I didn't. Actually, I didn't care for ice cream: the ice made my teeth hurt. And the pantry looked like Stop 'n' Go. The food was getting cold and Fi, of course, was getting a bit chilly herself.

'We've got to eat soon. I can't keep reheating all of this,' Fionna didn't bother to whisper.

'We will, just a second. As soon as David makes it up the walk, we eat. I promise. Just come upstairs. Let's watch one of the movies. Margaret left her book in the car so I already started running the previews.'

'No.'

'Do you need any help? I could be doing something.'

'No.'

'Would you like me to kiss you and hug you and make everything better?' Comedic failure. Fionna turned away from me. The hair on her head was straight and long, most of it even hers. Unable to leave without having something said that would make things better, I leaned against the doorway, watching her.

That was my punishment, it seemed we had wordlessly decided, for me to stand there with a frown, wanting her to talk to me, only to be ignored as Fi move around in an effort to keep the food warm. Lifting and placing and closing and waiting and then repeating. Each flash of upturned ass as she bent to remove a dish from the oven became an accusation, until I became content with my silent flogging and went upstairs.

Two hours can go by rather quickly. If you're watching *The Great Escape*, for instance, and you start counting from the moment the title comes across the screen, two hours is not even long enough for Steve McQueen to ride his motorcycle unsuccessfully towards the Alps, or for Charles Bronson to float to freedom in that little boat of his. Two hours was, however, enough time to realize you didn't know when a certain nigger was going to arrive at your door, or what to say to the wife he had deposited in his absence. And if she was by birth British, regardless of the fact that both her parents were born in Trinidad, her destiny would be to sit a rigid deposit of angles, frozen by embarrassment, unable to share the anger and therefore converting it into pain and humiliation. I tried to give her something to read, but the closest I could come to a mystery novel was my copy of 'Benito Cereno,' which made Margaret even more anxious when she found it lacked the correct formula.

Fi was downstairs, seeming to make more noise than when she was cooking for real, when the bell finally rang. I ran to it before Fionna could get a chance.

There he was—

'Christopher!'

—drunk already, falling in the doorway. In, oh God, a glowing cherry Kool-Aid British colonial officer's coat with blue shoulder pads, gold buckles, and a white wig—

'The red-coats are here! The red-coat is here! Revenge for the Empire.'

—reeking of something sour and strong. How did he drive

here like that? Pushing past me David dropped a duffel bag in the hall and headed for the kitchen. Fi came out, and I was studying her face to see whether she was going to smile or scream when David pushed by her, glancing her with his hip hard enough to make Fionna's little body bounce like a marionette being slapped. She didn't even have time to cry, she was too busy making sure she landed right, and David didn't stop, he just disappeared into the kitchen. I went to help her but Fionna slapped my hands away, fast. In the kitchen, David was at the table, an entire husk of corn in his mouth, digging into the mashed potato pile with his fingers.

'Fucking hell, David, easy, man! Easy!' I was pulling him by his arms and he was giggling. When he turned to me he held out a collection of mash-covered digits, each one waving at me. 'Good,' David said, letting the half-chewed husk fall to the floor.

I got some paper towels from over the sink and wiped off his pudgy brown paws, 'You're a mess, cuz.' David was still looking at the food, his body slowing. And then with another burst he started yelling at Fi.

'Luv, you are amazing! This is just brilliant! It's everything he's been on about.' I turned around to see her, David's messy hands still in my own. Fionna stood leaning into the corner, her knees slightly bent, her arms hugging herself.

'Lovely, this. I can taste the butter,' David said as he broke free from my hold and lifted the remainder of the starchy mess to his mouth. Laughing, looking at me and smiling as he continued to chew. I tried to get Fi's eyes, but she kept looking at him, her face nearly devoid of expression as her body rocked back and forth. No anger, no tension, just not there. When David stomped upstairs, calling Margaret's name, I reached for her. 'He's an asshole,' was the first thing Fionna said, coming to life, hot and wet and into my chest as I hugged her. I said I was sorry.

'Obviously not too sorry,' she said, shrugging me off. 'You shouldn't let any man act like that in our house.' But he pays for this house. And the food. It wasn't that bad, was it?

'I don't care what he thinks he pays for. If Margaret wasn't here I'd tell him to leave. I would, Chris. I don't know how she puts up with him.'

Apparently she put up with him by pulling him into a small room (like my upstairs bathroom) and first yelling (as if maple could contain such trebles) and then, after he attempted to sing songs over her shouts ('My One and Only', first verse), by just crying.

I stood outside the door for a while, listening, wanting to help someone inside. Wanting them to come out and fill their plates so we could all talk about what a pretty day it was and where are we going to take that group holiday we've been talking about? When the door didn't open, I went back down to Fi to help her get the dishes ready. The kitchen was empty. The door to my study was now closed and locked. I didn't bother knocking. I wasn't prepared to begin an entire apology session. I wasn't prepared to admit that my dreams for the day had come to an end.

Back out on the deck, I made the perfect beef patty with my hand and laid it on the grill. The peace of coals. Me, my meat, my park. What a lovely day to be in Brixton. Sunshine being replaced by red skies and air cool enough to make your sweat tingle. I pressed down on the hamburger with my spatula so it would sing its tribute. I heard slamming doors inside, but I didn't know if they were for me, or for him. Didn't matter, really.

I saw the fireworks about six burgers later. I heard the sound, got excited, and when I looked up there they were. The first thing I thought was, look at all the colors. They seemed so out of place in this sky, like a Cadillac on the M4. Ducking my head inside, I yelled frantically for Fi, but she wasn't answering. The house seemed empty. Margaret's pocketbook was gone from the living room. The study door was now open, but the bedroom door was now closed. When I heard the next rocket shooting up I grabbed my keys, a four-pack from the fridge, and went outside.

In the park, David was sitting on a child's wagon; I don't know where he stole it from. His white wig had fallen off and hung loosely behind him, the ponytail caught limply between his flesh and the back of his collar. The red coat was open now and the bear gut had appeared, dominant and hairy. As one firecracker shot upwards the next was pulled from the duffel bag, his little silver lighter igniting a moment more of life. The sky was in its blue-to-black phase, and David's fire laid pinks and reds and greens upon it.

'Surprise,' David said without pausing from his ritual. 'It's why I was late, this. I had to go all the way over to Peckham. In the Fiat. Try telling the missus, right?'

'Are these illegal?'

'Yes,' he said, lighting the next one, watching it shoot up in a tan line, curve into a fall, and then explode louder than a car backfire. I could hear the sound echo off the apartment complex behind us and pass us again as it flew downhill to the east.

FEEZZZZ!!!!! is the sound of the whistle as one of these babies (huge like hoagies) flies up in the sky. *POCK!!!* times ten is what it was like going off. Between these explosions the polyrhythmic silence, Monk-like in its pauses. In the sky neon spiders threatened their own constellation, an electric arachnid orgy. *SPEEZ* the lighting of a wick was a brushed snare. Above us, the last shudders of energy at climax, shooting pieces of itself randomly away from its source.

'It's this guy I worked on Iron Guard with, the camera man,' he was saying to me. 'He's got a licence because he uses them for videos, right? But they didn't come in till today so I had to run out there, for the surprise. You like?'

'I like.' My head was on the grass and I could feel the cold blades on my ears. I was thinking about how I used to hold on to my mom's leather belt buckle when we watched them on the Parkway.

'So I'm going down there to see my mate, to get the stuff, the soldier kit and all, and I see this bloke from the Patterson Group. My old job, right? Not really anyone, this. Just a messenger. Arthur. Used to run errands for me, type that will be there forever. So I see him and I say, "Hey, Arthur, what you like?"'

and I'm all happy to see this tosser and I'm shaking his hand. And then I realize: this man doesn't know who the hell I am. Two years it's been. I worked there for eighteen years, right, and two years gone and it's like nothing. I've put on a bit of weight since I left and mind you, this geezer's never been a genius, but two years and he doesn't even know me?'

'Guy sounds like a moron. Forget about it.'

'You know they made me redundant? After all that time, after all that love. Love is right, that's what it was! They just cut me off. Thanks for the blood, thank you for your life, now piss off, cowboy. Had to go it on my own after that, didn't I? How can you work for someone else after such a betrayal? Got to give it to the wife, she stuck by me, walked away from her own career to help me get mine back together. Of course, she and I working together lasted about three months, but she did it, right?' David said, looking at me, not even drunk for a second, 'Fucked up, tonight I did, didn't I?'

'Yeah, you really fucked up.'

There was more lager so we drank it, lighting the rest of what was in the duffel bag. Smoke lines drifting above and around us, hypnotizing. The explosions were getting bigger. Looking back at the apartment complex, faces were at windows, adult, child, each illuminated with every burst. Smiles. This is me, I said to them, with a pint can raised in salutations. Thank you.

By the time the cops arrived, we were back inside. David went upstairs to watch *The Great Escape*. I stayed in the kitchen taking care of the mess there, eating while I put away the feast that had been left undented. The small British fridge was unprepared for such gluttony, and most of the food ended up piled on top of it rather than inside. When I was done and the dishes sat next to the sink in a dripping mound of tin and plastic, I went upstairs. David was passed out on the couch; he'd fallen asleep before the tape had rewound. It was hot in there, the open windows and balcony door didn't seem to be helping. I took his wig off, and then went to his feet to pull the thick leather boots off of him as well. He could sleep the heavy of slapstick movies, but he woke while I was trying to sit him up, get that wool coat off of him.

'My head hurts,' David mumbled.

'Sleep it off,' I told him. When the coat was removed I laid it on the coffee table, headed for the bedroom. Fionna rolled over to face the wall when I came in. Her eyes were open and she was waiting for me to begin repentance. There was enough room in the bed that I could lie down without even touching her. Quietly, I leaned one knee on the mattress as I reached for a pillow, then closed the door behind me as I went to put it under David's head.

Crack

Fi wanted a chandelier for the living room, cast iron, the kind you stick actual candles into when you lowered it down by its chain, and damn if she didn't find it, only three hours after walking into that big warehouse at the edge of Camden Market It should have taken months. I only agreed to it because I thought we'd never find one (the woman always knew exactly what she wanted, so much so she rarely found the thing that met her image), but there the bastard was, just like she'd described it in bed the morning before, and for a price that would have hurt in dollars let alone pounds.

'Look, I'm just saying,' I said as the cabby swerved before us, leaning into curves as he negotiated them, trying to get past meandering North London alleys to the Thames, 'we could have waited. I can't keep spending like this. I've got no savings left.'

'I thought you wanted it,' Fi whispered, staring down at the oversized cast iron spider in her lap. Of course I do, of course I do. It's a nest we're building and I love every straw. No, you don't have to pay for it. No, I already paid for it, I got it. You're being silly, you're not even getting work right now. No, I didn't mean that. You look great. The house looks great. I don't need the money. I love it, really, I was just saying.

Victorious, Fionna leaned against me, my head gaining pain as the cab's meter gained fare.

When we walked inside my flat the answerphone's red eye

75

was blinking. 'Chris, it's David. I'm going down to the brasserie. Stop by when you get in.' I hit Erase but Fionna, coming in behind me, had already heard.

'Oh come on, Chris. It's Sunday. Can't he leave you alone?' But he sounded like crap, didn't he?

'He always sounds like shit, doesn't he?'

He sat near the front, at a small table by the bar, a full pint before him. 'That's yours,' David said, pointing at the glass, its small careful bubbles, its pale complexion.

'Cider?'

'Nice one. Big hand for the boy.' David showed his palm to me like a TV Indian.

'Where's yours?'

'That's what I want to know.' And he yelled over to the bar and one was brought to him. Twin beverages, both cold in hand, were raised so that they could clink together. 'To the women,' he said, before the glassy sound, and when the sides of our glasses had kissed he raised his glass slightly higher to the room before dropping it to his mouth. I looked around over my shoulder, but there was no one but us and the TV that remained on and muted behind me.

'How's your little lady, then?' he asked.

'Fi? Fine, really.'

'How's the whole living together part going?'

'Well, fine actually. I mean, she's not working right now, first the sprained ankle and then just a lack of work. She goes into the West End like every week for auditions, but nothing. I love it though. She's always there. She feeds me. The house looks great, like a home. I haven't been under a roof with a woman since my mom passed. It's nice coming home knowing someone loves you.'

'Isn't it, though,' David said, then drank again.

'Yeah, but like, shit, just now, she's got me coughing up mad cash for crap to decorate the house, right? So today I start in with the "maybe we should wait" line and the next thing you know

I'm apologizing in the cab from Kensington High Street to Stockwell, you know? And it's Sunday, too, and I know those damn cousins of hers are going to be coming by to eat my food.'

'The Nigerians.'

'Right. She cooks it and all, but who pays for it? I hate those bastards. They come over and talk in Yoruba the whole day. The only time they talk to me in English is when they're asking me to pass something or telling slavery jokes. That shit ain't funny.' David started giggling though, staring past me. 'Well, maybe a little funny,' I admitted. He was still giggling, looking over my shoulder. I turned in my seat to see the TV again and there was a commercial, not a very good one. I turned back, ready to critique and complain, but now he was staring straight at me as if the cathode ray had never been invented.

'She left me.'

It didn't help to ask who. I asked when but he just shook his head not listening. I said, 'I'm sorry,' but David shook some more, then took the pint to his mouth and drained it. I was sitting before him saying, 'Oh my God, man,' and he handed me his empty glass, interrupted my 'Jesus, I know you must be hurting—' with 'Fill her up for the boy, won't you?'

When I came back, walking slow and staring at my hands till I reached the table, he was excited again, joyous even. 'Look at that, Chris, look at that.' Pints safely rested, I glanced at the television. Someone had turned it to an American sports show and there was Jordan, still young and in an away uniform the color of cinnamon candies.

'That's why I hired you,' David said. 'That right there.' On the screen was the night after he returned from months of injuries, before the rings and most of the shoes, when he went to Boston and flew over Bird for sixty-four points. Ripping that tacky parquet floor up years before the demolition.

'Meaning?'

'Meaning? Look at that! Don't you even know what you are?' He was drunk already, I was suddenly sure, because sometimes when he was drunk he could get mad in an instant, start yelling, even if he wasn't really mad at all. He was already spilling his beer, too. I looked back at the TV, listening to him talk behind me.

'Do you see that? Look at him flying up to the basket, legs pulled so far behind him they're about to smack his bloody head. He's got that tongue out, right? And that ball, it's pulled all the way back, see? Like he's going to have to force it through the net.'

'Beautiful.'

'You're fucking right it's beautiful. You're fucking right. That's why I hired you,' he said, pointing up to the set. 'Only you lot can do that. Anybody else, anybody else would never even think of it. Anybody else would be like "Two bloody points? Who gives a toss how you make 'em." But you lot, you're fucking mad, you make everything this frenzied scream. It's the same with everything. Blues. Jazz. That's you. That's you, do you hear me?' He grabbed my arm. I turned back from Michael to meet David's eyes. Just glass there, yellow and brown glass; did he even see me?

'Nobody could do jazz but you, who would think of that? John Coltrane could never be English. We just don't think like that.'

'It's just an Africa thing.'

'Fuck Africa,' he was yelling again. 'Fuck motherfucking Africa. Who the hell needs Africa? What the hell have they done lately? It was you lot that put Africa on the map. It's about America, and it's about you, nobody else. Fucking exploding oranges! Oranges shooting all over the place!' David started laughing, spilling more beer.

'You guys aren't too bad. Reggae, that was y'all.'

'Fuck reggae. One man, Bob Marley, and he was a fluke. The rest is shite. And Red Stripe is a piss beer, too,' he added, giggling. 'And I'm not even that, am I? I was born in Crystal Palace. Fucking Crystal Palace! There's not even a palace there any more, you know that? You'd think they'd rebuild it or change the bloody name. Not even a decent football club. Chris, that's the last thing I know that you don't: nothing good comes out of this place, nothing has in years. This whole place is dead, it's true. If it wasn't for Margaret I'd be in New York. That's a place. This place, you can smell the rot, can't you? You love it, you think it's lovely and you know I'm glad since I've needed you here, but the whole place is a corpse, innit? And me, I'm its fucking mascot. I'm decaying right along with it. That's the only thing left I'm good for.'

'David, you're the man.' I clasped him around the neck, trying to pull his spinal cord into sobriety. 'You made me happen, cuz. I would have never got out of Philly on my own. I'd be nothing without you, I know that.'

'No,' he kept muttering, shaking his head violently and then becoming dizzy with the movement, eyes squinting the vertigo away. 'Shit, why do you think I needed oranges?'

The lido, three hours later, pints and pints down the road. I went over the wall second this time, pushing David's drunk ass first. We undressed over by the deep end, him at his leisurely pace and me frantic, just wanting to get it over with, get him home, into his bed and safely passed out. Pants, socks, shirts, drawers, I laid everything out neatly so I could get dressed as soon as possible.

'Two minutes this time, you fat bastard,' I told him.

'Right. A minute or two. You got a match?' he said, tripping on himself trying to get his socks off. I noticed the cigarette hanging out of the side of his mouth, bouncing as he struggled.

'Why the fags, man? Since when have you liked plain tobacco?'

'She left a carton, didn't she? I think I'm going to take it up.'

'If you want to take up one of her habits, why not try reading some of her books?'

'I did. But they were bloody awful, weren't they?'

The water was cold, but still free, freeing. So much liquid in my stomach, in my blood, affecting my head, and now all around me. I touched the bottom, felt around in the darkness for change, and then rose to the top and did the backstroke all the way down to the kiddie end. Above me was orange-red sky, like someone had vegetable dyed the clouds (or cloud, since it was just one slab as usual). Wouldn't that cloud make a great duvet? Hugging me like it seemed to hug this city all the time?

I hit the back wall with my knuckles, stopped floating and stood up, sat on the edge, and looked around. There were children's things scattered about: yellow flotation devices, bathing caps with rubber flowers. When I had my child, this is where it would play, I knew. It would have David's accent and call him uncle, come home from school in one of those green and plaid private school uniforms (or public school, or whatever). We would hang out at this pool, sober, all day, reading the paper and licking flakes. What better world than that can you imagine?

I didn't know David was going to dive, never thought he would be mad enough to. Up in the air, hands over the head, sucking in that gut of his for once. Boop and then gone. Nothing to the water but a slight ripple in surface, quickly vanishing as it forgot itself. Nothing in the water at all.

I walked back to the other end, looking into the surface, trying to make out some brown within the gray. I started counting. 1, 2, 3, 4 . . . 27? 38? And then I started running, bare feet on stinging concrete, to where he went down. And there David was. He was waving up at me from underwater, big tube-steak arm moving in an exaggerated 'Hi there!' Was he smiling? It was hard to tell because the wind was blowing and the surface rippled, and sometimes he was there, sometimes he was gone. Sometimes David, sometimes just dark wet space, nothing. I stood, above him, watching him until he rose to the surface.

'Ugh,' I could almost feel the air pulling back into his lungs, his chest getting wider. 'Wooh,' he said, spitting and wiping his palm across his face.

'What the hell were you doing down there?'

'Sitting.'

'Sitting and doing what?'

'Listening,' he said, looking straight to the sky and my sheet of cloud. Below him his arms and legs made circles.

'There's nothing to hear down there,' I told him. David nodded, but didn't say anything else, just looked down into the water.

Not a word. Not even after we'd gathered our clothes and dressed again, had climbed back up the wall and made it down once more. Out in the open emerald of Brockwell, David just started walking away from me, towards the direction of his home. From behind, I knew his shoulders should never look like that, a collapsed bow, his head disappearing into his chest until just a little bump of it remained. I yelled, 'Big man, I'm going to talk to my jawn, tell her we're going out of town, then I'm a come crash for a while, maybe a week or two!' David lifted an arm slightly to tell me he'd heard me but kept going. I was too tired to chase after him.

Back at my flat my keys were Spanish cymbals, my feet those sticks that beat Japanese drums. *TOM TOM TOM*. Walking down the hall, up the stairs to the bedroom, knocking shit over like it was my job. Don't stop, keep walking. And don't wake Fi up, no no, because good moods were needed for me to escape and compensate for Margaret's absence in the weeks to come. Sitting on the edge of the mattress I made it as far as no shirt, pants down to my ankles, shoes on. Then I started staring at Fionna's ass. Goddamn, look at that baby, it looking at me. I started laughing because the white sheet was trying to contain it, but hell no. What was it going to do? One thin cotton membrane vs. Africa, yelling at the top of its lungs, 'Whatchu got that can step to this?' Nada damn thing. And wasn't it lovely, she lovely? My house, my blessed house, lovely? The fat bastard, lovely? My world, lovely dovely. Yeah baby, my world. That's right. I earned it. If it was a dead land, I was a happy fucking maggot.

The next morning, at eight, Fionna whispering my name to me, telling me to turn the alarm off. I rolled over and extinguished the sound. Through my sleep I'd heard the phone ring, but when I checked the machine I saw that Fi, in her effort to discourage David's habit of late night message calls, had turned it off. My post-drink body felt as if small, angry men had beaten it with sand-filled whiffle bats. Standing in front of the refrigerator, I drained a liter of Fionna's bottled water.

Dressed, showered, lotioned, I cut through the park towards David's. For a while I walked behind a woman and her dog. It was a big thing, some kind of mastiff, its face the size and expression of a man's. I paced myself behind it, watching the prams and the obstinance of joggers until I reached the park's far wall and made David's turn.

I was slow this morning, I was late. David wouldn't care, but I did: I was already past due in routing the proposed titles for our Thompson Foods bid and I was too tired to stay the night working, so at his gate I hustled to the door. I pressed the bell once, and then again until the blood fled my finger's surface, knowing as drunk as David was the night before, getting him up would not be a simple chore. Satisfied with the length of my buzz, I stepped back to wait for him, accidentally bumping into something that blocked my way, a large burnt log. I didn't expect it, I almost fell back into the gate before I caught myself. That's when I noticed the rest of the small lawn. It looked like the dumb bastard had decided to have Guy Fawkes early, and on his front walk. The area was filled with burnt crap, pieces of all sizes thrown everywhere they could land (on Margaret's pink roses, completely covering the small patch of grass), big chunks of wood and plaster and, shit, pieces of furniture as well. One half burnt object was Margaret's reading chair, the one her grandmother brought from St. Kitts, with the intricate carved pears. Then I realized, those big chunks of coal strewn every-where – all over this yard and every adjoining one, littering the sidewalk and even the gutters of the street – those were Margaret's mysteries. Dispersed without care like crab apples. She was going to kill him. And the odor: the place smelled like a mason jar of burnt matches, left to rot in the sun. Insanity, and chances were I was going to get stuck cleaning it up. All of it, until every ash was disposed of, every black hunk carted off. I'd worn my blue pinstripe pants, too, the ones I dropped seventy quid on on Neal Street the week before.

Disgusted, I looked up, ready to see the bear open his window with his smiling faux-guilty manner, ready to send those keys flying towards me once more. But instead of fat boy, instead of arrogance, carelessness or pride, what I saw through that window was the clouds above. There was no pane, there was no glass, there was no ceiling or curtains there, only light, space, and a plane drifting slow and deliberate far above. Through David's window on the second floor I could see the morning sky, a pretty blue thing this day, the color of Captain America's leotard. Even the sun, a rare guest in this place, shone down through the space after I had been staring for a while. Above that window, the third floor looked like the charred ribs of a whale. Urgent Agency, the place that had been my office, the place I produced, where my computer rested, where there were folders filled with the best work I'd ever done, had been replaced by a bunch of blackened beams, a few patches of ceiling that had forgotten to fall down.

I knew that he was gone. My brother. I knew that he was the ash around me. That the only place his voice now existed was in my ear and in the heads of others who had heard him. I also knew that whatever I could have done last night to stop this from happening, there was nothing I could do now. There was no machine or service I could think of that could put pieces like this back together for you. But for some reason Chris Jones just kept standing there, looking up to David's window, the back of his skull fixed to the top of his spine, unable to close his mouth or look down again. David's false savior, the one who'd failed to rescue him from even this fate, just stood there. Waiting patiently for something to move above him besides the smoke rising lazily from the feast now over.

Crawl Space

David's funeral was a quiet thing, particularly for such a loud man. It was just us standing there on a slope of cemetery land. I thought it would be more – we got the call the day before and I was expecting a crowd – but it was just Margaret and Raz, the former in black, the latter in a purple suit, shirt, and tie. No viewing, no family flown up from the Caribbean, no friends standing as monuments to the lives he had acquired. We were all that was left of him. All that hadn't been lost or pushed away before now.

It was still sunny out, kind of hot even, and I stood, uncomfortably, listening to the preacher's prefab sermon and the silences when he gasped for air. Margaret stood across from me, the coffin separating us, and the only way I could manage that was by staring at her ankles, at the bottom of her dress. Unable to look away but even more incapable of looking up at her. Anger, despair, or a blank stare – it didn't matter what I saw there because I couldn't handle any of them, or the emotions they were symptoms of. Fourteen years Margaret took care of the man and he was just fine. One night under Chris's watch and this is our next meeting place.

I knew Fionna was somewhere behind me, so when the lift started taking the coffin down, away from me, I reached back for her, one blind hand hoping to grasp another, but I touched nothing. Nobody was touching at all. Us just standing there, a couple of people alone at the same place, the same time. More like people waiting for an elevator than bidding farewell. Margaret was still and straight as the shovel dug into the mound of dirt she stood next to. Getting brave, I looked up at her, to reveal myself in exchange for a glimpse of the face she wore, but there was nothing to look at. She had both hands covering the space from her nose to her mouth, keeping herself from saying something, damning someone. Her eyes looked as dry as oyster crackers, like she couldn't blink anymore.

When it was time to drop dirt down the hole, I got in line with the rest. Margaret used the shovel, skimmed a little soil off the top of the pile and let it fall down, and then Fionna did the same, letting the dirt fall as light as hourglass sand. After Raz went, he passed the shovel to me. It was a cold metal thing, its green paint chipping off the handle. I dug it deep in that brown mound, shoved as much blade as the earth would allow, then left it there, instead reaching for the dirt with my hands. The soil was loose, dark, and I got a good sum of it by cupping my palms together. I let it drop in one solid clump. It sounded like a bass kick when it hit the door of David's new home.

When I turned around, Margaret was already driving away from me. The red Fiat popped into gear and ran: no limousines had been hired, no expense wasted on mortal formalities. So that was it? A life was over? Apparently, because Fi was already halfway down the hill towards our rented car. Moving lightly, her arms swaying, staring at her feet so as not to sprain an ankle on the slope. I followed her. My hands were still heavy with earth so I wiped them together till they were just covered in dust like brown sugar, the tiny specks glittering back at me. A finger in my mouth, tiny particles of soil found a stream in my saliva, a delta in my throat. I sucked on the rest of my fingers as well, then along the callused lines of my palm, leaving my hand slick and glowing with spit's hunger. Before me, fifty yards at most, Fionna had already reached the car. She sat in the driver's seat, starting the engine and putting a cassette into the player.

This was not over, this death ritual. There would be more. Tonight I would buy some hooch, some good shit, too,

American (David would like that), and I would come back and pour it on the grave. A whole jug that I could pour down and know that it would reach the wood around him, maybe even seep through. I would buy one for myself, then bring a box—

'Fi, where the hell are we? This isn't Brixton.'

'Well, no. I was thinking we could drive by Ikea, pick up that wardrobe we've been looking at, the green one.'

'What the fuck are you talking about?'

'I'm sorry, it's just we've already rented the car, haven't we? And look, we're already here.' Fionna cut off two lanes of oncoming traffic and found a parking space before they stopped honking. 'Come on! It will cheer you up! You need a new lamp, too,' she said, opening the door. I didn't even unbuckle my seatbelt. The tears were finally coming: long awaited, much anticipated friends. It was good sitting with them.

I was so weak. After that first realization at David's door, I had found myself back at my own. Nearly an hour after I had done the opposite, I was sliding back in next to Fionna, trying once more not to awake her. There I remained for the rest day and most of the next one. Feigning sleep when Fionna came in the room and refusing to turn on the radio or television, I successfully escaped reality up until Margaret called and confirmed my description. When the phone rang so late that night I knew who it must be, and when I saw Fionna's face as she took in this dreaded information, I watched as she realized that this was no simple flu I'd been stricken with.

In the days after the funeral I made up for my original cowardice with a full-fledged inquiry. Keeping my alarm set for eight as it has always been, I used my new abundance of time to get up, go down to the newsagents on Brixton High Street and buy a complete and heavy set of the dailies. Now, at my kitchen table, underneath the banging of Fi's aerobics upstairs, I hunted through the obituaries to see what had been mentioned of the one I had disappointed. But I was too late. After a week of scouring *The Guardian, The Daily Mail, The Sun*, even *The Sport*, I found nothing. Finally, I admitted my latest round of failure and harassed Fi into calling Margaret's answerphone to ask which publication and date I should request a back issue for. A week later I received an envelope in the mail with no return address. Inside was a crisply folded clipping I knew must have been cut by the blessed widow.

The obit was insulting. From the paper stock it was hard to tell, but I think it was from the *Voice*, which should have known better. A brief record no longer than my thumb that basically mentioned David's two decades of work at the Patterson Group, that he was a resident of South London, and that he left a wife, Margaret Crombie, behind. The last line was 'The pinuncle of his career was the founding of Brixton-based Urgent Agency, co-chaired by the immensely talented American creative director Christopher Jones.' Pinuncle. Did the copy editor bother even reading the paragraph, or did he just assume that respect for the dead does not include proper spelling? Or were they just too fucking stupid to know that a life like this should not be reduced to this burp. The last line I declared aloud, apparently screaming, because immediately a response came back to me.

'What the hell are you yelling about? Will you shut up? Will you shut up?' Fionna running down the stairs, waving the sound away with her hands.

'Look at this shit!' I said, tossing the article at Fionna. She wasn't ready; she slapped it to the floor.

'Don't throw things at me! What is wrong with you? Why are you being such an ass? Why, Chris? Why?'

Enter standard apologies here and continue with 'This thing, it says nothing. Nothing. Like he was some John Doe who faded in the night. It's not an article, it's a damn list.'

'Well, considering, do you really want them to say more?'

'What the fuck does that mean?' Continue with apologies, even more. That seemed to be half my verbal weight these days.

'I mean, come on, Chris. Don't tell me you haven't thought about this. I mean, she leaves and then . . . poof.' The last sound comes complete with fully complementary visual effects: eyes bug, hands go from balls to wide receivers.

'David was a fucking slob! Everybody knows that! The man was a pig. And all those books – he might as well have filled the house with kindling. "He fell asleep smoking," that's what Margaret told you, right? That's what you said Margaret said. He was drunk. You have no idea how the man could drink. The only reason you're saying this shit is because she left him the day before. And that's stupid. If it had happened two weeks earlier, you'd be blaming it on the smoke detectors.'

'If this had happened two weeks earlier, David would have just killed Margaret too, in addition to himself, the house, and Urgent.'

'It wouldn't have happened two weeks earlier because some-one would have been there who could protect him.' Someone who could handle the job.

'Chris, why don't you get out the house?'

'What? I get out the house. I go for walks.'

'Twenty minutes in the morning. Maybe fifteen minutes to pick up some take-away at night. Why don't you just give us a break.'

'He didn't kill himself.'

'Just get out the house.'

'I'm going to call the paper. Fuck that, I'm going to go down there and get the little shit that wrote it! Fucking disrespect!'

Fionna walked out to the hall and into the bedroom, where she closed the door. After a few seconds I could hear her music coming through, the same song she did her routine to for hours every afternoon, the same thudding vibrations as she practiced her moves on the wood floor.

There was a bottle of vodka in the kitchen cabinet over the washer-dryer, a gift he'd given me that I'd never touched before. Loudly opening then shutting the front door, I took off my shoes and slipped back to the small closet underneath my stairs. Moving the vacuum cleaner, there was enough room to sit down and a bucket to pee in. Upstairs, for hours afterwards,

Fionna walked around, watched TV, made numerous phone calls, danced some more. That night, when she was in the shower, I climbed out with the bottle drained, grabbed a box of cookies, then crept into the bedroom and closed the door.

Left

My cover letters went out to every contact I could remember, everyone I had been introduced to or whose name bounced off David's lips for one reason or another. Each letter said basically the same thing: 'I have been employed by David Crombie as a senior creative partner for the former Urgent Agency and I'm looking to continue my experience as an advertising creative. David often spoke highly of your work, citing both its intelligence and creative power, and I would consider it a great privilege to be able to assist in furthering your vision in the future.' Afterwards, when the phone did ring it was for Fi. If I got a call, it was just an assistant calling to say 'no openings at the moment' and 'we'll keep your résumé on file' before hanging up and leaving me holding a dead phone. Every morning Fionna told me to call them, talk to someone and try and get an interview, and some mornings that seemed almost possible, that I could just pick up the phone and do that. But at the end of each day I found that I didn't, because without David, what was I? Just some newbie with a couple of lucky months on his résumé, an outcast from a third-rate town across the sea. Certainly nothing to pause from a busy workday to talk about.

At least Fionna, after a dry stretch that had lasted as long as I knew her, finally got a job. The unexpected pregnancy of Topsy in the West End's musical revival of *Uncle Tom's Cabin* meant that the company was desperate for a dancer who was both small and black enough for the role. Fionna now had a gig six days of the week, including matinees on Friday, Saturday, and Sunday, sucking up cash every time she put a toe on the stage. It was a sign. Everything was going to be all right now. After Fi came back from the audition, after they called and left their news on the machine, we danced across the living room like it was Juneteenth, shucking and jiving around the kitchen table as if legal tender was raining on us. The part wouldn't start for another month and a half, when the now-Topsy went into her second trimester, so Fi had time to practice the role before taking it over. It was work, something I hadn't seen Fi get much of, something I wasn't getting at all.

So to celebrate we were going to eat food, restaurant food, where we would sit dressed fancy as heavy plates were laid before us. 'This will make you better,' Fionna told me. Since it was decided that true celebration means having someone else at the table, she invited one of her oldest friends to join us. Devina, whose wedding I'd attended a few months before, was the friend Fi had finished her A-levels with, the friend Fi called when she had good news. Her husband was a rich thug, but Devina seemed cool. It was Fi's day; I didn't care as long as there was something to eat.

Fi said, 'Meet me at seven-fifteen at Kentish Town tube station. I'm going to come straight from rehearsal; the reservation is for half-past seven. And bring a bottle of wine, a red. Or a Champagne, if you can get it cold.'

I couldn't get it cold: I couldn't even get my ass there before seven-fifty. I overslept and then a bomb threat at Kings Cross meant that I didn't even make it past Holborn Station, and then I was stuck in the back of an underachieving black cab, staring at the meter, trying to make sure it didn't go past the amount I had on me.

When Fi saw me walking down the block towards her she turned around and scissored those little legs in the other direction. Jogging, leather soles down wet cobblestones, I caught up to her.

'You didn't even bring the wine!' Fi said.

'I got stuck. A bomb threat, y'know? Blame the IRA.' No laugh. There was an off-licence a street ahead. Fionna turned and started walking to it.

'Babe, I blew my cash on the cab to get here. You got any money on you?'

'No. I asked today; my first check is next week.' There was a cashpoint across the road, so I skipped through traffic to get in the queue. By the time it was my turn, Fi was saying, 'We'll tell them I was held up at the theater. We'll tell them rehearsal went long, that I had no control.'

I put my card in, as always. Tapped my code into its screen, trying to shield the keyboard with my body as my finger poked around. I selected the amount: enough to buy a wine so good that Fionna and Devina and her hubby would forgive all tardiness, enough to pay for the whole dinner if necessary, enough to put us in a taxi home after the meal was done. I was expecting that cash, too, that thank-God flutter of the machine counting my dough before it coughed it up, pushing those multicolored pound notes my way. That's what this world had given me time and again when I put my plastic into the insert-here hole. So when, instead of the familiar cash delivery, the machine sent an error beep screeching out into the street, it was immediately clear something was wrong. Fi jumped like a deer after the hunter's first shot. *Insufficient Funds*. Startled, I looked back to the screen, at the out-of-place, out-of-land Philly message staring back at me. Lighting the whole street blue in the glow of its letters.

'Oh shit, we're broke.'

'What?'

'That's it. We don't have any money.'

'What are you talking about,' Fi asked, pushing into my side to read the electric declaration.

'I don't have any more money. Game over.'

'What are you saying, you don't have any more money. Wasn't there money in there?'

'There was. I think we used it.'

'How can that be, Chris?' Fi asked, looking at it again. 'Don't you check? Don't you know what you have?'

'I didn't think of it. David always just filled it up. There was so much in there.'

'Then how are we going to get the wine?' Fionna asked, annoyed.

What we had: four pound seventy, counted out in loose, lint-laden coins pulled from the bottom of her pocketbook. Not enough for Fi to go alone, lie about my absence, order a salad, and go home, but enough for two tube rides back to Brixton.

We stood on the platform in silence, me following her to the far end, staring at the tracks until the train arrived. The car was crowded. The only reason Fionna stayed next to me was that there was nowhere else to sit down.

When we got home, I went to the study and Fionna went upstairs to the living room. Better to be in different rooms than in the same room not talking. That night, I could hear her making calls, watching TV, banging on the floor as she practiced for her role. I sat at my drafting table, head resting on its cool white angle, trying to think my way around my obstacles. My visa would be running out soon, and technically it was only valid if I was working for Urgent, so I had to get something going on. I needed to call up our old clients, get replacement samples for my book. At least Fi got a job; money would be coming from somewhere. After a particularly heavy thump from above, the bulb broke. An electric pop gave sudden movement to the room, leaving me in the darkness, listening to the wind swim over the treetops in Brockwell. Feeling my feet get cold, I thought, Someday, if I get up, if I ever find the energy or motivation to, I'm going to turn the heat on.

Fionna came down about an hour after she turned the TV off. I heard her opening the door. My back to her, I could feel her placing her hand upon my neck, and then her lips there. I remained as I had been for hours. On the floor, Fionna crawled under the desk, awkwardly unzipped my pants, and took me with cold hands into the warm wetness of her mouth. When I finally got erect, Fionna rose and led me by the hand to the bedroom. For a second there was only flesh in this house, no worries. Sweating, naked, I wasn't even cold any more. Alive for the moment inside her.

The next morning, at eight o'clock, I went to get the paper, but since I didn't have any money I just circled the park and came back. When I got home, Fi's cuz Dio was carrying the last of her suitcases into his car. She was already in the front seat, waiting for him. Rolling down the window Fionna said, 'I'll call you.' Dio was trying to shut the trunk, making sure to fit everything so they didn't have to come back for more.

Reality

When I heard her keys in the door it all seemed silly: the crying, the whole not-going-out-for-days thing, the feelings of despair and destitution, the hopelessness, the eating of dry cereal and cheese because cooking just seemed too much the bother. A click in the door and that whole period was just comedic absurdity. Pointless drama. Now the reality that fostered it was gone and my Fi had come back to rescue me. When the doorknob turned, there was even this insane moment when I regretted her reappearance, where relief was replaced by indignant fury, a flash of self-respect and optimism where I knew she was a cancer best removed. The door swung open and I saw Margaret standing before me.

'Oh, Christopher, I'm sorry. I thought no one was home. I rang the bell, didn't you hear?'

'I thought it was the Witnesses.' Margaret was different: wrinkle lines had fallen smooth and her long bangs had been trimmed above her ears. She wore a jumpsuit that was baggy and white, and when I fell to my knees before her, grabbing her legs in my arms, I could feel how soft the material was against my unshaven face. On the ground, hugging Margaret's calves, the material ate my tears as I cried, 'Oh God, I'm so sorry, I'm so sorry,' into them.

'Chris. Up. Get up. You're being silly. This is too much.' After she pulled away and past me, I rose, followed her inside, wiped the snot and tears on my sleeve as we entered the kitchen.

'How about I make some tea?' Margaret asked nervously, refusing to face me, instead charging to the cabinet.

'Yeah. I'm so sorry.'

'Stop. You don't have anything to be sorry for Chris. Really.' She closed the cupboard and quickly grabbed my wrist, nodding each word into my face. 'You don't. Nothing at all.' She was a merciful liar.

'Can I have a cigarette?' I asked. Margaret let me go.

'No, because you don't smoke. And I don't either any more. Have a seat. Milk?'

As we talked, Margaret was surprised about all the wrong things: the news of Fi's leaving caused little more than a side-of-the-mouth, eye-rise shrug, but the fact that the loss of David also meant the loss of my career credibility seemed a surprise.

'Don't overestimate David's weight. He was an odd one in that world. Did he ever tell you on what grounds he was dismissed from the Patterson Group?' I nodded no. 'Embezzlement, right? The senior partners said they were investigating David for stealing over thirty thousand pounds.'

'David wouldn't do that.'

'That's what he said, of course. That it was just an excuse to "kick the nig-nog off the job". Their last chance to keep him away from senior management. I almost wish he *had* stolen it now. At least we wouldn't have gone so deep in debt to start Urgent. We wouldn't have had to get so many loans. The bank wouldn't have seized the house. I wouldn't be in this situation now.'

'What do you mean, they seized the house?'

'Not much of a coup, the state it's in now, but they're taking all of our holdings until I can cover the back payments. I'm working a double shift just to get myself out from the hole I seemed to have been left in. I won't even have David's old flat at the end of the month. The bank's taking control of that, too.'

'My flat? The one I live in?'

'I know, Chris. Really, I do. I wish I could do something about that. Four weeks, then they'll have it.' My house.

Margaret looked at the table, at the nicks and grooves it held. She was waiting for me to say something but I kept my mouth shut.

'Chris, you know what you're going to have to do.'

'I can't.'

'You're going to have to back to America.'

'I don't want to.'

'I know.'

'Fine. I'll just go to New York, get a job on Madison Avenue for a year, and then come back again.'

'Don't worry about coming back, just go home. And move on. If you go back you're going to have a life there.' Margaret reached for my hand. 'You'll find new loves, you'll get a lease, obligations. Life will go forward. Don't fight that. You'll never be fulfilled that way. You just have to accept it.'

'No I don't.'

'It's the way of life, Chris. My father came here to work for one year, and after that he planned to go back to St. Kitts. He was adamant about it. Thirty years later he's still in Camberwell. And I know he was miserable till he accepted that reality.'

I nodded yes because she was someone whom I respected and cared about, but I wasn't accepting shit. This was the place where my life was supposed to happen. I wasn't losing that. If I had to leave, I'd just go someplace where I knew I could never get comfortable. Someplace I knew I could never stay.

Down at her Fiat, Margaret gave me a kiss, a hug, and twenty fifty-quid notes for my furniture. I tried to tell her she could take it, use it to replace her own, but she folded the paper into my hand, saying, 'It'll get you back, get you settled. I was going to give it too you anyway. Do what you need to do.' Margaret got into her car and closed the door; I kept standing there, trying to think of something that would prolong her stay. After she fastened her seat belt, she rolled down the window but didn't say anything. She just stared at me long, as if she wanted to remember what I looked like.

I followed her taillights down the street, and after she turned I kept walking. End of this block, end of this pavement, end of this world. Looking around, just a bunch of row houses on a wet street of a dark city, but to me everything I'd ever hungered for. A place without guns, where most violence was limited to the arm's reach, where it took them a year to murder what Philly could disposed of in an up week. My home. A city *in* the world as opposed to hidden from it, a land whose intersections led to every continent floating. Success was defined by how far I'd run from the place I'd been born to. And that's what I would lose by going back there. But it was pointless: I could already feel the other place pulling on me, the familiar tug of a gravity I'd thought I'd conquered. Rubber band delusions, all it was, because now the tether had reached its limit and was tugging vengefully back at me. You go up, you go down, boy. Dogs shouldn't forget their chains. Fighting to remain on this London curb, I stared down and could already see the terrain of pain that awaited me. It said, Did you think you had unfastened me? No, I answered. Then I began falling.

II

Fall

Visibility was clear. I knew exactly where I was going.

50,000 feet. Nothing but a slab of asphalt embedded with diamonds, rivers of tin wires leading into a sea of melted mirror glass. Highways were faint white hairs, barely visible at all. A white slate of cloud hung between us, too weak to catch me. Planes seemed nearly still as they floated above the ground, each at a different altitude. Slow targets as I plummeted to the earth between them.

20,000 feet. Gray stalagmite skyscrapers rose out of its earth to meet me. Miniature versions of buildings gave me orientation, reminded me where I was, like falling into a living map. A city of roofs: the long, linked tops of row houses, the brick boxes of schools, the swimming pools on Center City penthouses. The small green and tans of baseball fields linked together by deliberate straight roads. Toothpick bridges stitched Pennsylvania to New Jersey, trying to close the wound of the Delaware. The Schuylkill, a snake laying on trees. The forest of Valley Green was just a head of broccoli.

5,000 feet. Falling, I touched ground at City Hall, bouncing off the metal hat of William Penn and shooting further west, leaving him nodding in my wake, a colossal novelty doll. Skinned a knee clearing the lightning pole of Liberty One, *swish swish swish*, its point shaking like a car antenna after my impact. Flying west, past office windows as people with jobs glanced up and then continued working. Falling down, meteor boy, returning.

Smack. On the ground. Ripping a body-wide groove in the middle of Spruce Street, right along the yellow lines. Heavy chunks of concrete cracked and flaked as I smashed through them, a finger stroke through a pan of brownies. Face forward, arms at my sides, I would have been screaming if the asphalt wasn't filling my mouth, a solid stream threatening to push back teeth from gums, giving me Dizzy cheeks as it forced its way down. Hard spaghetti spirals pressing their way into my nostrils, spinning pigtails to my brain. Black road digging under my fingernails as if they, too, were entries, trying to leave my palms heavy with its indigestible burden. The sound of an army of drums being broken, beaten until their canvases became the battered victims of percussion. Even through my road-stuffed ears I could hear that, hear the echoes of it as skidded from 49th to 52nd Streets.

Landing ended, I rose from my hole, my clothes raining dust. In West Philly, life kept moving. As I stood between them, men drove cars both ways down the road. Nobody even honked at me, not even glancing in their rearview mirrors as they sped by. On the pavement, old ladies still walked slow and scared, hobbling from one leg to the other like windup soldiers with gray wigs on, pacing a triangle between the supermarket, the check-cashing place, and home. Drug dealers still sat on corners, waiting for their business to come to them. Nobody to notice me but the rats who paused from their hunt to stand on hind legs and bob their noses in my direction, the cockroaches and the yam-skinned man. Smiling at me from the curb as I stood in the traffic wanting to climb back into the hole I had made there.

How long had he been waiting? Sitting with his ass stuck in the metal mesh of a garbage can, his legs hanging over the edge and kicking loosely like a child in a shopping cart. How long had he been waiting, staring skyward, hoping for the streak in the sky that would be me, tumbling down, back into his jurisdiction? Oh, and wasn't he laughing now? You never heard a joke that funny, the way he was carrying on. Whiplashing his head as he filled the street with his joy. I could smell the rot of his breath between the passing cars. A smile of randomly missing teeth made even more horrific by the fact that his face was actually handsome, that beauty could be wasted on an existence like his. Pointing at me, the fallen, with both dirty hands. Ha–ha, ha–ha, Philly boy come home. He would feed for weeks on this moment, smiling at me from his putrid garbage throne. Letting his cackles bark me down the road and blocks beyond, keeping rhythm even as I banged on Alex's door. Silencing only after I collapsed into her unexpecting arms and lost awareness there.

Home

'So what the hell happened?' Alex asked me the next morning. I'd woken up to the sounds of her getting dressed, of cabinets being opened and closed. Her apartment was so small she'd banged the couch nearly as many times as she passed it.

'It broke.' The couch was narrow, too, and not long. My feet had been hanging over the edge the whole night and now they were bloodless and numb.

'I didn't even get my chance to visit. Was it any good?' Alex's hair was a bit shorter, her banana peel skin almost brown. It was October, but the summer clung to her flesh as always, giving her a moment of negritude before returning her to her octoroon pale.

'No, it was perfect. It was absolutely perfect,' I told her.

'Then why are you here? Why didn't it last?'

'Shit, it was better than this place.'

' "Philadelphia Freedom",' a women with a voice that cursed learns to sing lightly. ' "I luv-uv-uv-you. Yes, I do!" ' Alex screeched.

'I should smother you. Nobody knows I'm home. You ain't got no windows, monkey-love. I could get away with it.' Alex hit me on the head and walked into the bathroom, leaving the door open as she stared at herself. 'Where are you going?' I asked.

'To work. To earn some money.'

'You have a shoot?'

'No. I got a part-time job.'

'What, you prop styling? You doing some assisting for another photographer?'

'Green's Nursing Home. The one up Germantown, on Schoolhouse.' Alex rolled her eyes when I let out a sigh.

'You got a gift,' I reminded her.

'Don't start bugging; I know what I got. I got bills. I can't eat off photos right now, so that's just the way it is. It's not that bad. Some of the residents are cool. They have good stories. So, what's your plan, Chris? You're home.'

'I get my shit together. I get out.'

'So, you're going to look for an ad gig. The Sunday paper's in the trash at the bottom. Don't make a mess pulling it out.'

'I'm not getting into advertising around here. Two, three months tops, then I'm gone. I don't exist here any more.'

'So, you going to try to poke around and get some freelance work? I'll look out for you, see what pops up. I know about one gig, should be coming around next six months or so, a buddy from Temple's working at the Philly tourist board. They got grants, I know they're going to be looking for stuff.'

Pumping up Philly to the ignorant. Not going to happen.

Alex's apartment only had one room, and she barely fit in that one. She couldn't manage me there and I knew she shouldn't. Momentum I was having, I might rip a hole through her floor and drag her down with me. So I started making calls. The first agency I contacted let me see their place that afternoon. The listing said: *Sunny studio, 275+*. Cheap enough that I could take it and still pay off the lease when I was done. It was only a few blocks away. I met the landlord in front, a small man with too much hair on his body to be human. His clothes were dirty and so was the apartment; the hallway leading up was dark with grease, the living room windows streaked and crusted. In the kitchen, hollow brown cockroach shells lay on their backs across the counters and floor like beachcombers. 'I been fumigating, y'know?' the landlord told me. The place was shaped like a lollipop, the circle being the room and the stem the kitchen with the bathroom at the end. I could hold out my arms and reach from the wall behind the stove to the window on the other side, and did so, and then wiped the black grime from my knuckle. It was a hole I could climb into. The offer of a cash payment meant that by night it was mine.

I walked back from the realty place with a contract in my pocket and keys in my hand. At the bank my pounds were replaced with green play money, all the same size; everything could be obtained with just a few folds from my roll. I passed a yard sale that had a futon; a Penn student gave it to me for thirty bucks and smiled as if she was an humanitarian. Did I look that raggedy? Bobbing and swaying, I thanked her. I didn't say, I went to college, too. That I was a man once that walked upright, clean shaven. Thirty bucks was a good deal, and she could think what she wanted. Huge as it was, I folded it over my head and I walked back home. It tried to swallow me with every bounce. I saw where I was going by staring at the ground, hating that I knew this place so well that the pavement was all I needed for orientation.

I got as far as Clark Park before I had to lay it down. It sat getting dirty on a public bench as I waited for my strength to return. I noticed the other men sitting around me, a parliament of the powerless.

'Yo cuz, you hook me up?'

'Brother, brother' – shrug, shrug, hand held out – 'got a little something you can spare?'

'Give me some money, get some eats, cool?'

'Yo nig, you want some smoke?'

'How much?' I asked.

'I'm the man. How much you want?' asked the dealer-bum, eyes skipping from Baltimore to Chester Avenue to see if anyone was coming, sitting down next to my futon on the unbroken end of the park bench. Connecting my thumbs and forefingers before me, I made the largest circle I could with two hands. 'Like that,' I told him, trading another green note for a green-filled sandwich bag.

I kept walking home, the futon on my head massive and white as a corpse, up the hill towards 46th and Baltimore, to my new house. Moving guilty, scoping for cops with the limited vision that the mattress offered. Trying to remember what an innocent man walked like so I could imitate him. Outside of my vision, I imagined my succubus Fionna and her parasitic cousins lining the streets and staring my way, laughing and pointing and feeding off my misery as they once did off my hospitality and ignorance.

In the crib, I flopped the futon down, dirt shooting out from underneath it in angry brown gusts. It took up most of the floor. I kicked it against the wall, made enough room to walk around on the kitchen side. It was a bloated carpet: no matter where you stood in the room, if you fell it would be there for you. If my head was stronger, I would have gotten more. Tied them to the walls with cable cord, nailed them to the ceiling and in the bathroom and kitchen, too. I would make a suit of futon, wrap it around my legs, arms and torso, sewing it down with fishing cord. Then I would feel good. I would be safe and happy once more. Outside, gunshot ghosts thundered off in the distance, reminding me again that storms got closer – that's what they did you see. Eventually the *pop-pop* would catch up to me.

In just a few weeks, I discovered that my apartment was not actually a space in itself, but rather a hole between the four other homes of my neighbors. Below, living behind the thrift shop on the first floor: the screaming one. Late night curses into the silence of the building. His favorite word: *niggers*. Two syllables that could be belched in anger or surprise or sometimes palpable awe, *niggers, niggers*. It was hours before dawn when the screaming came and I turned over on my stomach and sat up, my heart becoming a noticeable component beneath my shirt. A new unit of time was formed in the darkness, hijacked from dream, waiting for the next scream to come. In the isolation of my hole I dialed Alex.

'What?' she said picking up.

'He's doing it again.'

'Chris, didn't I fucking curse you out for this shit last time? Remember what I said and then hang up on yourself.'

'I'm sorry, but the guy, he's screaming again.'

'It's three-thirty in the morning.'

'I know! And this guy, Alex, he's yelling. It's insane.'

'Then go tell him to shut up.'

'Hell no.'

'Chris, do you even know what day it is?' What day it was wasn't important. I went back to sleep curled up with the butcher's knife I borrowed from her two weeks before, dreaming of striped snakes biting the bones in my arms until I woke up and saw my elbows were gashed and painted in blood.

Right side: the guy who lived behind my toilet. In the morning, when his girlfriend stayed over, his metal bed frame slammed chunks of plaster from the wall, for weeks making me think it was a washing machine because I didn't know anybody boned like that any more (no slight change in rhythm, no moan, sigh, or recrimination). The last three beats slamming with deliberate finality and then gone. After that, sitting on the toilet with my ear pressed against the wall, all I could hear was the sound of *Live with Regis and Kathie Lee* being turned on.

Left side: one damn song. Never the sound of a toilet flushing, of a door being shut, or even a cough. Just one damn song. Coming on about ten o'clock at night and going till midmorning. The same Hammond organ intro, giving rhythm to the melody, to the light rain of a snare drum. The same crying voice, too, begging to satisfy some need long forgotten. I could never make out the lyrics, or even identify the artist (besides the persistent suspicion that it was a Stax B-side). No one outside that room had heard that song in a long time. Sometimes it was so loud I could hear the record's scratches. Torturing me with the hope that every time it reached its end that it would be the last time. A moment later, fingers on a Hammond started it up again.

Above me: a rarely present owner and his always present dog, heartbroken and crying just as I was, a high whimper that would go for a few minutes until transforming into a bark until, feeling sorry for itself, it would stop. Only to break down shortly later and begin again, running tiny circles above me, enjoying the circumference of the room. Hours of nails clipping into wood with pawpads thudding behind. Lying on my mattress, staring at my ceiling, I felt sorry for it. I wanted to comfort it. I wanted to take it somewhere pretty and shoot it in the back of its furry skull. I heard its owner taking it out for a walk one night, and as soon as they were downstairs I turned off the lights and poked out the bottom corner of my window. The dog was a beige dust mop. The guy being pulled by it was older, tall with hair unfashionably large. He wore a security guard's uniform and tennis shoes. At least he had a job. It couldn't have been his dog. Some woman had left it to him. Across the street the beast, stopping to leave its fecal mark, looked up towards me. I ducked before it could start barking me out to its owner, name me to this place, inciting a riot from the city I was hiding from. Pulling me from my world of sleep and smoke, where I dreamed of getting off the tube at Brixton station, going up the escalator to the street beyond, turning left and walking towards my true home. The dream didn't come every day, but enough to keep me satiated. In the best ones David was still alive and Fionna still loved me. Alex was there too: we had all escaped this and everyone was safe and smiling. Happy and riding the Victoria Line tube into South London. Each time, I looked for signs that this new return was the real one, noticing the curve of the train's inner walls, the speed of the escalator steps, searching for any clue of authenticity. When I awoke, Margaret's number tempted my phone. But I resisted. I wouldn't be dialing until the call when I told her I'd be coming home. Until then, all that was needed was to roll some spliff or order food so I could lie down again. Outside Philly rumbled by, hopefully forgetting my arrival.

Broke

Midway through the second Philly month, all I had was fifty-eight bucks. My roll of crisp, tightly fitting, bills had degraded to a rumpled collection of soiled notes sitting on top of my television.

'What happened to your money?' Alex asked.

'Well, I think that's pretty obvious. I spent it all.'

'How? You never go out your house.'

'I order take-out.'

'You order take-out. That's great, Chris. Real smart, real responsible. What the hell you plan on doing now?' From the tone of Alex's voice, borrowing from her was not the answer.

'I was thinking I could use the rest of my money to buy some Sara Lee cake mix. And some rat poison, as much as I can afford. Then I'll bake the whole thing together into one massive chocolate tart.'

'Get a job.'

'I don't want to get into the industry here. I'd much rather eat the cake.'

'Get a temp job. Make some quick money. I'll bet it won't be anything that could tempt you to stick around. As a matter of fact, it might even make you as miserable as you seem to want to be right now.'

'I don't want to be miserable. I just want to be gone.'

'Well, have you been working on getting out? You said you

were going to come up with some new samples for your portfolio. How's that going?'

Next morning, while right-side neighbor's bed frame slammed into my wall, I went downstairs and read his paper. The agency that listed 'immediate openings' in bold caps told me to come in the following day for some tests, run through some drills, dress as if I was interviewing for a job. That night, I started getting nervous, fucking around a little first. There was all that weed, left over from the last buy, and since I would be joining the work force again it seemed appropriate that I should acknowledge the end of my obsolescence by lighting the rest of my stash afire. Unfortunately, there seemed to be no rolling papers currently on my premises, so I was forced to make due with my baby-blue toilet paper instead.

I packed everything I could gather into one collective log and set it burning. Based on the power of the hit I took, the initiative was a raging success. The sheer force of the blow was strong enough to make me completely unaware that, in the process of ignition, I had set the entire contraption on fire, along with my hand and top lip as well. It wasn't until I opened my eyes that I saw that the Buddha wasn't the only thing burning, and by then I was forced to swat the stogie to the floor. Before taking my morning nap, I frugally ate the burnt remainders to make sure nothing was wasted.

Hours later, when my alarm went off at two in the afternoon, my lip was really hurting. In the absence of a pilled pain reliever, I decided to take shots of the whisky I had left over in the fridge as I got dressed for the interview. This strategy first proved faulty when I fell asleep on the number 34 trolley and missed my stop at 22nd Street (making me a full twenty minutes late for my meeting), and continued to provide difficulties at the temp agency itself. For one thing, along with the first-degree burns I'd suffered earlier, it made the typing test very challenging. My fingertips felt like greased plums; I wasn't sure what language was coming up on the screen but I was positive it had never been uttered before. While filling out the application, I found it nearly impossible to obey the thin little underlines that the form mandated my handwriting follow. Fortunately, though I was sure the whisky was slurring my speech during the interview itself, the red blisters covering my upper lip must have been sufficient distraction, considering that the agency actually called me the night after.

Yes, they had work for me, maybe as soon as next Monday. A position with the electric company, had I answered phones before? Shit, didn't I just answer this one? The secretary said, 'Nine o'clock tomorrow morning we'll get the drug screening out of the way and then we can get you out on assignment. Is that okay?'

At dinner Alex asked, 'How did it go?' We were sitting on her couch, putting a sheet over the two cardboard boxes that was her table. I could smell the food so I was rushing, trying to get the fabric down.

'It's screwed. They wanted me to take a drug test first.'

'So what, you got First Amendment issues now? You're clean. You've always been clean, don't worry about it.' Alex brought the plates to the table. Red, steaming, smelling of hot sauce.

'I've been smoking spliff daily since I got home.'

'What? What the hell is wrong with you? Aren't you a little old to be acting like a jackass?'

'Alex, you smoke pot all the time. Parmesan?'

'I don't eat dairy.'

'Yeah, but you smoke a fat joint, don't lie. What the hell is this?'

'First of all, you're rude. Pasta.'

'But what kind of stuff is this?' I asked, holding something up with my fork.

'It's texturized vegetable protein. It tastes just like meat.'

'Monkey-love, if it tasted just like meat, would I be asking? You're weird. I love you, but I think you should know this. Ain't no tofu allowed in the ghetto, what's wrong with you? Tell you what I'm going to do: I'm gonna go out there, climb up a tree, kill us a squirrel, a big fat gray one, and then we're going to eat the fucker.'

'You gotta get that job, boy,' Alex said, slurping spaghetti strings into her 'O' shaped mouth, getting flicks of red across her chin and neck which she didn't notice. I reached out and wiped them off with my thumb.

'Take the test,' she told me.

'Are you crazy? I'll fail it and then they'll arrest me and send me upstate to Holmesburg.'

'They don't arrest you for stuff like that.'

'They'll deport me.'

'Insane negro, this is your home.'

'They'll take my passport, they'll make me stay here for the rest of my life.'

'Oh God, please shut up. Just stop. There're ways to pass any test. I keep some pills in my cabinet, goldenseal. That'll help clear you out. I'll cut your hair down too. Sometimes they take hair samples and check those as well. When you're done eating my food, go get my clippers from the bathroom.'

'The job only pays six-thirty an hour. That's not enough for this humiliation.'

'Well, when you get paid, maybe you can put some pride on layaway.'

Bald, clipped, and razor shaved, I walked home. The half-empty pill jar recommended two a day for two weeks to 'properly flush the system of impurities.' Sitting in their container, the stuff looked pretty harmless. Like ground-up lawn grass, green and fibrous, compressed into small, hard, jellybean rocks. Not something that could hurt you. No white powder, multicolored beads, painted coating, or gela-tinous shells. Twenty eight pills required, thirteen and a half hours to go. I chugged the first two, swallowing them and their pickled-ass taste down. Two more every two hours. Flush my way to freedom.

Midnight: force two past my tongue, put a jug of tap water

out, set the alarm, try to fall asleep as their sourness replaced the saliva in my mouth.

Two o'clock: warm oblivion, but the buzzer kept coming and then I remembered. I took two more pills, a swig from the water nipple, and a piss so long and loud that I was totally awake by the time I flushed it.

Four o'clock: the ritual was repeated only out of respect to my conscious self. Too tired to get up for another piss, I reached for an empty Pepsi bottle lying among the trash that cluttered my floor. The plastic rumbled while I filled it, going from cold to hot.

Six o'clock: the sun had returned but too soon because I needed sleep, so much more sleep. Always. Putting the piss bottle back I squeezed it too hard. Whiz splashed all over my hand. Tears from eyes. Mouth saying, 'Damn, damn', as I reached for a shirt to wipe my fingers down.

Eight A.M. the bell went off. Eight-ten it went off again. Eight-twenty I got out of bed. In the bathroom mirror, my head was still bald and I splashed cold water to watch it dribble down. I spy. The only hair visible on me besides my eyebrows were the little strands poking out of my nose. I grabbed the biggest of those and pulled, looked down and saw coarse black disembodied strands between my fingers. They would never catch me.

Nine o'clock: staring at the nurse's closed office door, piss stinging like Drāno wondering if they could take a sample from the puddle I seemed destined to make below my chair. Trying to think bad thoughts. David pouring vodka over his nappy chest and dropping a match there as he tried to get a fag started or David lighting himself with no fag in his mouth at all, screaming *Chris* like it meant *Ayudame* as the flames engulfed him. Fi at Dio's, sitting around the kitchen table and laughing about me and my slave-descended pedigree. Right then I reminded myself to devote more of my melancholia to Fi's abandonment in the future. I'd been neglecting that anguish. Apparently, even for a lonely man like me, the pain of getting dumped by a lover was easily overshadowed by the guilt of mortally failing a friend.

Almost bursting, I heard the click. There was movement at the nurse's door. But it was just another guy coming out, looking as unemployed as I was. Sitting down beside me, I could smell cologne and leather upon him. That could be part of the test: they put you in the waiting room to the point of exhaustion with a mole. Just like in *Kiss of the Spider Woman*. But that was stupid. That was the pee talking. I wondered at the dreads that hung like willow branches along his cheeks.

'Did they cut your hair?' I asked.

'Nah,' he said, confused, staring at the way the fluorescent lights shone off my dome. 'Nurse Howard cut yours?'

'Yup. She's a rough one,' I told him.

The office door kicked open. She was as big as gluttony could imagine, covered in a plantation of white cotton, smiling like this wasn't a cruel world after all. Reaching out to me, fingers of overstuffed socks.

'You got to go, don't you? You really got to go. I know that look. You wanna go now,' Nurse Howard told me, smiling, pointing me in to her office door. 'I know you. You went to Northeast, right? I recognize you. You used to catch the number 26 bus.'

'A long time ago.'

'Uh-huh. Your skin really cleared up good. Used to catch the number 26 bus, got off on Chelten. You remember me?' She looked familiar, but she could have been my twin and I wouldn't have known. At 400 pounds her features had become bubbles.

The office was too small for her; there was no way she was going to fit between that desk and that wall. Where was I to piss at? At the sink left of her chair? I could do that.

'You can do your business.' Ecstatic, I started tugging on my zipper. 'Not here, eager boy. You crazy, you know that? Open the door.' A closet? That would be fine. But when I hit the lights it was a bathroom.

'Take a cup from the dispenser, let the beginning of your stream out into the toilet and give me a sample from the rest. Try to fill half of the cup.' Half a cup, half a gallon, I didn't give a shit.

I was already squared up in front of the bowl, reaching for myself before Nurse Howard closed the door on me. Ecstasy, the truest kind, my head bent to the right side, my eyes squinted as if witnessing the glory of the Lord, the rumble of my water hitting the porcelain pond almost loud enough to cover my groaning.

'Try not to spill anything on the container, I hate that. That's the nastiest thing about this job,' Nurse Howard said through the door, as if she could see me. 'So I haven't seen you in a while. What have you been up to? You still live in the neighborhood?' My whiz swirled around in the cup making bubbles. I squeezed myself again and aimed back down to the bowl, letting it go till I was shaking my dick and arching my back in shivers. Finished, the plastic cup felt hot like a morning lover. I put it back on the sink, shook, zipped, flushed.

Looking at my clean head in the mirror I thought, I got you, I got you on this. Smiling-face nurse even recognized me; that must be a sign. Reaching down for the cup again, I almost spilled it when I saw it sitting there. Something was very not right. Something was, in fact, very wrong.

After a few minutes, I came back out of the room. I didn't know what else to do; there was no window or back door to climb out of. Nurse Howard was grinning, coming towards me, reaching greedy for my sample. It wasn't too late. I tried pulling away, to drop it, but her marshmallow hands grabbed it before it hit the floor.

'Careful,' she said, in a voice too loud for the room. Nurse Howard put my cup on the counter and sat back down, filling a blank label out with my name. She knew it without asking. My bladder ached from its ordeal, but my legs were getting ready to run.

'You're a fast one. That last dude was in there for an hour, listening to the tap run.' Nurse Howard was having a good day. She looked at my cup. 'What the hell is that?' Her head bounced back, seeing it. Holding my product up to the light, she swirled it around a like a glass of Merlot.

'*Green*?' she said staring at it. 'Will you look at that?'

Please no. Nurse Howard's head was thick with braids, red plastic yarn woven into them. The gum she was chewing was spearmint.

'Well, look at it! I'm not going color blind here, am I?' She wasn't. 'You sure this ain't lime soda?' Nurse Howard added, thrusting my piss over to me. It jumped in its plastic cup.

I backed up. I could still make the door from here; she was too slow to stop me, a strong arm could knock her to the ground. Or I could reach both arms around her and pick her up by her panty's waistband, throw her sumo-style. Find the stairs, keep running till I got underground to the trolley tracks. Go hide in the darkness between stations until I figured things out.

'Look!' Held by long, multicolored, cubic zirconia – embedded claws, the cup of urine came so close I could see my breath on it. Nurse Howard could feel it burning in her hand, I knew that. Hung before me, my juice looked like water from a fish tank after all the fish are dead and it's been left to rot for months.

'What's wrong with you boy? Is it St. Patrick's Day.' Nurse Howard giggled, her mouth a display of gold fronts. 'You trying to be slick, right?'

'Huh?' There was something familiar in her face, the way she popped her gum. I could see her getting on the bus at Wayne Avenue, dropping her token before her body walked on. I remembered a big girl, hanging against the wall, smoking, her eyes on me till the number 26 would come. Eyes still fixed on mine amid the chaos of the public school halls, a round baby face you didn't have to look at to know it was focused on you. This was my chance.

'I was thinking, it's really good to see you,' I said. Nurse Howard's smile elongated, its tips rising up towards her ears. I could do this. 'Yeah, it's so good to see you. Like back in the day, right? So just seeing you, I was thinking, why don't we make sure we don't leave our next meeting up to chance. Maybe we could plan on getting together real soon.' I was nodding my head and Nurse Howard was nodding with me, her pupils going from dimes to quarters.

'Like maybe we could go over to Walnut Street and check out a movie, stop by one of those Indian places around the corner.'

'I could deal with a little something like that.' She was blushing. I enjoyed making her happy. I think she even forget she held my piss in her hand. Maybe I *was* a mack, I had just never applied myself before.

'So afterwards, you could come over my place, we could have a drink, relax. I could get out the oil, give you a massage or something. Because, you know, I really got to pass this test, right? I really need this, to pass this test. I'll do anything. You know what I mean?'

Nurse Howard knew exactly what I meant. I could tell because she had simply frozen. There was still that smile on her face, but it represented nothing but muscles in flex, the leftover remains of an earlier emotion. I was not the mack, I was an asshole. For a moment, there was nothing moving in that room. She used to wear high-top basketball sneakers with big fluffy socks, I remembered now, and a long blue Georgetown jacket she would hide her body in even when it was hot out. Now there was nothing moving but our chests: we were breathing together, me and her. After a minute, our gusts could have ruffled the papers tacked to the wall, our ribs contracting and expanding like mice caught in glue traps. The part of me outside myself, the part that was a better thing than the sum of my actions, cried out for her, and for itself, that it was related to such a bastard.

'I'm sorry, really. Forget the test, I'll get another job. This Sunday, maybe we could go down South Street for breakfast or something.'

'Stop! Please.' Her words barked over my own until mine ceased. That other part of me, it was wailing in self-pity.

'I'll sign that you passed, just go. Just get away from me.' Nurse Howard turned from me and threw my sample to the sink. Who knew she could move like that, like Steve Carlton when the Phillies won the pennant. Upon impact, an emerald tsunami splashed over the sink, counter, her desk, the floor, and all the things each surface contained. Eager for redemption, I darted for the paper towel dispenser to repair the damage my juices had caused. I would have wiped my conscience clean, too, but that momentary disorientation, that brief loss of vision and facial numbness, that was Nurse Howard smacking me. That's what that was.

'Go!' she demanded. I heeded the directive, holding my jaw as pain and blood began pouring. Doorknob in hand, I turned back to her. Nurse Howard was facing the mess, her head aimed down and her eyes closed to everything. 'It's me,' I explained. Nurse Howard gave no response to this. 'I'm fucked in the head. Really,' I offered, but she wouldn't look up at me. So I went and caught the trolley.

Training

Whatever delusions any of us had that this was a real job, a true beginning, were extinguished upon sight of the others who populated the room. Our thrift shop suits, our pleather shoes, our poorly chosen handbags, makeup, and colognes – all meant to conceal that same look of undeviating decline, of limitless promise for failure. Even among temps, we were exceptional. I felt so at peace sitting there, in my street-vendor tie, my face covered with twenty-cent-razor scars, because this was the job I always knew was waiting for me. Now I was here and the vacuum of this empty seat had been filled. All pretension of other fates was now over. I'd finally come to the place I belonged. With nothing left to fight for or against, I was a free man. This was a job you never had to worry about losing.

Our trainer, Rosalita, spoke with the hum of electric can openers. Sitting there, her gray suit shocked to be off the hanger, reading from a manual with the electric company logo. There was no syllable she judged worthy of emphasis, nothing to denote the individuality of a page, paragraph, or word. For Rosalita, the dots at the ends of the sentences were decoration. Her only pauses were when she ran out of air. The most exciting sound she made was the dry flutter of a page turning. When we heard it we all leaned forward in our chairs, trying to see how many more were left to go.

Apparently, we were going to assist poor people get govern-ment grants to pay their electric and heating bills. They would call, we'd pick up the phone, write their information down on the application, then send it to them to sign. Six of us, three in each row. Guys in front, women behind us. Me in the middle.

At my left, Reggie Sizemas stayed awake by picking his dandruff, wiping his glasses clean with his tie, waiting for his beeper to vibrate. When it did, Reggie took it in his little hands, squinting as he brought it closer to his gumball head. When he identified the number, Reggie whispered either 'Business' or 'Pampers', depending on the call. Nodding his head fiercely enough to make his frames dance down his nose, shaking flakes from his scalp like dull glitter. In between those moments, Reggie kicked his stunted legs out from his chair and tried to impress Rosalita, answering electric questions with the vigor of Tesla. Clive did it too, trying to get on Rosalita's good side, but he did it by winking at her, complimenting her small, deep-fried hair, or the way her black lipstick made her skin look lighter. As Clive stared, he trimmed the wires of his mustache with tiny scissors or straightened his sideburns with a comb small enough for lice. Going 'Uh huh' every time Rosalita breathed in, nodding at her ass when she went to the blackboard and nudging my right arm going, 'You'd hit that?'

At the top of every hour, Rosalita stopped to smoke. The three women in the back went with her, as if it were part of the job. Quick steps to the glass lobby, out the revolving doors, onto Market Street, light up. They stood and laughed with cigarettes snug in the corners of their mouths, their eyes nearly shut. Beneath them, thighs sloped into calves and then shoe-capped ankles. When the ash crept down to their filters, they reached into their handbags for gum. One person pulled out first and the rest shared. They rolled the empty wrappers into balls and dropped them on the sidewalk.

Coming back into class, they were still laughing, their clothes stinking with the burnt fiberglass smell of menthol. The biggest one, Cindy, came first. Her face a big egg, her body an even larger one. Strutting past our desks, holding her purse to her hip as if there was money inside. Yvonne followed, lint in her hair and smelling of project rot. Natalie trailed them, silent, bent over, her buckteeth guarding her bottom lip as if you might want to take it from her. They had all just gotten off public assistance and they were not happy about it. They stayed awake during the training by whispering DPA secrets. *Lie about being on the pill and when he's in the shower get his social security number so you can sue him later. Send your bills in without signing the check, keep your utilities on. Take your kids to the emergency room and claim they feel dizzy for a free checkup.* Reggie called them the Welfare Bovines, but not loud enough to hurt or be hurt by them. Turning back, Clive tried to flirt by begging for a taste of whatever crinkly-bag goodie they hoarded, whatever oily, salted thing occupied their desk at that moment.

Training was as unceasingly tedious as high school. With remainders of my intelligence and will still intact, I could barely acknowledge its ramble. I stayed awake by thinking about Brixton. How the people would know what I had conquered when my train arrived in the station. How the trumpets would blare as the tube doors slid away. How the lord mayor would step forth with his speech prepared and I would accept his ceremonial key, then move on to the escalator that would carry me back to the life I should be living. Besides that, I thought about eating. Every day on lunch break, I walked across the bridge to 30th Street Station, got a fast food meal and hunted for a good seat on the wooden benches. I sat, staring up at the giant Greek columns that held a roof so high that pigeons spent lives flying under it, grabbing fists of fries while watching everybody who walked by. They were the best looking people in Philly because they were from someplace else, going someplace else. Every one of them lining up at the soft velvet ropes for the Metroliner. By the time I was back in the basement of the electric company, they would be in other states, this one a blur behind them. They would be sitting in soft chairs, eating food from the dining car. There was a special train car that just had food on it; that's what kind of world they were living.

Yam-man was in the station, too. It was November; the cold

had forced him in from the wild. He sat by the door at the southwest side, forcing the commuters to ignore him, ready to run when the transit cops arrived. He didn't bother to approach me any more. Some days he seemed almost sane, tortured by his situation and exhausted by what his madness had done. Other days he stormed around the station growling, chest forward, furious, angry at no one. Too crazy even to beg, insanity popped off his head like carbonation off freshly poured soda. On the better days he stayed in the station until five, I knew, because then he walked over the bridge to stand outside the massive black skyscraper that housed my job, sticking his dirty hand out to employees who tried to elude him on their way to the trains.

I went back to work hungry, rechecking my bag for missed fries, sucking the salt from my fingernails as I walked. Reggie bought his food from the pizza place on 22nd, every day something red and greasy wrapped in white. He never opened it until lunch was over, when I had no food or money left to buy more. Waiting for Rosalita to reappear, Reggie read the *Daily News*, and took baby bites, only bothering to touch half his sandwich, leaving the other side to stare at me. The meat: shredded dark brown, blanketed in a thick membrane of white cheese, a chewy orange roll holding it all. On top, a thin layer of pizza sauce. At the bottom, seeping out, a pool of grease I knew would be hot if I took my tongue to it. Reading his paper, checking his beeper, Reggie ignored me and said things like 'I think I'll wrap up this second half for later,' when he saw me looking too long.

After two weeks, Rosalita was gone and now we had our boss, Mrs Hutton, a tall white woman whose short brown hair streaked down her skull like snow on a mountain top. Her skin creased and tough, her teeth yellow and crushed upon one another so she could smile and still get you nervous. Clive winked at her. She asked if he had something in his eye.

For the rest of the year lunches would be exactly one half hour long, any time longer would be taken directly out of our checks. 8:00 A.M. meant 8:00 A.M., not 8:15. She would be monitoring our calls not to punish us, but to maintain quality control for the good of the entire office.

We got phones, large black boxes with lights to tell you how many people you had on line. They came with headsets that consisted of cushioned earphones and a clear tube that curved to the front of our mouths. They looked so professional. That morning I learned that if I cupped both hands in front of it and breathed through my teeth I could sound like an airplane pilot. Clive could talk to the ladies in the back and still pay proper attention to his grooming habits. Reggie figured out that if he aimed the end of the tube at the base of his throat he could moan like Prince's guitar solo from 'Purple Rain.' But then Mrs Hutton turned the phones on.

Reggie was still eating his grease, so when the first call came through he told me to get it, hooking his headset in so he could listen.

'Electric company,' I said.

'Hello?'

'Yeah?'

'Hello, is this where I call about getting the money for my bills?'

'I think so.'

'Well, I need to get me some of that.'

'Okay.' I was breathing heavy. I tried to start bringing up something on the computer but my fingers had gotten all thick.

'Is this the right number?'

'Oh yes, this is the right number I'm just going to help you through right now.' Reggie started laughing. Choking on his food, but still laughing. I was hitting the computer keys, hoping something would come up, when I realized I could hear myself hyperventilating into the microphone. It sounded like someone was getting mugged on my end of the line.

'Mister? Are you all right?' I hit mute. Reggie was really choking now, his eyes dripping tears and the veins in his throat bulging out. Blank faced, Cindy leaned forward and slapped

Reggie's back hard enough to knock his glasses off. Throat clear, he grabbed me on the shoulder.

'Cuz, you don't know what the hell you're doing, do you?' Reggie asked.

'Hey, I was taking care of it.'

'Holmes, you didn't listen to a word Rosalita said all last week. I saw you. You was just sleeping and doodling.'

'Yo money, you need to step your midget ass back.'

'Just let me take the call.' Reggie switched our headsets so that he was talking and I had to listen. He got her name, pulled her account up on the computer, got her an application for the aid, then hung up the phone and laughed at me some more.

'See, that's how a real man does it.' Reggie nodded till it was time to push his glasses back up. F real men. I returned to drawing circles in black ink on an empty aid application and planning what memory I would think about as I cried that night. Mrs Hutton came pounding out of her office.

'Who was that on the line?' When Reggie realized accolades were not to follow, he pointed at me. Apparently, I had the worst phone answering skills she'd ever listened in on.

'What are you thinking? Don't you know your job?' Mrs Hutton was getting madder at me because I was smiling, thinking it better to reveal my ineptitude to a boss early rather than fail them in the end.

'You keep working like this, okay? Watch the repocushions.'

Repo cushions meant that I was getting sent up to Outreach for the rest of the day along with Natalie and Cindy. Outreach was something new. Just from the way Mrs Hutton pronounced it, you could tell it was labor intensive. When could I come back? 'When you get your phone manner down.'

Going up in the elevator, Cindy stared at the lit numbers above the door and said, 'I don't care. They ain't breaking my ass.' Natalie looked more scared than usual: her front teeth nearly covered her chin. She was creeping to the back corner of the elevator as if she didn't plan on coming out.

The room they had us come to was almost as big as 30th Street Station, filled with cluttered desks and the people who sat behind them and stared at us. On the table before us were three large metal boxes with numbers, lights, and faded instruction stickers. Mrs Hall, the old white lady who was the supervisor, plugged me in first, putting earphones the size of turtles over my skull.

'What's gonna happen here is,' Mrs Hall started, 'I'm telling you'se because it's your first time up here, what's gonna happen here is we're going to turn on these machines and what they're gonna do is start calling a list of numbers we put in there automatic. First you're gonna hear some ringing and then you'll have your customer, and then when that person hangs up the machine will have already called the next person on the list and told 'em to hold on for you, so all you got to do is start back up again.' I raised my hand.

'Yes?'

'Can I go back downstairs?'

'No.'

I looked at Cindy, waiting for her to go Denmark Vesey on the woman, but all she did was shove a few more onion rings in her mouth and mumble, 'Hit me.' Natalie's earphones were almost as big as her head. They looked like they were trying to swallow her.

For the next three hours, the voices on the other end of the line kept coming. I couldn't get them to stop. I wanted to hit one of the buttons on the box, but I was afraid I would break something or it would shock me, bulge my eyes out of my sockets and leave my body smoking. A chorus of the broke, phones ringing across the ghetto, me on the other line. *I ain't got no money to eat, I ain't got no money for you. Screw you, turn off my lights, I'll learn to see in the dark. Please don't turn my heat off.* During one call, after giving my lines, an old voice said, 'I can't feel my toes.' I tried to wave to Mrs Hall across the room, but she yelled back, 'You can go at lunch time,' and the rest of the office stared at me from their cubicles. There was a click and then the call was gone, replaced by another confused voice on the line. 'Hello, I'm Chris from the Philadelphia Electric Company, and I'm calling to give you money.' Their poverty was a vacuum, devouring my voice before it even got down the line, their hunger so strong it could suck the flame from a candle.

Five o'clock came around just when I stopped believing it would. I walked home fast to kill the workday, but didn't catch the trolley because my apartment was a closet of dishes, soiled clothes, and trash. People drove by me in their cars, their radios on, going places I wouldn't know about. Close to home, I bought a forty, a gallon of milk, and a box of imitation Oreos. In the crib I washed out one coffee cup from my collection of crusty dishes, poured the milk to the very top, then sipped it. Under the milk, the cookies got soft except in the place my fingers were holding, and until it got dark I practiced dipping them correctly, getting every part equally mushy. I finished the whole box that way. I was tired of cookies two-thirds of the way through, but it seemed weak to quit without finishing the job. David would be so proud. See, I *was* a hard worker. Afterwards, the forty came out of the fridge and into my hand; my first time touching malt liquor since high school. When I got really drunk my apartment seemed smaller.

The Piper and the Pope

On Monday, a week after Mrs Hutton arrived, fifteen thousand postcards, red and yellow with a cartoon of a white guy with a big nose and scarf hugging himself above the sentence *Are You Ready for the Cold?*, went out in the mail. Two days later the phone started ringing hard. I handled a hundred and twenty calls each day, telling every person the same thing: how to get the government to pay their electric bills. Each call lasted an average of three minutes and I could handle fifteen an hour. I helped them through their applications, asked them all the financial information needed, then put their applications to the side to be sent to them. The phone was never not ringing; often I was cleaning up the last call with the new caller on the line. Nobody in the office talked to each other. We came in and went straight to work, took lunch at different times, and at the end of the day we were tired. Nobody brought the newspaper anymore.

After a few weeks, I could identify types of customers even before I got the information out of them. I could recognize the welfare voice that sounded as if the person was so tired they couldn't even move their jaw or lips to talk, that they couldn't even stand up, that they were lying flat on their beds, their arms at their sides, the phone rested upon the tops of their faces because they were too tired to hold it to their mouths. Most welfare voices didn't sound like this, but everyone who did was on welfare. The only energy that could be heard in the room was the sound of children and television in the background.

Some of the callers spoke Spanish or Polish or Russian or Korean or Vietnamese, and I figured out how to get a translator on the line. Those were good calls because they were always confusing and took a long time and even with Mrs Hutton eavesdropping I could get away with staying on for a while. In her office she had two lights for every employee, a green one if we were taking a call and a red one if we'd been on that call for more than five minutes. Clive insisted that you could tell if she was checking your line because you could hear a slight clicking, but Clive was a moron.

At night I dreamed I was answering phones perpetually. I tried to censor my thoughts, because I knew that I had callers on hold, inside my mind. When Alex rang and I answered, 'Customer service, how may I help you?' it fueled her 'Chris, what in God's name is going on with you' line. But I didn't want help, I didn't want to come over and talk about it, I didn't want to go visit a good counselor her friend used. I just wanted to sleep. I wanted more but that's the only thing I seemed prepared to accomplish.

When Mrs Hutton realized we were losing calls because of the half-hour wait just to get through, she brought in some new people. One girl named Angela was real sexy, and she sat in an empty seat between Reggie and me. Clive kept trying to poke his head over and get in our conversation. She had a short brown 'fro and earrings like silver tears. She listened to me talk with people all day. At night I lay in my bed with my hand on my dick staring up at the ceiling, thinking about her. I planned a whole future. I would take her back to England with me. She would be surprised to see how much more I was. I dreamed of coming home from work and us trying to make babies on my lunch hour. Unlike Fionna, she would love me, and if I ever fell she would catch me, too. The next day I went in to the job wearing the polished black three-quarters shoes I had bought in Camden Market, my stone thin-cut khakis and rust velveteen long sleeve gull-wing collar Armani shirt. The chair was empty:

Angela was gone. Cindy saw my clothes and said, 'The bitch failed the drug test, you sorry muthafucka.'

The next day, in Angela's place, we got this tall skinny guy who wore patterned socks as thin as panty hose. His name was Lynol. He was supposed to be listening to Reggie's phone calls but, even though he had the headphones on, he spent the day reading a book. I couldn't see the cover so I asked him what it was about. Lynol said, 'An inspirational novel based on the life of Jesus,' saying the first syllable of Jesus like it was a declaration. The next day I came to work and he was sitting in the chair next to Reggie again, so I sat over in Clive's.

Clive was gone for three days. Apparently he didn't call because Mrs Hutton pulled me aside and asked if I had heard from him (since I was the other complete wreck in the office, she assumed that I knew Clive intimately). While he was absent, Natalie sat in his chair. On the phone her voice was a whisper she hid in her hand over her microphone. I sat on the side of her bad arm and had to be careful not to bump it. She had fallen on her apartment building's front walk; it hadn't healed right; the lawyers were still talking. She swallowed painkillers with chocolate milk.

When Clive did show up he looked crusty and dirty, like someone had used him to wash dishes, leaving him to dry without rinsing him out. He came back for two days then disappeared for one more.

'You know that nigger's on crack,' Reggie told me.

'You're bugging.'

'For real. I seen that shit too many times not to know. My cuz was on crack. My old girlfriend from high school, she's a piper now.'

'Your girl's a crack ho?'

'My old girl, my old girl. Way back. Old school. She wasn't even my girl: I just kissed her.'

'You think Clive's on the pipe?'

'Shit, can't you smell that stuff on him?'

'That's his cologne.'

'Not unless he's wearing Eau de Crack.'

'Nigger, stop lying.'

'That muthafucka is smoking rock. Watch. Watch. Smell that muthafucka.'

'I don't have to smell him. Stop lying on the man.'

'He's all skinny too.'

'And his nails were burnt,' I remembered.

'For real?' Reggie asked.

'Yup. I saw them when he was on the phone, they were all brown and shit like he'd been smoking.'

'Damn. Now I know. That nigger is on crack.'

'Clive's smoking rock, huh?'

We told basehead jokes the rest of the day. When anybody asked where Clive was, we said, 'Smoking crack.' Some woman called for him and after she hung up Reggie said to the dead receiver, 'I'm sorry, Clive's currently sucking the glass bone. Can I have him call you back between rocks?' Natalie actually whispered for us to shut up, but the word 'crack' was too funny not to keep saying. Immediately, Clive rose beyond my original estimation. Crack cocaine. None of this succumbing to the ebb of destiny and letting life do its inevitable damage for Clive. He was diving right into it, gloriously! Head first and smiling, stoned, all the way down. Clive had conquered his instinct for self-preservation. I didn't even have the endurance to get a halfway decent alcohol dependency off the ground.

When Clive, my crack hero, reappeared, his clothes were dirty and he smelled like clear plastic burnt to black bubbles. He was sitting in his own seat, so I had to kick Natalie out and sit next to Lynol. At the end of every call Lynol said, 'God bless you', even though Mrs Hutton had already specifically asked him not to. I wanted to go rat on him, but I was too busy and lazy to get up from my chair, so I said, 'Hey man, you still saying it.'

Lynol chuckled. 'Well, I do believe I am!'

'She might hear you. She listens in on the lines.'

'Thank you. The spirit must have come over me.'

'She fires people. She fired my girlfriend.'

'Fool, stop lying, you never got nowhere with her,' Reggie piped in, hand covering his microphone.

'Oh, don't worry. The Lord protects his sheep,' Lynol smiled. Reggie was looking at me from the other side, wagging his head as if I was doing something wrong. When preacher man went to lunch Reggie leaned in. 'You shouldn't mess with that dude.'

'I didn't do anything to him.'

'It just ain't right.'

'So you got religion now?'

'I been had religion,' Reggie said, unbuttoning his shirt and showing me a thick three-dimensional little man on a cross. 'See.'

'How much did that cost?'

'Three hundred ones.'

'You go to church?'

'How am I going to afford church after I spent three hundred ones on this time-saver?'

'You don't like him either, you're just afraid of going to hell.'

'So?'

On the mornings when Lynol came late and I asked him why, Lynol would tell me that Satan messed up his alarm clock. How? He tricked Lynol into setting it to 6:00 P.M. instead of 6:00 A.M. Or the devil would have made him miss the express sub by misplacing Lynol's transpass. Or the devil would have simply plagued him with sloth. But then he would get happy and make a fist in the air and say, 'But I have conquered him this morn!' and I would root for the devil just as I had rooted for the bad guys as a kid watching Batman or James Bond.

Once, at around two in the afternoon, the peak time for calls, when customers usually had a forty-minute wait, Lynol just put down his head set, unhooked his phone, stretched out his arms, and yawned. Me: going call to call, looking when I could as he casually lifted his backpack to his lap, unzipped it, and removed an apple, browsing some of the loose papers in the sack before zipping it up. Lynol wiped the apple with a napkin he'd stolen from Reggie and then bit into it with a loud crack. I was on the line with a welfare woman whose depression had slowed her vocal cords down to a bored fog and all I could hear was crisp treble of Lynol chewing through my earphones.

'What are you doing?' I asked him. Lynol smiled.

'Having my silent communion-with-God time.' Lynol took another bite and I could feel juice or spittle spritz my arm.

'You're chewing an apple, not talking to God. You're chewing a fucking green apple. You might as well shove a carrot up your ass.' I didn't know what it meant, but I had the fire of the righteous. Staring at me, Lynol put the apple down on the desk, slowly ground the contents in his mouth, then swallowed it down.

'I love you, black man, just like God does. And it's obvious you suffering like a sinner. The question is, are you gonna change your ways before you plummet down to hell?'

I started giggling, because wasn't it a bit late for that?

The next morning I came in early to trade seats with Natalie so I didn't have to deal with Lynol any more. Clive came in right after I did. We were the only ones in our row. He sat down next to me. His fingernails were clean again, well trimmed, but his clothes were the same ones he'd worn the day before.

'You see, don't you?' Clive asked me.

'No.'

'Boy, I see you looking. The clothes. They're the same ones I wore yesterday, right?' Clive said smiling.

'They are?'

'Yup,' he confirmed. I smiled and nodded my approval.

'You want to know why?' Because you sold the rest of your wardrobe to pack your pipe.

'Why?' I asked.

'You know.'

'No.' Yes. Because you're on crack, and this is your new uniform.

'Cindy,' Clive said, lowering his tone but enunciating every syllable and looking over in her direction of the room, as if she could see his lips moving through the cubicle walls.

'You did that?'

'All night, brother,' Clive laughed. 'That was me.'

'Damn.'

'Let me tell you, that's a lot of woman too. I climbed that mountain.' Clive went to slap my hand and I let him even though I thought he was going to get Cindy juices on me. Between my eyes and his smiling image I saw a picture of Cindy's inhumanely large pecan butt, naked and aimed towards the moon. Clive would be tense and gritting, banging away from behind like a chimp in a nature film as she snacked on pork rinds and watched *Martin* on the black-and-white on the other side of the cluttered room. Children would be playing too loud in the hall and Cindy would yell at them to calm down or she would kill them, and Clive wouldn't notice any of it; his only concern in the world would be keeping his rhythm and controlling his load.

Cindy walked by a few minutes later, and when she passed she was giving an honest smile. For that moment I knew I could love her, that I could lay naked on a bed cupped in her arms, listening to her hum. She was wearing a new blouse today, a blue one; after three months I knew her whole wardrobe. Next to me Clive smiled big again and held up a plastic container of food the size of a shoebox.

'And that bitch can cook, too,' he added.

Philly.

Outcall

'Come on, we'll go down the Art Museum. It's Sunday; it's free till one.'

Nope.

'Then we'll swing down to Penn's Landing. They're having music today, this afternoon.'

I shrugged that away from me.

'Then what? It's a pretty day and you're in a rut. You should really get out of the house.'

Why the hell should I do some dumb shit like that? America is TV and I'm sitting right in front of the damn thing already. Nothing exists that isn't held within its cathode eye. Like Philly could offer anything to distract from its brilliance. Channel to channel click-clicking.

'Aren't you going to stop on anything?' Why stop – 21, 22, 23, 24, 25, 26 – when the next image might be better and yet no sight is worth settling on? When the chance to forget your self, your guilt, your pain, lies just one button away?

'Al, you know what we need on TV?'

'What?' she asked me.

'More obese black matriarchs.'

'Chris, why don't you go for a walk?'

'You just never see them on TV, do you? I mean, in real life we're surrounded by them, these rotund sassy black mamas who break everything down to a wisecrack and a baked-potato hand on a turkey-loaf hip. How come there aren't any of them on

TV? They should have a sitcom with one. That's a novel idea – they should have a sitcom centered around a loud, asexual negress, she could yell at her family every week, roll her eyes, you know how they do.'

'Sure.'

'Don't laugh, it's true – there hasn't been a good chocolate mammy on TV since *Tom and Jerry*, and then they just showed her feet.'

'Are you trying to piss me off? You know, you can go home. It's not raining any more.'

'I'm sorry. I didn't mean it like that. Not the woman thing. I was just telling funnies. It's not just mammies, what about the coons? How are all the spades going to support themselves? Used to be when a brother could bug his eyes out a bit that was worth something. How about this – check this out – I got a brilliant idea: why not put a coon in a fish-out-of-water comedy? Like this: take a jigaboo and put him on a set surrounded by literate white people not hip to his negro ways. He could jump around like a confused monkey for a bit, then they could all come to some mutual understanding. How about, for example: me. I could be that coon, fair lady. That could be my new job. Fuck advertising. Maybe that's how I'll get out of here.' I turned the TV off. I wanted to throw the remote against the wall, watch the black plastic crack and see the batteries roll across the floor. It wasn't my remote to throw, or even my wall, so I just sat there, hoping maybe Alex would wrap her arms around my neck, explain away my suffering and tell me how everything was going to turn out fine. Instead, after silence retook the room, she walked over to the window and adjusted a tear in the screen.

'So you've just given up then. You're not going to let me help,' Alex said.

'I wish I could tell you what to help with.'

'You get any work done yet, Chris? Any progress on your portfolio? Any movement towards anything that's going to get you out of this place you're in?'

'No. I can't think.'

'Well, when you going to start thinking? I talked to Saul, the guy who works for the tourist bureau. You could get on him about doing some work.'

'Alex, I can't.' I can't even explain myself. All day I think about getting out of here, and then, by the time I get off, I'm starving because I can't afford to buy a big lunch. Then once I get the food in me, all I can do is lie down. All I'm good for is sleeping. When I get up, it's time for work again.

This morning was to be different. Mrs Hutton was sending us out into the community to sign people up for assistance. Me and Cindy were to be the ambassadors. Cindy was chosen because she was fast and she wouldn't take shit from anyone. I was chosen because Mrs Hutton considered my presence generally disruptive and she needed the break. 'The only reason you ain't been fired is 'cause you sound like white folks on the phone' was how Cindy put it. So we had two days going around the ghetto in a mobile unit seeing what the folks we talked to on the phone really looked like. Like we couldn't just look around the office.

Eight A.M. was me standing in front of the electric company building with my too-light jacket on, my hands in my pants trying to steal heat from my balls. Cindy stood next to me, bobbing up and down holding herself to fight the last of the spring cold. When she pulled out her cigarettes I asked for one. She said, 'A quarter.' All my pockets had was three nickels and ten pennies, which I counted out in front of her.

'Don't you have a dime?'

'Nope.' I pushed my change closer to her.

'I don't want your dirty-ass pennies,' Cindy said, but she gave me a cigarette anyway, taking the nickels from my palm. I sucked on that thing hard, hoping I could get cancer before noon, cut short my tour of the land I was trapped in. Stealing its opportunity to gloat.

A white motorhome with the blue company logo stretched along its sides stopped in front of the building. Inside there was a miniature office, and we seated ourselves behind the desks as it drove on. I'd never been in one before, but when I was a kid my favorite show was an adventure about a group of scientists who drove an RV around the ruins of the post-Apocalypse. It was easy to remember as we drove through the post-industrial ruins of Grays Ferry, South Philadelphia. Redbrick tract housing with small, trash-laden yards, streets lined with large American cars in need of paint or death, telephone wires that bore sneakers like strange fruit on poplar trees. Too little space for too many things. White people who didn't look like any white people on TV or in magazines, broken teeth and hair cut jagged and crude, too-bright clothes made of materials nature never intended. White people as far from what they were supposed to be as fact from story. I'd heard about this place all the time growing up but had never been because there was no reason to go to someone else's ghetto.

Our driver's face was red and covered with wrinkles, redundant and overlapping like the lines in an etching. He looked like the people outside. His name was Bill and he offered us donuts from a white bag on the dashboard. They were all powdered and small, and after I ate a couple the sugar clumped around my tongue. Bill stopped driving when we arrived at a parking lot of broken concrete and faded parking lines, pulling up to a small row of shops at the back of the lot.

'I'm going to call in, tell them we're here.' When the door closed behind him Cindy expelled air like Houdini coming out of the water trap.

'I don't believe this shit!'

'What's your problem?' I asked.

'Grays Ferry? I didn't know they wanted us to come down here. That bitch Hutton, she didn't say nothing. Nothing.'

'Where'd you think we were going? Society Hill?'

'This is where that kid got killed.'

'What kid?'

'That kid, last summer. This is where those white people shot him.'

'Why'd he get shot?' I started lifting the blinds on the window, looking for bad people.

'Are you sure you're black? There was stuff about the fighting down here the whole summer. This is where the mayor came down. This is where Farrakhan was going to hold the rally.'

'Word?'

'Where the hell were you?'

'I was out of the country.'

'Where?'

'Out of the country.'

'You was upstate?' Cindy asked.

'No!' I yelled. Cindy bust out laughing, her eyes growing wide as her head pulled back and her finger pointed me out to no one.

'Nigger, you was upstate, you was on lock-down, don't even lie.'

Bill came in and drove us towards the front of the parking lot by the street, next to the McDonald's. We opened up the main door on the side of the vehicle, sat behind the desks, and waited for people to show up. It wasn't even nine yet. Cold air came through the screen, carrying the smell of fried pork and melting cheese. Cindy started talking about how hungry she was and got Bill to go get food for her. If ten dirty pennies would have bought anything I would have gotten something, too. My paycheck was two days' coming. 'You want some of mine?' Bill asked, and I said no. I couldn't play myself, begging from a white dude, but I kept looking at Cindy's food sitting next to me as it disappeared in a quick numb moment while she read a romance novel.

When she was done, Cindy shoved everything back in her bag, crushed it into a ball, and threw it in the trash on her way to the bathroom. When its door closed, I pulled her rubbish from the bin and took out her sandwich paper. Orange hunks of cheese sticking to the paper like melted plastic that I ripped off with my teeth. Buttered muffin crumbs I collected, balling them together in my fingertips into one caked salty mass.

The first people started coming an hour later. They poked their heads in and when they saw us sitting there they looked to Bill, who motioned back to them that it was okay to go to us. They were polite, though they often didn't want help, just the application, which they stuck into their coats or pocketbooks or bags as if to say 'You never saw me take this.' At eleven a short, skinny, brown-haired woman sat across from me and told me in an educated, out-of-place voice about her brain tumor. She was taking an application in case she lived long enough for them to turn her electricity off. 'Death brings odd comforts,' she said. 'All my life I worried about bills.' I wanted to give her something, but all I had were blank applications and pencils. When she walked out the door I thought, Like Schroedinger's cat, she's dead now. She would see David before I would.

By one o'clock a line had formed outside. We had built up a rhythm and the day was going faster than when we were hooked up to the phone lines. I liked working with Cindy because she was rude and it made whoever I sat with nicer because they were happy they'd avoided her. She was also fast since she never explained anything twice or entertained rambling questions, so while I took my time talking with people, Cindy whittled down the line.

During a break between customers, Cindy complained that she needed a smoke. She wouldn't go outside because she was afraid the white people would come out of their houses and hang her from the telephone lines like a pair of used Pumas. To torture her, I borrowed cigarettes from the carton Bill kept in the glove compartment. I stood by Cindy's window, puffing up a fog and smiling within it as she gave me the finger. Sucking poison never felt so good. That kept me going until I saw some tattooed pink men in jeans and white undershirts coming down the road. Throwing my half-smoked cigarette down, I ran back on the bus and locked the door behind me as Cindy laughed at me.

The next day we went into West Philly. I tried to do the job right since it was my home, filled with my people. I walked to the meeting spot from my house, happy to get inside the bus before the dark clouds above could fulfill their promise. Out the window was: trash like nobody had invented cans; kids running and screaming while their book bags bounced on behind them; men without hope even at dawn waiting at day-labor lines trying to be asleep while standing in the cold; the smell of grease (food, hair, body); stores that had opened and closed and opened and closed until the titles on the marquees said nothing about the contents. Trolley tracks where there were no more trolleys, just broken and twisted metal embedded into the road. Occasional cobblestones appearing amid the asphalt as stone zits, sidewalks that buckled and cracked underneath the roots of dead trees, maroon broken-brick sand and the sharded glass of alcohol-escape sprinkled on the ground. Every surface covered in the fading graffiti of written screams. Wee-ha, my fucking home, my fucking people. Wee-ha, my fucking source, my own fucking kind. Everything I was, loved, and wanted to run away from.

I was polite but fast so we could help as many folks as possible, because by eight-thirty there was already a line. I wore a tie, hung from a shirt with a collar, so I let my accent shape my words so they would know I was one of them and not a part of the machine, so they would stop being so damn humble and polite to me, like I was an ofay. 'Excuse me Mr Sir. Excuse me?' No, fuck that, I'm here to help you. I am you. Spit on me as if I was yourself.

At ten I had my first voice-box in person. She had no teeth and she held the device to her neck like it was an electric razor and she was shaving her throat. I wanted to lift her onto my back and carry her somewhere. Her face was unwashed, and I could see the flaky white lines of tears and saliva on the midnight softness of her skin. So skinny, so small, and she listened, staring, to every word I said. Her face nodding between her wool hat and the faded scarves cloaking her neck and chin from the cold. Eyes that kept looking until they hurt, until it was, Mama, please turn away, Mama, please walk away and heal or die because whatever void is there I can't hope to fill, whatever pain I am useless to erase.

There were three wheelchair customers that day. They knocked on the door and I went out to the street with the applications to explain it to them. The last one came when the rain had started and I hovered over her to cover her from the drops while she finished the forms. Done, I stood inside the shelter of the doorway as she wheeled herself back out. It was a long open parking lot filled with unpaved stretches that she maneuvered. I should have followed her, held something above her as she went. I should have gone home and cooked something for her to devour, a soup thick, salty, and green that made her fall asleep every time she ate it. Cindy yelled for me to come inside and close that damn door.

With the rain going, nobody else arrived. Listening to it hit the roof, I sat in the passenger seat next to Bill. He smoked with the window down and his hand hanging outside, his knuckle hooding his cigarette. When he pulled it in for a drag, the water dripped from his fist onto his shirt.

'This is my old neighborhood,' Bill told me.

'Yeah? You used to live in West Philly?'

'I used to live right there,' Bill said, pointing. 'You can't really see it from here, it's behind St Mark's. I used to go to school' the hand shifted, 'there. I used to buy my groceries from . . . there. I used to jump on the back of the trolley into Center City . . . there.'

'I live here now.'

'Yeah? Nobody I know does anymore. No more jobs.' The man could take half a fag down with one puff. 'Y'know, it hurts, really, seeing it like this. I'm not the crying type or nothing, but it hurts. It's hard to deal with.' Of course it hurts. It's pain. Nobody's feeling happy. Maybe you never should have left. Maybe we never should have come here. Maybe everybody should run so far away they don't have to see any of it any more. Leave it vacant like half the homes that line the street already are.

I walked back to the main cabin and sat next to Cindy, and

she rolled her eyes at me. 'Why you talking to that honky?' she asked as she got up for the bathroom. When its door locked, I walked to the trash. There were a few cold fries at the bottom of her lunch bag. Nice and chewy in my mouth.

Dancing

The women's checks bounced. The temp place messed up, didn't switch enough to the proper account. The brothers were protected from the error because we always went to the agency to pick up our pay in person instead of waiting for them to mail it out (we were usually broke first). We felt bad for them, but excited and lucky, too. It was decided we should honor the good fortune by getting drunk.

'I know this jawn, it'll be perfect. They sell forties for four dollars. They got a little show going on, you ain't seen nothing like this shit. It ain't the type of place you tell Lynol about. And the cover's hardly nothing,' Clive told us. Reggie said he wasn't going up in no North Philly gangsta bar. 'Don't worry about it, this jawn is cool. I'm telling you,' Clive insisted. I sided with Clive until Reggie relented, then we were off to Sodom with a tour guide. I was going to get wrecked tonight.

It was dark, it was humid, we were at the front steps of an abandoned row house. Clive knocked on the front door four times and a small wooden window opened up at eye-level.

'I got three coming in,' Clive said into it. The window stayed open silently for a moment, then there were sounds of the door unlocking. I was suddenly tired. I wanted to go home to my hovel where the only danger was myself. There were too many locks for anyone to have on one door, endless clicking and absurd disengaging until it finally opened to let us in one at a time.

There had to be three of them on the other side, grabbing us with their thick hands and feeling us down. The smell was as strong as the musk in the lion's den at the zoo, just not as nice: sweat, the overriding heat of too many bodies in an enclosed space, sperm cold and liquid and going bad on the floor like sour cream, perfume that lays cheap over stank like sugar on shit. No windows, no light but the sparse colored illumination coming from the top of the stairs. A gutted row house, no furniture or separating walls. Space without obstruction except for the black outlines of folding chairs, some with people sitting in them. Shapes that seemed old and accepting of the situation. A few alone but others with female bodies on them, slight liquid movement in the dull darkness. Once we had been searched the guard said, 'Stay here' and walked over to the stairwell, shining a flashlight beam along the angle of the steps three times. Another three light flashes down and we were given the clearance to go up.

'Give ten dollars to the man at the top,' the guard with the flashlight told us. It was too dark to see his face.

On the second floor we were searched again by a tall, overweight bald brother who rose from a lawn chair to do so. 'Gimme twenty dollars,' he said. Even in that light I could see Clive flinch, but he pulled the money out, so me and Reggie followed.

There were women in the room. The round brownness of their bodies blended into the shadow, their shapes revealed only by their movements and the reflection of the few muted lights upon the sides of their wet flesh. There were men. Seated with the expressionless silence of subway riders. The smell was strongest on this floor, its source. Clive started walking to the back of the room and we closely followed. The floorboards hummed with the music, plaster dust fell from the walls to its rhythm. I almost tripped over a patch of plastic lawn grass raised on a platform four inches off the ground; a lady was dancing on it. Leaning away from the mini-stage, I brushed the knee of a woman sitting on a man's lap. She was leaning forward, her back to him, her hands on her thighs as if she was peeing. I excused myself but she didn't look up, concentrating instead on the small round circles she was carving into his lap.

We stopped and seated ourselves at a loose cluster of chairs. It began to register that the women in the room were topless, some apparently naked. The surrealism of the nudity of strangers, of their panted breaths.

'What do we do now?' Whatever it was I was getting it done and getting out of here.

'Five dollars, y'all. Five dollars and they grind on your lap for a whole song. Five dollars more for anything extra. Try to get them just when the music starts so you can get your booty worth.'

The room was small, thin, and long and filled with couplings of seated men and the women who pushed their asses into them. Slow-moving crotch riders grinding slurred versions of the beat of the room. Clive waved a folded five-dollar bill to an incoming shape until he had a woman before him. The bill caught between her teeth, her legs spread over his lap, one hand on the back of the chair and another at his groin.

'You got any money?' Reggie asked me.

'A little. I got like ten ones. Fifteen maybe.'

'I got ten.'

'I ain't trying to spend it,' I told him.

'Shit, *you here.*'

'Yeah, but I'm trying to eat on that.'

The woman on Clive's lap thrust her tailbone into him like she was trying to slam her asshole through to the chair. She stared at the top of his head like she was landing blows. A young one, long hair that even in the dark looked like a wig, her thin upperbody flanked by the bulbous weight that exploded past her waist and kept going down. She looked like a cousin I had, from Delaware, the one who went to college for accounting. Song over, she stood up, almost getting away before Clive found the next five in his pockets. Past him a woman was holding an old man's dick in her right hand, his leg the pivot of the flurried flapping of her arm. He raised a wrinkled hand to her face and she kissed it quickly, then lifted her gaze to the ceiling until he slid his claw back down. Old man, old clothes, wearing a hat as if people still wore them any more. I wanted to save her, then him, somehow, from something, but then they kept going, flapping and moaning.

Reggie had a woman on him. Her calf rubbed against mine with the rhythm of her dance, but she didn't seem to care. Ladies without partners circled the tight space, weaving slowly between the chairs, waiting for one of the seated men to pull on their arms so they could earn some money. Some wore small black G-strings from which hair climbed out. One woman, older and large, wore thick white underpants that glowed in this darkness. Cottonal Y-fronts, I recognized. Must have got them in the West Indies; they didn't sell them in America. I bet she was comfortable.

Because I was alone, ladies began to orbit. When one came close I would turn my head and look past them. Reggie sat like the Lincoln Memorial while the woman on top of him bounced, her small pancake breasts flapping in front of his eyes. Over to their left, a couple stood, her leaning against the wall, panties pulled down to her thighs. She was looking over her shoulder, telling him to hurry up. His hands were on her waist, his ass vibrating like humming bird wings.

'Hey baby, let me get on there,' a voice said as she began to straddle me. Fingernails on my neck, weight bearing down on my thighs.

'I don't have any money,' I told her. It didn't come out as loud as I wanted.

'It ain't all about money, baby,' she told me, pushing her crotch into mine. I could feel it reaching down into me, searching, looking for something to take hold of. A thick arm brushed by my face on its way to the chair and covered my cheek in cold liquid that stunk of spray deodorant and pointless masturbation. The next song had a fast beat, and she leaned forward trying to shake her breasts across my face, showering me in the dead liquid that coated her body. It slipped between my lips and tasted of nail polish remover.

'Come on, baby, how you feeling?' My rider reached down at my lap and was greeted only with the empty loose material of my pants. She pushed her hand deeper, farther, eventually locating the flaccid thing that avoided her. She walked off without looking at me.

'Wow, she did that shit for free?' Clive asked.

'Yeah,' I told him.

'You the man,' Clive said. But I was not a man. I was a thing in a hole. Shivering, wondering why I dug myself down in the first place.

I got up to leave. Nobody said anything, so I didn't offer an explanation. I just concentrated on not touching anyone. I walked by the bar on the way to the stairs; there was a light beneath it that guided me. When I got to the steps the bouncer stopped me and flashed the light downstairs once to clear my departure. While I stood waiting, I saw the woman who had ridden me crouched beneath the bar. She was still naked, looking older in the light. She kneeled like a squirrel, in her hand a large yellow bag of peanut M&M's that she dug into, throwing the candy up to her mouth. One after the other, tiny mortars, all caught and crunched with joy. She didn't look at what she was doing, she didn't even care what color they were. Just staring down at the floor like there was a book there and she could read it.

There was a bar about four blocks away, a place of old men. I sat on my stool, watching the Sixers get knocked out of the playoffs again. Around me, they talked about the past as if it was the one true world, as if the present was a shard of a broken destiny. I felt at home. Within the mix of their words, between the overlapping conversations of this small place, I heard a collage of David's voice calling. Buy me a drink, you bastard, he said, and when all my bills had evaporated into change, Come to me, David was saying.

It was hotter outside than when I came in. I focused on walking a straight line. I was going somewhere, it just couldn't be back to that apartment, its filth and clutter, or the life it was the home of. There was someone in front of me at the street light, hiding underneath the shadows of the el tracks. Yam-man, don't come at me now, because I will kill you. I'll kick you in the head so hard, I'll use your skull as a sneaker. But the form was too tall for the yam-skinned man, and it was another shape. When I got closer, it wasn't him all. Just another brother walking in the dark, coming from trouble or moving towards it like I was.

He was dressed like a child. High-top sneakers and brightly colored sports paraphernalia. A quilt of logos. His jeans were so large his legs looked like an elephant's. Through his earphones and five feet of Philly space, I could hear his music's rapid vibrations, see his head nod to its beat in forward circles. If you wanted to hear what the music said, you would be happy, because when he saw me standing next to him, waiting for the light to change and the few cars exploring the night to pull off, he started rapping along with it. It's amazing how loud some people can talk without fully screaming. Isn't that pleasant, him giving that gift to us? Out here on this hot spring night, going on three o'clock in the morning. So charitable of him, freeing all the open apartment windows above us from the tyranny of silence. The lyrics delivered proudly, his lips snarling in defiance as he gave his rhymes of power: people he was going to shoot, women he was going to bone, products he was going to acquire. As if power had anything to do with guns any more. As if it had something to do with the amount of weaklings you took advantage of, pussies your dick touched, or brand names you draped yourself in. As if power meant being free of empathy, compassion, self-control, or any other distinctly human emotion. As if power meant personifying everything the people who hated you were afraid of.

'Nigger, what the fuck you looking at?' He turned to me, prison haircut showing underneath his baseball cap.

'A living archetype of black mediocrity.'

Redefinition. Power was a punch from a ring laden hand to an unprotected jaw (gold ain't that soft). Power was a foot kicking into the stomach of a man already on the floor. Power was, on this street right now, hitting someone in the head with a trash can lid, slamming again until the metal was dented and the target had stopped trying to get up from the ground. Power was spitting on a man's face that was already covered in blood, then continuing to wield that lid some more. Power was not a broken fool, lying at the corner of 51st and Market, giggling because he doubted his assailant even knew what 'archetype' meant. Rejoicing in his pain because it meant his life might soon be over.

Sick

A busted lip, a goldfish eye, ribs that felt barbecued and a pinkie too swollen for bending. For no reason, I was still living. I sat at my desk, listening to a British voice named Suzanne Patel, making me feel for a second as if I weren't back in Philly answering phones for the electric company. At the end of Ms Patel's application process I started asking made-up questions just to keep her on the line. Trying to fall into her voice while Reggie tapped against the aching that was my body's side.

'What the fuck is wrong with you, can't you see I'm sore?' I asked, hitting mute as Ms Patel kept talking. Reggie was the gray of frozen meat. 'Trash,' he said, reaching frantically under the desk by my knees.

'Reg, why are you bugging?' But Reggie was silent, bent over, staring into the bin.

'Yo, Reg, what—' A wave of slop exploded from his mouth, the stench immediate. Hot bile hit my lap. On my thigh, a partially digested tomato. Lynol jumped from his seat to place his hand on Reggie's back. I plucked the red clump of tomato off me, watching it stick to the wall.

'That's it, boy, let it out.' Lynol made circles with his palm on Reggie's spine as Reggie breathed hard until again, sudden movement, the sound of liquid splashing against the trashcan's plastic walls.

'That's it, boy, Lynol said. 'That's the Lord our God pushing

Satan out you.' From inside the can, Reggie said, 'Blaaaaah.' 'That's it, Reggie. Devil be gone!'

Everyone came from their desks. Reggie pulled his head up, waving Lynol off, and we all stood there watching him. The front of his shirt looked as if he'd been bobbing for pizza.

'Goddamn!' Cindy came over and the only thing she saw was me. 'Damn, you look fucked up! Fucked *up*.'

'Then go fuck me down again.' I waved her off. 'Excuse me' came through my earphones. Ms Patel, still holding the line.

Going home, my pants hadn't dried, so people stayed away from me on the trolley. Only $2.36 left from the binge of the previous night, I picked up another family-size can of Beefaroni for $2.09. It was the size of a small drum; it would do the job. At home, every dish was dirty, every pan or pot, so I peeled the red and white paper label off the can and sat it directly on the fire. Then I took a nap.

Awake, I remembered my hunger and ran to the kitchen to turn the burner off. I was afraid to touch the can. The top of it had popped out, giving it the shape of a torpedo. The sides were streaked black, the metal bubbled around the bottom. There was no more money, so I finished it off.

Three hours later it still felt heavy in my stomach, like I'd just swallowed it. I tried sitting on the toilet but nothing, so I lay back down, listened to the dog's fuzzy swirls above me, the screams of 'Nigger' below. I dreamed that I was back in David's Fiat going up Brixton High Street, trying to drive from the backseat, straining to reach the wheel and pedal as the car kept moving onto Effra Road. Struggling to touch the brake with my fingertips.

I woke up. There was a brick in my gut. I could feel its squareness, its porous red sides, its chipped corners, the weight sitting against my spine. I rose and the brick hung in the air with me. I would give birth to this, name it Fred. Fred, someday you will be a part of a great wall. But slowly Fred began to crumble, its edges breaking into hefty sheets that hailed on the floor of my rectum. Something spiraled through my intestines. I dove for the toilet, landing on it sideways with my feet hanging out the door.

I knew they could hear it through the walls, feel the vibrations like the MOVE bomb. The first explosion was relief and fecal shrapnel. The second, liquid propulsion. The third, the lining of my stomach, strings of flesh still clinging to my rectum walls. The next wave, acid, splashing through my anus and burning everything it touched, sizzling as it began to eat through the toilet's porcelain bottom. So hot that I stood up, and I had begun to think I would never move again. Wiping it off me, it felt as if I were taking skin with it, revealing the orange fat and sore red muscle below. Steam rose from between my legs. Looking through them, the bowl was black like a roofer's vat of tar. An obsidian nugget the size of a cat's eye slid down into the soup below. Staring at it, my self-disgust peaked. The rest of the food that was still in me exploded from the back of my throat and out my mouth. The bottom of my stomach slapped the back of my tongue. I kept my head between my legs and into the bowl, looking at red vomit on black shit. Liquid strings linked my lips to the mess I had born. My climax of shame and suffering had finally arrived. I would die with my pants around my ankles.

Back on the futon, I tripped between consciousness and sleep like a thin rock skipping across a dark pond. Images repeated and twisted upon themselves, resurfacing after being mutilated to reassert themselves again. I would be on the Victoria Line tube but, arriving at Brixton station, the doors would not open and the train would pull out again, going further into darkness. Or I get out into the station, but the escalators only run down. Or I get out of the station but instead of staring across the road at the HMV or the Body Shop, I am in Camden, the New Jersey one. Even in my dreams, pain. I needed drugs: country hay domes of marijuana and Hershey Park rivers of hash, Cough syrup bottles held in a beer hat with straws leading to my mouth. Thick Pepto-Bismol cream to be drunk from pink half-gallon cartons.

Cola syrup in brown medicinal bottles put in the fridge over-night.

It was suddenly very hot. As fast as my pores sweated, my flesh melted the beads to steam. My apartment had moved inside a radiator, the walls were hot plates, burning the blue paint in streaks of brown. Flame burst through nail holes. The glass of lightbulbs liquefied and oozed to the floor. The windows were clear taffy; if you wanted you could reach right through them. The smell of wood burning, of my flesh melting into the floor. My skin, soft butter, my eyes chocolate dots. They will make pancakes with my remains, sell them to better kids than I was so they can grow up strong. In the kitchen sink, china cracked from overbaking, silverware at the bottom forged together into one clump. Whatever was in the toilet bowl boiled over, malted septic sludge. Even the roaches were dying, a whole city under the sink going down like Pompeii, too busy with its own life to notice my disaster. This is what I've become, filth to burn in the fire. This is what I've built for myself. This is where David was, fire racing up curtains, floorboards buckling from heat. These were the flames that took that life. The specifics of his death didn't matter because even the construction of this place was a form of suicide in itself. David, you bastard, you did it to yourself. Chris, you ignorant fuck, you couldn't even learn from his mistake, could you? You had to blame yourself for it. You had to follow him here.

'You've just got a fever. Now sit up.' Alex held a glass of orange juice to my mouth. I didn't remember calling her. Juice made my lips soft again and dripped across my chin. Rolling down my throat and cooling the cauldron. Citric acid burning whatever set me afire.

'I'm going to make you get better,' Alex told me, but I had just realized that it didn't work that way. A place like this you built for yourself. Not Alex, not Margaret, not even Fionna if she had wanted to, no one could take someone else from their place of self-destruction. And not me, even if I'd moved in with him after he'd driven his wife away, tucking him in every night

and waking him with tea in warm cups. Nobody could decon-
struct this place but the one that built it. In this room, the sin was
with the victim, the sin was the walls. So if I couldn't blame
myself for David's edifice of ruin, why was I building my own to
match it? Why not dream myself a wrecking ball?

Awake, the heat had deserted me and my body was mortal once
more. My head hung off the edge of my futon and the back of
my skull rested on the floor. Both windows were open, Alex was
sitting along the wooden edge of one of them, reading a
magazine, her shirt pulled up slightly on the side so I could
see a roll of flesh easing out above her belt. She was digging in
her nose and when she found something she wiped it on a tissue,
made a face, then lobbed the paper into the trash. I closed my
eyes again, waited a minute, and woke up officially by letting out
a yawn.

'Hey,' I said, sitting up. Alex pulled herself down so that both
feet were on the floor. Her hair was now in a bun, her head
leaning against the glass of the window. A glance at my angel
revealed a more beautiful image than any casual observer would
be blessed with.

'Well? How you feel?'

'Better. I'm going to get better now.' My shirt was off, I don't
know how that happened.

'Well, I'm glad you've decided that. Who beat you up?' Alex
was looking at my ribs, grimacing.

'Some dude on the street I had words with.'

'You're lucky you didn't get shot.'

I stood up, nodding my agreement.

'I'm going back to London now.' I told her from the kitchen.
The fridge had food; thank you, woman. There was more
orange juice in a carton, and the angle of the hallway was good
enough that I could drink it from the top without her seeing me.

'Well, if that's what you think you need to do, then do that.
'Cause this is bullshit. This place was a fucking mess. This
building looks like a crime scene. Your apartment is a pit, even

without your touches. Unbelievable. I can't believe you've been living like this. You know you could have stayed with me.' I walked back to the living room. Alex was staring at me. The place looked as if she had swept. The newspapers were in a pile, so were the magazines. By the door were three full bags of trash. When I got out of here, I would find a way to treat her this well.

'Lie down with me,' I said. Alex kept staring back. 'Just lie down with me for a second. I'm tired.' I reached out my hand and walked to her and Alex reached back for me slightly. I tried to keep holding hands as I put myself on the mattress, but lost balance and couldn't.

We lay on our sides together for a while. I put my arm over her waist and it sunk lightly into the softness there. I was no longer part of the room; I was something inside it. Alex drifted off and I leaned in closer to her so I could touch her warmth. Her shirt hung open and I could feel the flesh of her stomach in my palm. As she adjusted her body, the edge of my hand slipped in the front of her pants, feeling heat and fabric. Pinkie finger brushed against her pubic hair and I let it rest there, waiting for Alex to tell me to move it. When she didn't, it twirled her tight black curls. Floating between us, my dick filled and hung firm and disembodied. I felt its heat rising over my belly, she felt it climbing the line of her spine. It was the only movement between us as it beat with my heart until, growing complacent with its own presence, it subsided. Alex leaned her back closer into me. David would have liked her; they would have had fun. David would have liked all of this, even the electric company. I could see that. In minutes, Alex's breath became heavy and steady with dream; I could feel her sound through her back. An oblivious whisper underneath the growl of cars, the *pop-pop* of local guns, the sustained thunder of jet planes trying to distance themselves from this ground.

Running

Straight up, I was getting the fuck out. I borrowed thirty bones from Alex, a small enough sum that I could pay her back if I didn't miss any days before the next check, and I knew I wouldn't because Mrs Hutton said if I did, I'd be fired automatically. 'House rules,' she dismissed. For lunch, I cooked ramen noodles in an electric kettle plugged in underneath my desk, three bags at a time. Cindy complained about the smell, but how else could I patch my gut for sixty cents? After work I didn't even go home, walking instead in the opposite direction into the city and started researching.

My plan was practical: hit every bookstore in Philly, get as much information on the current state of the British advertising industry as possible. Target a new location every day, head over with a pen and pad in pocket, ready to work. Claim a chair or corner and inhabit it. Even in Philly, British business and advertising magazines were available for my perusal. Their covers ripped from the rumpling of too many hands, but still there for me to search articles and ads for the name of firms that seemed viable.

Information copied, the next step was to call the following morning, setting my alarm for six-thirty to do so. Get the number from BT, then tell the secretary that I was calling on behalf of an American business interest. Yes, we're planning on expanding into the British market and we're looking for an advertising agency to assist the transition. Could you send a portfolio over, a client list and such? That's attention C. Jones, Suite 4, 213 W. 46th Street, Philadelphia, PA 19146, USA. And could you tell me the name of the head creative? Thank you.

Every day a different bookstore, every morning more calls made. New agencies I'd never heard of, bigger agencies that had turned me down before. When I ran out of places to contact, the next step was the rebuilding of the great portfolio. I called every company Urgent ever made a dime off of, begging them to send me samples of my work. What had I been doing since David died? Freelance projects, Stateside. But I'm returning to London soon and will be making myself available. If you hear about something promising, you can pass my number on.

Then it was waiting time. The apartment was clean, so I didn't want to hang about and mess it up. There was work to be done, places to be walked to. It was June, summer had arrived again, a year had moved forward without me. My brain had congealed like cold grits and I needed to warm it up, to get ready for the stunt that would get me out of here. Whatever it was, it had to be now: my lease would be up in two months. I knew there was no way I could re-sign it. That I would not survive another twelve months here was undeniable.

I would come up with some new ads, something fresh to bring back from the colonies. I would pad my portfolio with imaginary commissions from fictional American companies. Or even better, I would create my own ads for brands so well known that even in Britain they would be common knowledge. Concepts without the limitations of client approval: unhampered, they would be the best I could conceive of. I just wouldn't mention that I hadn't been hired to do them. I would never get caught. These were different worlds, I could get away with almost anything. The air was barely the same chemistry in these two lands.

With all the clippings I could muster collected, I made copies of my portfolio and sent them out. I could only afford six books, instead of the nine I wanted, but didn't it feel good writing London, U.K. on something, knowing that in a few days these pieces of me would be there as well?

After mailing them off at 30th Street, I was so excited I walked over to the Borders at Rittenhouse Square. It was there, browsing British magazines to prepare my mind for the culture shock of reimmersion, that I saw her on the cover of the latest issue of *AdForum*. Plaits poking around her head like an asterisk, barefoot and dressed only in a burlap sack. My Fi. Look at her there, that face I used to kiss and put food in – and singing, no less. The headline said '*Making Yourself Heard.*' Her mouth was open so wide she could have swallowed herself, or anyone else foolish enough to get too close to her.

The article barely had anything on *Uncle Tom's Cabin: The Musical*; it was focused on West End and theater advertising in general, but it did have a sidebar that mentioned the show. The smaller article was about the importance of shying away from the use of individual members in promotion, due to the reality of rotating casts. 'This April, Apricot Advertising learned this rather painful lesson when the visual focus of much of their print advertising, Topsy, portrayed by actress Fionna Otubanjo (see cover), was replaced by Alice Collins, who held the role the previously.' I was smiling. Big. Not because I was happy for Fionna's misfortune, but because I didn't seem to care at all. With that knowledge, my smile grew grander. If the silence of books wasn't sacred, I might have screamed my joy aloud. Then, when I saw what was across the page, I almost did. What I took at first to be another random ad turned out to be much more. A contest. My sign had been delivered.

It was Lionskins, the condom company, trying to expand their market to the next generation of fornicators. The challenge was to come up with an innovative campaign of print ads to be aimed at the male 16–34 demographic. The sole qualification necessary was that you were a member of an independent British advertising firm. The award was £4,000 and the celebrated glory of public victory. Finally, something worth contacting Margaret for. I would ask her for the permission to use her address and the name Urgent. It was on.

Alex said I could borrow her camera equipment; it wasn't like she was getting any opportunities to take it out. I would still need to pay for film, development, scanning, and the rental time plugging away at a computer to get the job done. If I stayed on the ramen diet, I could make that happen with the next check. Those damn noodles had proved particularly cost effective: not only were they providing a cheap lunch, they were also ruining my appetite for dinner as well. But for anything to happen, I needed my money. My check had to clear.

Office rumor said: the temp agency didn't screw up account procedure last pay, they just didn't have any money. That sounded pretty crazy, since we'd found out from a temp in accounting that the agency was paid $12.57 for every $6.30 hour we made, but we could all sense it was true. The broke can smell the broke. To make it worse, this week the agency not only had to pay our money for this check, they were going to have to cover the back wages for the two-thirds of the temps who'd been stiffed the week before. Reggie started taking bets on the checks not clearing, but then realized that if he won nobody would be able to pay him.

Pay dispersal time was one o'clock Thursday afternoon, over on 33rd and Arch behind the railroad tracks. If we were going to play musical chairs with the cash, nobody wanted to get caught standing up, so at twelve-thirty the office cleared out. Lynol and me were supposed to stay, but ten minutes after the rest of the temps had left, Mrs Hutton took her purse and walked out to lunch. Lynol followed, telling me he was going to the bathroom. Thirty seconds later, when I snuck out, I could see his lying-ass running a block in front of me.

Everybody was there; we could barely fit into the office. Every temp from the electric company had turned out. Some people I hadn't even known were scabs until I saw them there, hungry for their money. Temps from other sites too, maybe from the gas company, crowded in as well, looking just like us but with different faces. Clive, who hadn't bothered to show up for work that day, had decided to make an appearance here instead. He wore a dress shirt, but only the two buttons at the bottom were done. That skinny chest had more hair than I would have thought it did. For pants he wore pajama bottoms. For shoes, his bare feet sat loosely in black rubber galoshes.

Instead of Mary, the receptionist, just handing out the checks from her desk drawer, smiling and waving and not even having to bother to get off the phone, reinforcements had arrived. In the eye of the mob of eighty some people who surrounded him, a big white guy waved a fist of check-filled envelopes over his head where nobody could reach them, his stomach hanging over his waist like a trash bag filled with water. Seeing the money, the room got quiet. The boss man started the discussion by apologizing for the previous week's mistake, mentioning the possibilities for repayment of insufficient funds fees, how the agency's greatest asset was its workers, how he would like to give his sincerest apologies—

'Is that all?' Cindy asked. Cackles and laughs. Aqua-belly blushed.

'No. No, it's not. That isn't all. I also brought donuts,' he said. Mary went into an office and pulled them out. They came in large pink boxes that seemed awkward in her arms, but nobody bothered to help her. When they were placed on a table at the far wall Mary turned around and said, 'Dig in,' but the only person who went over there was Clive. His hair was knotted and unpicked, his eyes thick and glazed like the donut he grabbed for, all pretense of hiding his piper status gone. Reaching for another before the first one was completely in his mouth, he ate standing, staring at the blank wall as if it were a goldfish tank. I don't think he knew where he was.

Somehow it was decided that alphabetical order was the fairest, then the checks were handed out. Adams. Snatch, run. The sound of feet banging down carpeted floor, doors slamming behind him. Anderson. Snatch, run. The sound of feet

banging down carpeted floor, doors slamming behind her.
Anthony. Snatch, run. The sound of a man banging his knee
into the corner of a desk as he ran for the door.

'People, people, I can assure you on this, there is enough
money in the account. The last pay was an anomaly. Everyone
will be paid. I can guarantee all of you that everyone's check will
clear. I haven't even paid myself yet,' he said, holding his check
up to the room. I tried to see the name on it through the
cellophane window but the type was too small. 'Honky needs to
get busy before I plant a foot in his ass,' someone said beside me,
followed by *hmmphs* in the affirmative. But that was lazy. His
being white and us being black didn't have much to do with
anything; there were tons of bourgeois negroes in this city, more
than most, and broke-ass crackers were everywhere. It was just
that he was full, and we were hungry. That was the pain of this
place to me: not that I had been full once and had been reduced
to hunger, but that hunger is what I always was and no matter
what I consumed, this reality would always be a paycheck, a
payment, a meal away.

'Chris Jones.'

Check in hand, damned if I ain't running. People between me
and the bank were casualties to be apologized to later. I didn't
want to be Clive any more. Out in the street, my sprint gained
form. Head down, nose to my chest. Aiming north up 33rd
Street towards Market, pushing off the balls of my feet, hoping I
wasn't pacing myself too fast but refusing to slow down. Carlton
Jones, who got his check right before me, pulled up in a black
Jeep, air fresheners hanging like grapes from his rearview
window. Slowing briefly at the stop sign beside me, he looked
my way and I caught his eyes. Ride? Wheels started spinning,
skidmarks writing themselves on the road in front of me. F you,
too.

At Market Street, I turned left and headed downtown. The
agency's bank was the main branch of CaneState, by the
Clothespin and City Hall. If you were to shoot an arrow from
my face straight seventeen blocks down, it would land on the

middle of its front doors. Oh so free, running like God made me to. Business shoes slapping and tie blowing over my shoulder like a dragon tongue. In my hand the glorious crinkling of paycheck cellophane, the kind that had my name underneath it. People in cars looked at me as if I was doing something important. Move man, move. They could feel it, too, that I had to win this one. White people checked to see if there was a cop behind me. Passing 30th Street Station, I thought of catching a taxi, but cars were slow, cars had laws. And I was keeping all this money, had to: couldn't be giving away magic beans. Look at me. I was running, finally moving again. Oh shit, am I alive? How long had it been? Knees so high they tagged my nipples, hands chopping the air to punish it for getting in my way. Check in my hand. Best part of the day because there it was, right there, in my hand.

Temps I was passing. First some of the old ladies, some of the Browns and the Davises, I recognized them from the office. Cindy was in there with them. Seeing me coming, she tried to speed up her walking, but it was useless. Her legs had forgotten swift movement and she had on high heels anyway. One of the women, last-named Baumen from accounts receivable, tried waving me over, like she had to tell me something. *Chris, wait, you forgot* . . . She wasn't playing me for a sucker. I waved back happy and kept going going gone, running through a red light and dodging a SEPTA bus, the number 64. It honked, I kept moving. We were both happy.

At 22nd and Market, I passed a bunch of young guys, Douglasses, Jeffersons, and Hamiltons. Look at how content they were, smoking and laughing as if their checks had already cleared. Weren't the Washingtons screwed? Crossing to the other side of the street, I tried to run silent, keeping behind a UPS truck that was going about my speed. Hugging its side, making sure not to get squished between it and a parked car. I had just made it past them when the truck stopped. Flying out beyond it, I was revealed. When I looked over my shoulder they had seen me.

'Yo black, wait up! Wait up!' Giving the nationalist fist, I kept running, leaping over a pothole the size of a sauna before it could take me down. A couple of them started to run after me. There was a guy getting out of a car ahead, his door cutting off my path. The sidewalk was crowded, the gaps between the parked cars too narrow to reach it at this speed. Moving my legs faster, I cut in front of the moving car to my left and made a racetrack out of the meridian, one foot for each white line. Taxis swerved at me, cars honked, people cursed, but it was all worth it because at 16th Street I looked over my shoulder and the brothers were gone, lost in the crowd. On the street, Carlton Jones's black Jeep circled the cop-infested block, searching for a place to park. I pushed through the bank doors, my chest was thumping like it held something living inside.

Under the Bridge

I got bit. Lord have mercy, got bit two times. Got all excited about the first one, planning my office and running off to the travel store on 22nd Street to search for Lemonlight's address in an *A–Z* (I could take the Circle Line to the Victoria Line from Durban Road, Back to Brixton, Back to Brixton). When, boom, I come home two days later and there's another letter in the box asking for Christopher. This time, a major player. Sublime Advertising. Ain't that something? Both letters with the same message for me: interested, possibility, make an appointment when I cross the Atlantic, soon. Look at that. Two pieces of paper from fairyland, one for each back pocket. All I had to do was win the Lionskins contest, collect the prize money, get my ticket, and the world was mine again. As tight as she probably was, Margaret would probably buy me a ticket if she knew that prize money was coming to pay her back. So, again, all that was left was doing this. All that was left was to win.

Selling men condoms was too easy. There was so much shit out there you could catch, it was a wonder boys didn't have them grafted to their foreskins. A book in the library, amid the section on infectious diseases, featured a whole centerfold of clinical shots of inflicted genitalia. Thick multicolored secretions, pus-filled blisters, painful bloated distortions as virus-mutilated flesh. There was one disease that bore canals from your urethra through your dick's head. They showed a picture of the afflicted taking a piss. The top of his cock shot liquid from twenty different holes like a sprinkler. Forget death, *that* shit was scary. If I could have, I would have had that photo scanned and laid out. Even the British ad council wasn't that lenient. What I needed was an image that invoked the same unmentionable dangers of unprotected sex without resorting to shameless scare tactics and putting people off their tea. More than that, what was needed was an image that could put forth the unquestionable 'reality' that Lionskins was the only condom to get the job done. An image that immediately represented sex, illicitness, and expertise of the intimate. It was hooker-hunting time.

Clive was a big help: he was the only one in the office not pissed at me since they found out my check was the sole one that cleared. Lack of funds had forced him into detox; broke never looked so good on a man. Reggie, on the other hand, was coming back from lunch with nothing to eat but a bag of barbecue potato chips and a peach soda. He wouldn't even look at me. Loose, well-worn Help Wanted sections from the *Daily News* and *Inquirer* were strewn carelessly around the office, but nobody had quit so far. A job you might get paid at was better than no job at all.

Clive provided me with a thirty-minute lecture on the history of prostitution in the Delaware Valley, not stopping till Natalie sat down next to us and he got embarrassed. There were five-hundred-buck-an-hour hookers doing private visits on the Main Line, there were two-hundred-dollar-hookers in brothels on Race and Vine that you could look up in the phone book, there were fifty-dollar-an-act hookers on Spruce Street after ten o'clock, and there were five-bucks-a-tag crackheads under the El in Kensington. When I told Clive what I was planning, and my price range, he suggested buying a token, head over to Kensington tonight. Monday was usually slow, they might even lower their price to three bucks a pop.

Alex hooked me up with equipment, making me promise on the grave of my moms that I would get it back intact. From her crib, I walked down to the El on 46th Street past homes that begged to collapse, shedding paint and splinters and concrete chunks the size of cupcakes. On their porches sat clothes, newspapers faded by light and rain, and poor people. Hair sticking out over their heads like black cotton candy (if you took it into your mouth, it would taste like the popcorn on the floors of movie theaters). Looking back at me walking down the street, too broken even to pace their cells, knowing nothing I can do (dance, sing, give out free cigarettes) is going to change that.

On the El, I sat alone, pretending to be too bored to be mugged, arms folded across my lap and my head down. By my feet, liquid ran along the black grooves of the flooring, ebbing to and fro with the momentum of the car. I kept touching the camera to tell myself that it was still there, rubbing my finger over its smooth sides until the plastic was warm and I felt like I could bend it like a tin spoon.

We were aboveground, then we were underground in Center City and screaming through the hollow, then we were back aboveground again, in the white ghetto now, among the white hungry folk. Ghetto to ghetto, negro to trash, and all for a dollar fifty. Forget the Chunnel.

Kensington? This isn't Kensington. The real Kensington was down Notting Hill, over from the Royal Albert. Kensington was travel agents taking you anywhere in the world, the back-yard of the queen, cute little shops and American tourists young and loud and buying things. Philly-Kensington was all wrong. It was people with bad skin and brown cooked teeth and thin gold chains, hair forced to attention high over female heads and violent boys with harsh mouths. Hooded sweatshirts covered with flannel shirts, jeans too tight and sneakers too dirty (but still brand-name, baby). Mouths spitting out 'you'se' and 'we'se,' a community subject to its own internal grammar. This is a place where niggers die, where field reporters come on TV talking about tragedy and then interview neighbors who stand in the cold and say 'It's a shame' in steamed vocals into the camera, then rush home to see themselves on television for the first time.

Front Street, under the blackened frame of the El tracks. I walked for near an hour, determined to either get the picture or get mugged. Streetlights extinguished by gunfire or shame provide bubbles of darkness, sections between functioning poles where reality was soft and crack ghosts haunted. Cars came down the road and crack hos emerged from the shadows like cats to can openers. Clusters of them, hiding in the vacant lots and buildings that lined the road, waiting in shadows, whispering to their habits that the next headlight was going to be the one. Dreaming about a bit of cash, a taste of food, another pebble in the pipe to remind them why it was all worthwhile. Me walking down the street was nothing to them because tricks came in cars and I was too big to rob, weak as they were. If they had ever had a gun or knife they would have smoked it by now. Buy now. More love. Suck it down with a Bic lighter.

I needed one alone but couldn't get them to come out, and I was scared to get close to a group for fear of being pulled into the darkness by a collective of bony hands. Getting desperate, when the next car pulled up and one of the creatures climbed inside, I followed it around the block to the alley between 2nd and 3rd. A close distance behind, listening for the footsteps I expected to come after me, I waited in the doorway of an abandoned deli for the car door to open, for the crackhead to emerge. The vehicle actually bounced. As soon as it was still, the white Buick opened its big-ass wing and she got out. Drinking water out a Pepsi bottle as she walked my way. I stepped towards her.

'Excuse me, miss?' My voice weak from hours of neglect and fear. I cleared my throat. She jumped. Aqua blue velour V-neck with grease stains on stomach and black denim cut-offs (its gray strings bouncing when she did). She was a man, I could see from her neck, and from her feminine walk. The real women out here moved like stiff-kneed infants on their first strut.

'Watchu want? I didn't do nothing,' she whined, stomping her foot down.

'No, I'm sorry, I'm a photographer, I'm trying to get—' Camera lifting up, she didn't like that. Pepsi bottle came flying, hitting me over the eye, making me certain it was a brick despite the fact I saw the blue logo before impact. Realizing the camera wasn't in my hand, I dove forward. Sliding into the ground, somehow Alex's baby was safe in my palms. Just the skin under my arms was gone. Crackhead ran in front of me, back towards the shadows of Frankford Avenue. Not too fast either. Pausing repeatedly to turn around and see if I was dead.

Retreating, I hit a pizza joint back by Kensington station. The guy wouldn't give me the key to the bathroom without buying something, so I got a slice. Going on two A.M., there was nobody in there but coffee drinking SEPTA workers and the two crack hos sitting by the window. Sharing a medium soda a sip at a time, their ashy hands pushed it back and forth between turns.

'That's what I'm saying. That's what I'm saying. I go up there and I'm like, "Yo", banging on the door and shit and the bitch don't answer, right? Yelling her name and shit and nothing.'

'How you know she there?'

'I know this shit. Bitch don't go nowhere, she don't, that's why I gave her my kids in the first place: bitch don't go out. So I'm like, "Yo"!' Hand drumming against air. Her arm was scraped like mine was. ' "I'm here to get my babies, open the fucking door," right? Nothing. And I can hear the TV on, so I know she's in there. Trying to keep my babies, tackhead bitch can't get a man to make her own, okay? Bitch too fat to even get down the stairs, and you know that elevator don't be working, right?'

Laugh. 'Yeah.' She couldn't have been more than sixteen', she even wore an adolescent's gumball band to hold the bit of hair that stood atop her head, giving her dome the shape of garlic.

'So I'm like, fuck this shit. I'm beating the door, I'm kicking it, I'm like Bruce Lisa, ha ha. You know what I'm saying? You don't know me, I'm crazy. I don't care how long stank bitch got my kids, they mine, I'm the one that birthed them. Ain't no amount of babysitting going to change that. Can I get some respect up this mawfucka? That's what I'm saying.' Mama had no front teeth. With nothing to stop her S's, they flew past her wrinkled top lip and sizzled before her.

'You say you got toys?' the girl asked.

'I yell it. I'm out there with that whole bag a stuff I bought with Saturday's money. Jelly Babies, Thundermen, a bootleg of *The Wonder World*. I'm saying that, right, into the door. I'm pulling shit out of the bag and holding it up to the peephole in case somebody's looking. But nobody there, right? She probably got my babies in her room, locked up, hands on their ears. Telling them all type a lies on me. It's my daughter's fifth birthday. How you not going to let me up in there for my daughter's fifth birthday? Then some nosy bitch from down the hall tells me she called the cops, they coming. What's that about? So I just leaves. Forget her.'

'You still got them toys?' the young one asked, hopeful.

Only air coming up the straw, Mama went back to work. Out the door and across the street, staring up Frankford Avenue for headlights. The girl she left behind turned to an old exhaust-coated SEPTA worker sipping his coffee and said, 'You buy me some food?' I got up and headed for the street, taking off my lens cap.

The shot: wild woman hanging out by the curb, leather dress on, red T-shirt stretched so much that her left shoulder hung out the top. Little blue supermarket sneakers at the end of charcoal legs. You couldn't even tell that her shoes didn't have laces, that she had no stockings on, or how bad her ashy skin thirsted for lotion. It was across the street, it was dark, but most important it was real. The face that stared back at you, that hunger, desperation, the sex and danger, that was real, too. And that was all you cared about. At the bottom of the page, the copy provided the mortal blow. *This is Karen. Karen services six men an hour, thirty-two men an evening, 192 men a week, 9408 men a year. If Karen trusts Lionskins Condoms to protect her life, don't you think you should, too?*

It took nearly two weeks to get the picture developed, scanned, and sent back to me in a digital format I could negotiate. Sitting up in Kinko's on 40th and Walnut, trying to rush their slow-ass, money-grubbing computers to get the layout done. Then there it was, emerging from my long-dormant womb, another Chris Jones original in my classic style: knockout image with deadly copy that jabbed you bye bye as you fell to the mat. Follow that with the roaring Lionskins logo in the bottom left corner along with a miniature photo of the product's box, and we definitely have a winner.

'Yo Al, check it out.' She'd just come in to give me the contact info for the Philly tourist board.

'I'm double parked. Take this and call Saul. He's good people. I talked to him yesterday so he knows who you are.'

'Look at this, love of ages, and glance upon the face of genius.'

'Shut up. What? Where is it?' I pulled it up, the hard drive struggling to assemble the file. God, it was even better than I remembered. What a sublime choice of fonts.

'What the fuck is this?' Alex asked.

'This is the condom thing, the Lionskins contest. This is only one shot, I got a ton more. I told you about this.'

'But what the fuck is this?' Alex demanded, pointing at crack ho mama's face, at those eyes staring from the screen at everyone in the room.

'That's what I shot the other night, when I went to Kensington. You get it? I'm using the projected sexual risk of prostitution to plug the product.'

'No, you're not, you're using her,' Alex said, still pointing.

'Al, it's just a contest, nobody is going to see it but me and the judges.'

'And what if you win?'

'When I win it will be over there, in Britain. Lionskins don't even sell in the States. Nobody this woman knows will ever see this. Ever.'

'So tell me then, make me understand this: how is that not fucked up? This is how you're going to represent us to the world?' God I wished she would put her finger down. 'You couldn't just use some clip art instead?'

'The point is that this shit is authentic. I didn't hire a model and have her pose for this shit: this is reality. That's what gives it its power. I mean look at you, you're mad. That's why you're mad.'

'You know why? You're a fucking sellout.'

'What!' Copy center boys looked nervous behind their counter. Security man was talking on the payphone, annoyed that he might have to get off. Now Alex was yelling too.

'There's not enough sick, destructive images of us out in the world that you got to go put out another? She has to be black? She has to be from Philly? Why didn't you just come take a picture of me getting out of the shower?'

'So if it was a picture of a white hooker from Boston, you wouldn't be bugging?'

'You're bullshit,' Alex said, getting up and walking out. I popped out the precious Lionskins disk and followed. Running next to her, talking to her face even though she wouldn't look at me.

'How am I bullshit? How am I bullshit, Alex? Explain that to me.'

'You know what? You been talking down Philly for years, busting on the place, bugging on the people, and I've always tried not to take it personal, okay? Even though sometimes it's been really hard, Chris, really hard, I've always tried to take it in stride, I've always tried to remind myself that you're just as much a part of this place as I am, and that deep down you love it as much as I do. Right? But you know what? The truth is you would sell it all out in a second to get away from here.'

'What is it that you think I'm doing, Alex?'

'You know what you're doing,' she said, trying to grab at the Santa-red diskette that I quickly pulled away from her.

'That's right: I know what I'm doing,' I told her. 'I'm creating. I'm giving everything I have, my world, myself, to do it. That's the only way I can. I'm not good enough to hold anything back. Everything or nothing. That's the only way I'm going to escape.'

'Escape what? Getting up and going to a job you hate, just like everybody else? You're so special, that's too much for you? You have to do whatever you can to get ahead? Even if it makes us look like animals?'

'To who? White people? I don't care what stupid white people think. And really, I don't give a shit what stupid black people think either. The image is a negative statement about humanity, and, yes, we're human. If they want to jump in with their coon issues, that's their problem. Honestly, do you think it's really possible to click a lens in this shit-hole town without the subject being offensive?'

'You wrong,' Alex said, and as mad as she was, you could see it was as if I had offended her personally, which just made me madder.

'That's it, Alex. That's what I don't understand about you. How the hell can you, a smart, educated, somewhat rational human being, love this.' I motioned. Arms wide, I motioned to everything. The telephone poles crucified with endless staples and pamphlets waiting for rust or rain to release them, the knuckleheads bobbing down Chestnut with their shirtless, chain-gang struts, fucking yam-man, who was standing in front of Burger King pretending to be the door-man and now (Oh God) coming over here: I held it all out to her. 'How?' I demanded, not surprised by the tone of jealousy seeping through.

Alex was writing me off with sideways nods. 'You look around here and as soon as you see ugly, damn if you see extra. All those things that you should appreciate, all those things you should be thankful for, you can't see any of it. You go blind. It's pathetic. If I was like that, how the fuck could I love you?' And as if this was a play and that was his cue, yam-man appeared beside her.

'Hey, can y'all hook a brother up with—'

'Yo, just get the fuck away from me!' I was suddenly yelling.

The throat-shredding, barely intelligible kind. So loud that I was as surprised as he was by my reaction. When the echoes of my scream had died, my face offered a demonstrative apology to yam-man as he shrugged an understanding forgiveness my way, but then both silent gestures were enveloped by the next scream. Female this time, the simple conjunction 'Ass-hole!' followed with the punctuation of a slam from a rusty car door.

In the driver's seat, Alex had sat down so quickly that a bit of her hair was caught in the jamb. She didn't bother to free it. I ran out to the street, but she wouldn't look up at me. Automotive coughs as the wreck tried to start itself, gears shifting angrily into first, and Alex was screeching away from me. Standing in the street, my 3.5-inch floppy in hand, I watched her go through a red light just to put some distance between us.

Independence Day

July. She wouldn't answer my calls, no matter how many times I dialed the number. She knew from her caller ID box that it was me. *Ring-ring* for Christopher, no pickup except for the recorded dismissal of her machine. After a few days, I started calling when I knew she wasn't there just so she wouldn't be sitting, listening to me babble. Pleas sat on her answering machine like sloppily wrapped presents, waiting for her to get home and open them. But all I was getting in return was silence, a conspicuously quiet phone. She knew that my holiday was coming, what firecracker lights meant to me, that I needed to recharge on them to last another year, she knew that there was no way I would go out there alone, unescorted and unprotected, to face the mob of Philadelphians that would also be present to witness the glory. I even had her camera, and regardless of the fact that she wasn't getting any work, she loved that baby. I knew that was eating at her. But that's was how tight the door was shut.

On the morning of the Fourth, I realized I was going to have to go over to meet Alex in person. Let her beat or scream or chastise or whatever she had to do to me before we headed down to the Parkway to watch the sky combust. I bought some flowers in Reading Terminal, figured they might soften her some. Calla lilies, long and white like she liked them. Only three but shit, they costed. At the thrift shop on 44th Street I picked up a vase, a long orange glass cut like crystal. Back at the crib, it took an hour in hot water to get whatever gunk was in it cleared out. I was just trying to shove those stems in when—

Pop pop pop poppop pop

—the familiar sound of a community coming undone. It had finally come for me. This time, no faint ghost. This time, right outside my window. So loud I dropped the vase in the sink and broke the bastard, only two hours after I bought it. So shocked that instead of hugging linoleum like a sane man, Chris Jones was hanging out his window, poking his head through that big rip in the screen that the mosquitoes had been flying in for months.

Outside, an absurdly large American car, too damn long to be taking that curb that fast, screeching out an angle in front of my building. Hanging out the passenger window, the upper half of a shirtless well-built man, all I could see of his head was the top of his baseball hat (maroon and white, the old school Phillies kind). He was going through great lengths to point something out behind him. But it wasn't called pointing when you had a gun in your hand. *Pop pop pop* goes this weasel, bangs even louder than the wheels screaming a turn underneath him. It was the only thing screaming though: everybody else standing around the intersection was too busy getting down on the ground to make a sound. *Pop pop pop.* Hiding behind telephones poles and stationary automobiles so that the next *pop* wasn't for them. Look at the weasel, his gun pointing everywhere as if he wasn't even aiming at anything at all, just trying to see how many times he could pull the trigger. *Pop pop pop.* That gun looked like part of his arm.

It didn't matter how bad it wanted to, there was no way that Caddy was going to make that turn. *Pop pop pop pop.* Even when the nose cleared the parked cars below my window, the ass just flew out to greet them. Thin metal crunching, plastic cracking in long dry lines, glass going from one unified plane to many smaller individual ones. The car it clipped jumped up onto the sidewalk. Weasel man, not prepared for the impact, flailed around like a mouse in a cat's jaw, then went limp against the side of the Caddy. Arms flailing towards the ground, chest banging against the passenger door as the smoking wheels took him through a red light at Chester Avenue and beyond. Leaving bodies hugging sidewalk behind him.

I ran down the steps, calla lilies in hand. Outside, people were already rising from the ground, checking for newly opened orifices, searching their clothes for signs of wet maroon. Once satisfied that they had gained no new holes, they looked around at the others. There was a woman thirty feet from my door, lying next to the parked car that the Caddy had slammed into. She was still on the ground, forehead resting on the pavement, hands loosely hanging away from herself. Just as motionless as the car she lay beside.

I ran over, knelt by her. It was an elderly woman, a skinny one. The scarf she had tied around her head had slipped off and sat limp over the back of her skull, revealing a freckled scalp and a loose collection of white hairs. I brushed the material aside and reached for her neck to check for a pulse. Life had battered that skin soft. A hand shot out to slap my own. I jumped back, startled.

'My neck's ticklish,' she said, staring up at me. I helped her rise off the ground.

Looking around, we were all standing there, the whole neighborhood. People were talking, nodding their heads, people were brushing themselves off.

'Is everyone okay?' I yelled. All present seemed to think so. A group inspection showed there was nobody left on the ground, nobody hiding in the bushes, nobody left bleeding in a car that we didn't know about. First-floor apartment windows opened and everyone was fine in there, too. Nobody seemed to know who the guy was shooting at, but whoever that was had disappeared like the rest of the madness. And in its place were smiles. Wherever people had been hurrying to go five minutes before was forgotten. Giggles and grins. A block party without music or potato salad, just us celebrating being alive. It was like we all hit the numbers at the same time.

'Now that's a good omen!' the elderly woman said smiling, retying her scarf around her head. She danced up and down as she did it. When her bonnet was set, I handed her my flowers. She smiled so big that the top row of her dentures fell down, clacking for me. Chris Jones, the recluse, for once so proud to play the part of the Philadelphia Negro.

The *pop pop* had finally come to me and still I was standing. Not just alive, but standing, calm, watching the dust return to rest. Look at me, not even sweating on this humid afternoon. I was unshakable; I was. I was invincible. I was determined. So I was fireworks bound.

Near sunset, I got off the number 34 trolley alone, joining the current of pedestrians marching north towards the Art Museum, protected only by a T-shirt and shorts and the camera that hung before me. Together, we, the city, walked to the Parkway, feeling as if the clouds were boiling, our clothes heavy with sweat. T-shirts that would be outdated by tomorrow and flags that would be forgotten even before then, left as litter for someone getting paid overtime to pick up.

Legions of temporary nomads trudging forward in the spaces between traffic-stricken cars, the screams of drunks and infants and the overwhelming feeling that something was about to happen, something good, something free. Amateur arsonists letting bottle rockets fly over the crowd by lighting the fuse and launching them from their hands, toddlers staring at the tin sparklers they held, fantasizing about eating the flame. Cops on bikes glided down 22nd Street towards the action, their tight blue butts hanging over the seats. As they coasted, they tapped on car doors and told young men to turn their music down, trying to bring peace in the battles of sound. Yam-skinned man canvassed out on the corner of 24th and Waverly, smiling and putting his hand forward like a Tuesday morning politician, waving at children, dancing to whatever rhythm was loudest to his ears. 'Hot!' he said to me when I passed. If they packaged whatever fire burned in his skull, we'd be addicted to that, too.

The Parkway is a full mile of wide street and grassland

separating the lanes, its main road lined with flags of every nation worth arguing about, colored banners I used to stare at as a child and wonder if they existed beyond names. At the end of the street, making the whole thing look like an emperor's driveway, sits the Art Museum. That's where I was headed. A public palace complete with Greek pillars as thick as redwoods and steps so wide they seem to invite the entire city to climb them simultaneously. By the time my section of crowd poured out onto the Parkway, the museum's orange stone was illuminated in floodlights, its majesty accentuated by the fact that it was deserted and the street before it was heavily packed with worshipers. That's where the fireworks would be coming out of, so that's where I kept walking. When the flow of the crowd died I continued to charge on, armed with a sharp elbow and endless self-pardons.

Two blocks from my target, the crowd had compacted into a sweaty wall, people packed so tight they couldn't move their arms or balance themselves if they were falling. The cops had us jammed in like this, stuck on the grass partitions. They were clearing the roads for ambulances and important people. It was hard to see anything but heads. Short folks and children were scampering up shoulders, lampposts, and telephone poles. Standing confidently on streetlight boxes until mounted police rode up and told them, on eye level, to get down. I wasn't short but that's what I needed to do: climb up, get a vantage point, somewhere I could not only get a clear view of the festivities but also some good overhead shots of the crowd. Through pushes and will, I made it to the side barrier, ducking underneath the wooden horse when the cop closest wasn't looking. When he turned around, I was already walking towards him to ask how I could get back to the press booth. Nodding, he pointed me down the street towards my goal.

I made it all the way to Eakins Circle, directly across from the Art Museum steps, when the PA system started announcing tonight's celebration. The sky was as black as North Philly. On the podium, a local diva was reinterpreting 'The Star Spangled Banner,' prancing about the notes, determined to make the song hers. I tried getting a shot (maybe I could dish it off to her publicist later in exchange for cash), but the crowd wouldn't spread for me. I still needed higher ground; there was a fountain about thirty yards away I started pushing towards.

Its ornate bottom was shaped like a square, a life-size copper animal guarding every corner. Each beast was currently being ridden by spectators who'd had the foresight to arrive earlier than me. At the center of the monument, atop a massive granite podium, sat George Washington on his perpetually trotting horse, its metal muscles bulging from the weight it would continually bear. Besides George, the space went unclaimed. I could get shots of everything from up there.

Climbing into the fountain's dried basin, I pushed through bodies as the crowd continued to condense in anticipation. At the base of Washington's podium, it was clear why it went unclaimed. The bastard had to be fifteen feet high. The singing had stopped; the mayor was talking; it wouldn't be long now. I had to get up there. My only chance was a waterspout further along the side, an old painted thing that probably didn't even work any more. It looked solid: it stuck out about two feet from the ground. This was it, this would be my final victory.

The crowd around the pipe spread for me once it realized I was about to do something stupid. Using the yard of space I had as a runway, I thrust forward. My left foot landed squarely on the spout's top, my calf coiled and aching to be sprung. In an instant, a leg that was bent shot into straight rigidity. I was flying. My hands reaching upward, my body stretching so fiercely that sections of my vertebrae no longer connected. Higher I floated, the distant pedestal above becoming close, feasible, nearly in my hands. And then it was becoming distant again, as far away as Brixton, moving more beyond my capacity the further I fell to the ground. Landing, my feet stung, Alex's camera banged hard against my chest. I tried again. Up. Down. I tried again. Up. Down. I tried again. Too dumb to stop. Certain that my ancestors would witness my struggle, bless me with the gift of flight.

'Yo cuz, you need a boost.' He was a short brother, muscular. Behind him his girlfriend seemed annoyed he had offered to touch me. In three seconds, I thanked him so many times he already regretted his offer. My booster cradled his hands and leaned against the stone for balance as I stepped into his palms. Up, up, I was reaching. Still a good six feet away but getting better. The strong little bastard was pushing me higher as I balanced myself against the granite, lifting his hands from his waistline to his shoulders. I could hear him grunting over the noise of the crowd. Above us, all my fingers twinkled for something to hold on to. General Washington remained in his saddle, motionless and nonplused. Wedging my foot against the wall and bending his knees for support, booster had pushed me above his own head now. He was a superhero. The crowd had turned from the mayor's final words and it was booster they were watching. Two hands over his head, his arms trembling, balancing my one sneaker in his palms. I almost didn't care that I was still about three feet from touching the top. There was a great view from here; maybe he could just hold me for an hour till the fireworks were over. Maybe we could walk like this home together.

'You got it, black,' another voice yelled up to me as a brother as tall as a Sixer stepped forth from the onlookers. His skin was so sweaty, the gold chains around his neck looked dull on his flesh. 'Come on here,' he told me. He was someone I would never risk slightly nudging, let alone stepping on, but he stretched out next to me, arms over his head, making a higher stair with his hands for me to walk into. I did, shifting my weight to the next leg. 'Reach!' he demanded, and I couldn't deny him. Grabbing hold of the metal hoof of Washington's steed, I pulled myself onto the structure. 'Go, go, go,' they were chanting below me. Forgetting the consequences of gravity, I rose, stood up, grabbed on to Washington's oversize left thigh and pulled myself onto the back of his saddle. I had never ridden a horse before. One hand around the president's waist, I waved in victory as the crowd thundered its pleasure around me.

That noise. The sound of every praise I'd ever been denied

bursting forth as the roar of a city. My shirt ruffled in their wind as I reached out for it, feeling myself grow big in places I'd assumed were hard and impenetrable. The main stage was forgotten: the acres of faces were on me now, the crop of arms wagged in my direction. Inflate me with your joy. If they could've seen my tears, they would have known they were thank-yous. Together we cheered as the symphony began to play, as the sky finally exploded in my honor.

Lightning pastels shrieked above us, electric rainbows streaked reflections along skyscraper walls, glass becoming canvas, sonic bursts bouncing off the buildings' bodies like twenty-five-cent pinballs. *SKEEZ*: shooting up from the ground as a hopeful white light. *POW*: the drab nomad exploding into a nation of resplendent fires. They are brilliant, each dot its own sun, growing dimmer as they fall, until they arrive back at the surface as mere embers. Ash rained around me as I rode my metal steed, the orange glow eating at charcoaled paper. Above us stars were coming into creation, universes no less significant because of their size or brevity.

The amazing thing: that wasn't the most stunning sight out here. What was above was brilliant, but what below was divine. Look at how beautiful we were. Faces turned to the sky, illuminated and glowing, screaming into the light. We were there, all of us. South Philly, North Philly, Germantown, West, Chestnut Hill, Main Line. Every culture, every shade, every class we had to offer, unified by eyes that cheered louder than mouths could, allied by the celebration of fire and birth, of destruction and life. All screaming because we understood what it was about: for one hour, on one night, we had beaten the world. For one moment, this was the place where existence raged brightest, where each instant was spent without past or future in consideration. We were the winners. There was no place else to be but here, no other land that could tempt us.

I took lots of pictures that night, several good enough to be used as promotional advertisements. I got them scanned, had the copy

and layout planned for them by the time they came back from
the processor. They all came out well; they were all work I was
proud of, strong additions to pad my portfolio, but there was one
in particular that rocked me. It was taken aiming down into the
crowd from my statue-sitting vantage, a photo of a throng of
faces, their skin and clothes bathed in the powder blue glow of
whatever was combusting above them off camera. Mouths open
like expecting chicks, retinas ravishing light, hands waving
miniature flags as if they were trying to fan the fire. Something
about their jawbones or clothes or posture: they were so easy for
me to recognize, these people I belonged to. The tag line, bold
and right justified at the bottom of the page, was all I wanted to
say about it: *Philadelphia: Celebrating a Local Holiday.* It made
everything I ever did before look disposable.

The morning after it was completed, I walked this and the rest
of the creations into the Philly tourist board in the municipal
building over on Broad, dropping it with the secretary and then
heading over to the electric company to pick up phones. By the
time I got home the message was on my machine: 'Can you
come in tonight?' I didn't make it until nine o'clock. The guy,
Saul, was the only one left on the floor; his office was the sole
light on.

'It's fantastic. It's absolutely what we want. You don't know
how many freakin' images of Independence Hall and the Liberty
Bell I've had to see on this project,' he told me. 'This work was
done by a real Philadelphian, someone who knows this place.
That's why we opened the bids to local independents in the first
place.' Saul was about the same age as I was, mid-thirties. I
recognized him from the schoolyard of Henry H. Houston
Elementary, but didn't tell him so. He had my favorite ad in his
hand.

'There's love in this piece, y'know?' he said, nodding at me.
'There's love.'

Love Park

'So I didn't get the job.' Rat poison. Sara Lee. Send my ashes to Brockwell.

'Chris, relax. They just want to see another example of your work,' Saul was saying. 'Listen to me on this. Usually they would just request another look at your portfolio—'

'They're overseas. I won't get one back for a couple of weeks.'

'Right. I understand that. I explained that to the board; they understand that. That's why I'm asking you to put together another sample of your concept so they can make sure. We're a city-funded organization. Money's tight. We only get so much for the year and they just want to make sure we're not wasting it. I don't think we would be, but they just want to know that.'

'So I invest more money, more time.'

'This is what's going to happen: you shoot one of the ideas you submitted in your proposal, how's that? Then, when the board accepts it, you can just include the expenses in the final budget. That sounds fair, right? You need the money quick – that's not a problem. I'll cut the check the second they give the okay. All you have to do is get it in by a week from tomorrow, Friday, and everybody's happy.'

'What happens if everybody's not happy?' I ask, but Saul doesn't have that answer. I do. No London job because no plane ticket money and get-settled cash. No electric company job because if I cut another day I wouldn't have one. No staying in my hovel because getting this done meant blowing the rent and food budget just to pay folks a fractional down payment of what I would owe them later. Searching trashcans for food professionally and arm wrestling bums for corner rights.

I put the red disk that held my Lionskins dreams in a manila envelope and went by Alex's place, dropping it in her mail slot when I knew she wasn't home. The disk was broken in two and said 'Sorry' in black Magic Marker on both halves. Four days went by. Nothing. I thought of calling, telling her that I had this shoot, that it could be a big gig for her, a portfolio maker, but didn't. It would just insult her further, me pretending that money was an appropriate enticement for her reappearance. Accepting her absence, I prepared to photograph this sample ad myself.

I scheduled the shoot for Monday, the only sunny day forecasted for the week. We would do it at Love Park, lots of space; if you came early enough there was nobody there but the few homeless dudes who slept in its bushes, and great views: besides the LOVE statue, you had the tower of City Hall behind you, the Parkway's Fountain of Angels and the Art Museum in front. I found a stylist in the back of *Market Edge* who gave me a low fee that I could pay later, and he even knew a model I could book through him. They would be coming down from New York together. Minimal risk, maximum potential, that was the idea.

Tuesday, five A.M. After fifteen minutes a trolley finally wandered up to 46th Street to take me downtown. A pathetic, waddling thing, I sat with my equipment bags willing it to become rapid transit, cursing myself because I knew I was supposed to *be* there at five. That moment of dawn, when the universe gave you better lighting than any mechanical device could manage, was only 40 minutes away. With rain clouds scheduled to arrive before lunch and make a guest of themselves for days to come, there was no way I could blow this time. Arriving in City Hall, I ran up gray stairs and left an exit gate spinning in my wake, jogging the short distance to the park, where they would be waiting for me. 'I'm here!' I was prepared to say. But outside was empty. Just me, Love Park, and a hot dog vendor.

Around now is when Alex would tell me to stop bugging, to remind myself that those guys were driving all the way from Brooklyn, that they were doing me the favor of bringing the extra equipment, too, so they could be a minute or two off. Actually no, they really couldn't, but it was too late to fire them now.

Growing tired of torturing myself with the sight of an empty road, I walked off to pick up trash. For the sake of the photo, we could at least pretend we kept good house. Checking back to the street after every bend down, no parked car appeared. In ten minutes I'd already filled the mesh can affixed to the Love Park ground, and still no show. No life appeared at all: it was too early even for rats. Then, standing in the hedges, while reaching for an empty Krimpet wrapper, I heard something. Splashing coming from the fountain in the level below.

There he was, my poltergeist, standing up to his shins in a pool of his own saliva, rabid froth pouring from his mouth and covering his body in white foam. But that was wrong, that wasn't it. Those were soapsuds coating his flesh; I could smell the perfume from here. The yam-skinned man was taking his morning bath, admiring the views as he scrubbed himself down. It was a sane version, this one, escaped from madness and enjoying a moment of freedom before he was rediscovered. Splash, splash, splash. Putting the wrapper in the bag, Yam-man heard the crinkling and turned up to me, every bit of him dripping as he looked to where I was standing in the hedge. We stared at each other, alone out here, motionless except for the wind on my bag and his body's dripping. Then, ending the draw, I waved. Yam-man waved back at me, lowering his salute when he reached for the dishwashing detergent sitting on the fountain's edge. I watched him pour the yellow liquid onto the hairs of his chest before I walked back to my bags.

I should have had food with me for all the participants, but the kiosk across the street, with its smells of eggs and butter, of pork fat burning endlessly on a steel grill, would have to do. Too preoccupied with paying the others, I forgot to bring extra cash for myself. A pocket check revealed no MAC card and only four bucks in change, enough to buy a cheese and egg sandwich with ketchup and onions: the way I liked it. It was big, it came on a hoagie roll, the yellow substance of its contents overflowing on to the foil. To wash it down, a bottle of chocolate milk had been recruited. With my last quarter, I picked up a soft pretzel to serve as an appetizer, and I was walking back to my pile of equipment, proud of my bounty, when the stylist pulled up in his purple mini-van. He got out alone, slamming the car door behind him and walking towards me as if I had caused some problem.

'I know, he's not here, he did not even show up, I waited for him for over a half hour but he didn't come, I couldn't even get him on the line till twenty minutes ago, I do not work like this.' Stylist Man told me as he put an open cell phone into my free hand.

'What the hell are you talking about? You recommended this guy!' I yelled at his back, him holding up a hand to shield the back of his head. I put the phone to my head. It smelled like it had been deep-fried in activator. A voice said, 'I'm so sorry—' before I had a chance to hang it up. I should have never hired a New Yorker to pose as a Philadelphian.

'Christopher, don't fret.' He had taken a seat on the closest bench and was stretching his legs. 'I have a few contacts with models in Philadelphia. I brought their numbers. I've already been calling. Eventually, someone has to pick up on the other end. I'm sure we can get someone by noon. I won't even charge you for a full day shoot. I promise.'

'It's going to rain! At noon, it will be raining here! And even if it doesn't, later they'll be too many people walking around here for what I want.' Stylist man flinched again, and regaining confidence, motioned for the return of his phone.

I went down by the fountain to eat, to think. It was ten after six. The stylist made calls from his cell phone, waking pretty men across the city who might do the job. The light was still good. It could be a sunny day; maybe the dark clouds would get lost in transit. We might still have a little over an hour to work with. So I sat, unwrapping my food, trying to think only of how good that grub was going to feel between my teeth, on my tongue, and then going down. I had the sandwich in both hands, ready to bite an isolated moment of bliss, when I heard that fool splashing towards me.

'Why you here?'

'I was supposed to take pictures,' I explained for no reason.

'Pictures, pictures,' Yam-man said, stepping out of the fountain. Water streamed off his legs into dark puddles of concrete that looked like shadows, clear bead diamonds dripping off his body to join the darkness. Naked, his skin was a thin elastic membrane hiding cabled planes, sheets of muscle defining themselves in places rarely seen, transforming from wires to balls as he wrung his hair in his hands, popping in small brown mounds as he shook himself dry like a dog. I covered my food and eyes. When I looked again, he stood before me, shoulders back like bad news, chin forward like future dues, water evaporating off arms that looked as if they could carry whatever was placed in them. Even this life he was living.

'Gimme some money, man.'

Seeing the vision, I put my food down. 'You want some quick money?' I asked him.

'Yeah. Gimme some money.'

'I'm not just going to give it to you. I got something I need you to do. Some quick, easy work. What's up? You want to earn it?'

Yam-man stood, dripping, looking at me for a moment with his head slightly cocked, then said, 'Nah', and walked away from me. Back into the fountain, his soap in hand. I went after him.

Yam-man knew I was coming as soon as I splashed into the water behind him. Revealing a startled look over his shoulder, he began wading out of my way. When he saw I was getting closer, he started running, staying inside the fountain circle as if his feet wouldn't work on dry land. I splashed after him, struggling to keep my footing on its slimy bottom, but gaining still, and after a few times around the circle I was nearly on him. I dived forth, catching his legs, and we splashed down together.

'What the hell's wrong with you?' he asked. I'm sure that question had been asked of him countless times before.

'I want to give you money. I want to help you out.'

'Well, gimme the damn money and leave me alone.'

'No. No charity. You take care of yourself this time.'

The yam-skinned man was the perfect size; even the shoes fit him. He was so good in that suit, his dreads clean and brushed to order, looking like a redbone Frederick Douglass. This was the man somebody had wanted him to be, the one some mother had imagined. As people started walking by to work, you almost expected him to join them, to grab a suitcase from under a park bench and follow. You could almost believe that somewhere there was an office and a set of responsibilities he belonged to. Click click, make it last forever. And didn't he love getting his picture taken? Turn this way, a little, a little, good. So many people focused on him, he blossomed with the shutter's every clench. Prancing about as if he were the only monument in this town worth noticing. Once I got him to keep his teeth hidden while he smiled, we were grooving. I could see the billboards already. When I saw the Polaroid proofs, I could already hear Saul's voice telling me that I had the job, I could already feel that check being passed into my hand, could see myself looking at it, knowing that my imprisonment was over. So clear was this vision that, a week later, when I went over to the meet with Saul and all of that actually happened, I felt as if I was living a rerun. It was anti-climax for me. Those Polaroids in my hand, I already understood that I was gone.

We broke at eight o'clock. Things were going so smooth that I suggested we head up to Strawberry Mansion to get a jump on the park shots. Yam-man nodded OK. A day like this should be prolonged. I could work with what we'd accomplished through a week of rainstorms. We just had to pack, get something to eat, and then we'd drive up to North Philly and continue. Even the stylist seemed cool with it.

After locking up the van, I finally retrieved the food that had been crying for me, my mouth overflowing with desire. Yam-man sat on the nearest bench, so I joined him. My hands trembling with hunger, I ripped the bags open. On the other side of my feast, Yam-man sat with his suit on. He was staring down 15th Street, watching the cars stop at the red light. From his face, it looked as if the craziness was catching up to him. Seated, the fact that he didn't have socks on was evident.

'Nice, shiny day, right?' I remarked, ripping tinfoil desperately away from the still warm sandwich. Even in August you could see the steam rising. The salt dried my nostrils as I sniffed it into me.

'Yup,' Yam-man said back, swiveling his head around and immediately noticing the food I had acquired. I gave him the money right after we'd finished shooting: I could still see the twenties hanging out like a handkerchief from his breast pocket.

'I got it over there,' I said, pointing. 'From that guy.' Yam-man kept his eyes linked to my bounty. Maybe it had been so long he didn't know how to use bills any more, particularly of this denomination. I pulled open my chocolate milk and I took the paper off the straw.

'Drinking,' Yam-man said, staring at it.

'Over there. Look' – he didn't – 'over there.' I kept pointing until he glanced away from my beverage and towards my finger. As soon my hand dropped, so did his eyes, watching me get the lid off.

'Starving' Yam-man said as saliva stretched from his bottom lip to his lap, making a charcoal pool in the gray herringbone.

'I gave you money,' I reminded him, poking at it in his breast pocket. His body rocked with my push, then came back again.

'Need some eats,' he added, his eyes watering.

'Yam-man, go buy some of your own.'

'Name's sir.'

'All right, sir,' I smiled.

'Sir Love.'

'Shit,' I said, and gave in to him. Pushing my food his way till he reached out for it. Nudging my drink over so he could wash it down.

You never saw somebody enjoy food like that. Taking that sandwich in bites the size of his hand. Gulping half the chocolate milk at once and then sloshing it through his teeth like mouthwash before swallowing it. When the brother was done, I handed him a napkin to wipe the ketchup and grease off his mouth. He used it and handed it back to me. We were just sitting there, two Philly boys, content to lean back where we were and feel the sun lay down upon us. Comfortable with our destinies, our place in the world. No other life to run to, no lot to run desperately from. Funny how much nicer this town was when you couldn't feel it sitting on you.

My Sign

I had a gig and a check to prove it. After I left Saul's office I kept peeking at it, peeling back its envelope in the crowded elevator: I see you. It was a little, thin piece of paper, but it was real; this I kept trying to believe in. Insubstantial in weight, yes, but if I rolled it into a ball and threw it in the eye of that security guard at the front door, it would hurt him: it existed. If I opened my envelope and took out my check and folded it into a paper airplane, it would fly: it had properties. If I planted it in my checking account, within days it would sprout cash that I, in turn, would have access to. I would have access, too. That was the reality I had the most difficulty accepting.

For days after it was deposited, to procrastinate from my real duty of preparing for the campaign to come, I dialed the bank's number to see if my promise had bloomed. Limiting myself to one perusal each hour, never boring of the same automated denial because I knew eventually I would call and my dream would be true. The absurd yet standard-rate price I was being paid to oversee the creative of this marketing drive would in one moment appear. Boom. Cash. That was magic. In anticipation, some of that imaginary money had already been spent. These ghost dollars whose power had no relation to their physical substance. Because of them, the travel agency already had my tickets on reserve, the checks for overdue bills had been mailed (to P.O. box addresses in boring states, it would be weeks before they would be deposited). Because of them I wasn't going crazy from the absence of one stubborn buck-toothed female. Because of them I could at least spend time investing in a plan to make that reality an outdated one. Maybe that was the purpose of the Alex Reconciliation Agenda: to keep me sane with the illusion that I had some control over the matter. To let me focus my anxiety on to a physical thing, a series of tasks that I could handle.

Of course, the Agenda was not a particularly elaborate plan – I was just going to get my Philly ad for Sir Love the Yam-man blown up to poster size and present it to her – but the goals of the mission were modest as well. True, the ultimate success determinant would have been total conflict resolution, complete forgiveness, but that was neither realistic nor dwelled upon. The stated victory parameters were much simpler: I just wanted her to know that I was trying, that maybe I was even changing also. Even if she decided not to let me back in her life, I wanted her to base that decision on the man I was and not some outdated reality.

It was this necessity that motivated me as I called to order the poster from the lithographic shop over on Arch. They were talking size, dimensions; I was talking passion, sincere emotional angst! Do not speak to me of this 1' by 4', this 3' by 6' nonsense! What do I care of abstract measurements? Give me size! Make this poster so big that there is no way Alex can ignore either one of us. If an extra inch improves my chances, so be it.

My former job seemed to be a problem. Apparently, Mrs Hutton's comment that 'If you miss another day, don't bother coming in' was not as literal a statement as I had originally interpreted it. Regardless of the fact that I called the night before my absence to offer my sincere apology for leaving the electric company on such awkward terms, there was still a misunder-standing. It was explained to me (by my former parasite/temp agency) that Mrs Hutton was not entirely pleased with my behavior, and this displeasure had manifested itself in her refusal to sign my time-slip until 'you go in there and quit proper.'

While I barely had the time and no longer needed the money, in respect to the week I spent working for that cash, I decided to take up the challenge and right there, right then, walked out the door.

My trolley was, as all trolleys are, a slow thing. Bicycles whose riders used no hands glided casually past us even as we attempted full speed. By the time I actually arrived at 23rd Street, my bravado had evaporated like the mist it was. There was, I realized now that I was close to making contact, a chance that Mrs Hutton might yell at me. What if she yelled at me and then didn't sign my check at all? What if she got Cindy to hold me down as she slapped me around a bit? For a brief, unexplained moment that seemed entirely rational, I decided that a more prudent action would be to delay this confrontation as long as possible, and it was this that led to the first of the miracles that would happen that day. I walked over to an ATM to check my ghost balance, to try to get out more cash than I thought was yet there, and I actually heard *it*, that near forgotten song, the – thank God – flutter of real cash coming back out at me.

I damn near expected Fionna to emerge from hiding behind a parking meter to rejoin me. Motivated by this newly realized fortune, I decided to further delay my appointment with the electric company by picking up my poster.

It was at least a three-mile walk, but I was prepared. Of late, I'd been walking everywhere, taking in paths I'd been content for years to see blur pass. To ensure a random mugging wouldn't make the act impossible, I even swung past the travel agent's on Samson to take care of my reservations. So simple, I trade my paper for theirs, and then I have tickets in my hand, a promise that on a certain date, at a certain time, I could fly out of here. Not even earth-moving news any more since I could already feel that gravity lessening beneath me as I took Aldrin hops down the road, seeing things around this town I hadn't noticed since childhood. I was almost disappointed when I arrived at my destination so soon.

I stepped up proudly to the counter and declared I was there to pick up my order. Soon I was whipping out a book of checks that floated instead of bounced. Yes, the price quoted seemed quite obscene. I would not be ordering from here again anytime soon!

'So, where's your car? If it's in front you'll want to pull around back. We can load it on there.'

'Naw, that's cool, I'm walking.'

'Walking?'

'Yes. Well, eventually I'll probably hop the El, but walking there and back, yes.' What was wrong with that? It was a nice day. My shoes were comfortable and showed good sense. People don't walk enough any more. A door opened from the side of the room and another attendant (they all had the same blue tennis shirt, wasn't that nice?) came in pulling a dolly holding a dozen absurdly large cardboard graham crackers. When he said my name I hopped with glee to meet him. Mine? I asked of the sheet on top, and he nodded, so I grabbed my poster, thanked them both for doing good business, and headed for the door. My booty was a large thing, as tall as I was, and I was taking care to balance it as I tried to open the door, nearly succeeding before I heard, 'Yo cuz, when you gonna pick up the rest? We close at seven.'

'What are you talking about? This is my order.'

'You sure?' the attendant asked me, and apparently I wasn't, because when he took my package from me, laid it on the counter, and lifted half of its cardboard packaging off and away, what was revealed to me was not the yam-man in all his glory, but merely a huge tile of the elephantized foot of him, a blow-up of that spot of ankle between his shoe and cuff that I had PhotoShopped to make it look like he had socks on.

'So, money, how you gonna get the rest of them?'

I am stupid. I looked at him like he might tell me.

I walked back to Center City, trying to negotiate the inconceivable but true: the Alex Agenda was threatened. This could not be tolerated, my pace increased just thinking about it. I needed to commission a photographer soon, and if it wasn't her, I would need to book in advance. It had to be her. I tried to remain calm as I ducked in the electric company building. Instead of being met and escorted in by armed guards, the front desk trolls barely noticed my arrival. With swipe-key in hand, I slipped through the entrance as if I still worked there, petrified that maybe that was true, that the past weeks had been nothing but a glucose reaction spiked by one too many lunchtime visits to 30th Street Station for a super-size drink and fries. But the delusion didn't take hold. I couldn't feel it: that pull, that dull tugging of my ass to that gray seat in there, that mute demand of the monotonous life from which five P.M. only provided a momentary reprieve. I was a free man – I knew this as I pushed open my door to the familiar office and saw the room of those still in captivity.

They were all there, sucked to their seats. The phones were barely ringing; it was July, even back-due heating bills had been taken care of. Relieved to be able to pause from trying to look busy, they looked up at me. It was after lunch, but all Reggie had on his desk was a bag of pork rinds: for shame, they still hadn't been paid. Reggie pushed up his glasses to get a better look and yelled, 'Chris boogie!' before Mrs Hutton came out of her office to greet me.

I was to be berated publicly – fine. As Mrs Hutton had perceived it, I had undermined her leadership, so I appreciated her need to reestablish authority. 'You don't just disappear, one day you're there, the next you ain't. There are responsibilities . . .' This too was warranted. I knew I was an awful former teleservice agent, although I would have accentuated the 'former' if she gave me the chance to open my mouth. Vent your months of frustrations. Yes, I was truly incompetent at this job, so wasn't it fantastic that I would never have to do it again? Wasn't that just the best outcome for all? This is why I was smiling, not because Cindy was giving me a wink of support behind Mrs Hutton's back, and certainly not out of any desire to belittle my former manager, and yet my pleasure seemed to make her yell louder. Her angry face, with its heat, its engorged eyes, red nose and cheeks, was a scary thing. But when you know you'll never have to deal with it again, it can be such a joyous sight. That's when I felt myself kind of bouncing, rocking back in forth to my life's song. I had thought it an ever so slight movement until I saw the way Mrs Hutton was looking at me: *What broke in him?* Chains, darling! When Clive – he was looking so good today, must be four weeks rock-free – started snapping his bony fingers along with my rhythm, I just fell into it. This joy. I was dancing. Very odd but true, I was moving with glee, with freedom, and I must have been doing something right, because Mrs Hutton stopped talking, instead taking out my timesheet in slow, cautious movements; without missing one of Clive's digitally produced beats, I watched her sign it.

Who knew, if I took this to the temp agency, if it would one day clear? Who knew if I would see any of these people again? Who knew anything? At the exit, hand on the knob of a door already opened, I turned back to them. Natalie was smiling at me, those oft hidden incisors punctuating her grin.

'You all should come with me!' I insisted. Mrs Hutton shook with my words, spun around and stomped to the back room, presumably to call security.

'Nigger, you better make a break for it,' Cindy offered.

'I've got work for the day, for you. I'll pay you. I'll pay you as much as you make in a week.' They all just kept looking at me, not knowing what I was. But I saw them: people I wanted to give something to, people who could help me solve my Alex needs.

'Come on, you're not even getting paid! You might as well get some money to hold you over while you look for a new job. I'll give you what you make in a week to just get up and come with me right now!' I would give twice this just to see it happen. I reached into my pocket and held the emerald beacons up to them.

At the site of the cash, Reggie stood up so fast he nearly knocked his monitor over, but I knew Reggie and understood that this was a purely physical reaction. But then Natalie got up, too, grabbing her fake leather pocketbook and keys off the table, and I realized something was happening here. Forget Lynol, who sat in my old seat laughing at me; I could see how his stare was caught on my hand. When Cindy and Clive stood up in unison, pushing their chairs in behind them, I raised the mast of my arm higher, proudly waving my herald.

Reggie and Cindy got the billboard. Natalie was sent to get packing tape and hoagies. Clive and I were off to 43rd Street to get the wood that would allow us to hoist it up. We were to meet back up at the abandoned supermarket behind Alex's block. Everybody knew the one.

At the lumberyard, I asked to use their phone and got the proper measurements from the printer. What I needed was not a permanent structure, nothing to be mounted on some wall to last for months of inspection. Alex just had to see it, take it in for as long as she needed to. My goal was to nail together one beam to go across its top, four more to hold it up in the air. If I had something like that, then we could tape the image's panels together from the back, and hang it like a curtain.

Clive agreed, it was a brilliant idea. Wagging his head saying, 'You got something here, you truly do.' All in all, he was very supportive. While we waited for them to retrieve our order, Clive asked me for a twenty-buck advance to hop around to the store. I slipped a crisp one into his ashen hand and didn't even regret it until fifteen minutes later, when I was standing next to my new two-pound hammer, a box of long nails and these wood beams, and homeboy had yet to reappear. When my cab arrived I was thinking, The son of bitch jacked me up for twenty ones, he couldn't even wait to juice me for the other 180, but here Clive comes through the entrance gate.

'Yo cuz, long line,' he said, strutting towards me. 'That line, it was like . . . yo,' He reached for the beam I had in my hand but then tripped forward, landed on his knees, and then jumped back up again. Watching the whole thing through glazed eyes, giggling it all away from him.

The smell of the dust falling back to the ground, the smell of the wood we had recently found, the smell of burnt plastic from the man who'd once abandoned it.

Everybody else was at the lot when we got there. As I untied the wood from the hood, I could hear them arguing behind me about who got what sandwich. When Cindy saw Clive stumble smiling out of the back of the cab, she paused from her denunciation of egg salad to walk over and give him the greatest left hook landed in Philly since the retirement of Joe Frazier. Clive made like a top, arms out, round and round, centrifugal force keeping him standing. Behind them, the others quietly reached for whatever hoagie was closest and sat down.

I could tell they'd been talking about me, most definitely using the word 'crazy' and reassuring themselves that they really had seen the money in my hand. They looked to Clive (who was somehow managing to eat between spits of blood) to see if he had discovered something in his extra moments with the suspect.

'So, what you want us to do?' Cindy was the first to ask, wiping the mayonnaise off her lips with the lightest dabs.

'I want you to help me hold this picture up for a second. I need to show it to this lady. She has to see it,' I told them.

'That's a lot to do for some ass' was the only response I got, and after Clive said it, nobody laughed but him. Cindy started getting up and Reggie quickly scooted his butt away from Clive in case she came charging, but all she did was throw down her cigarette and start giving orders. Her audience was responsive.

A big task literally, but a simple one. It was the only job elementary school had prepared us for. The others were nearly as eager as I was, and they mixed their labors with conversations on which creditor they would pay first. On all accounts, it seemed the cable man would be very fortunate next week. Reggie laid out the billboard sheet by sheet upside down, reading off the numbers on their backs to see the order. Natalie hung behind him, stretching tape out to the proper size, ready to lay it down. I watched her take care that the sheets were properly aligned and there was no gaps between them. They were perfectly straight; Natalie was good at this, much better than she was at answering phones. Yes, she'd bought the wrong tape (the silver electric stuff instead of the clear kind), but since it was going on the back it didn't matter.

'Stop making so much fucking noise,' Cindy yelled at Clive, but how else could he hammer? Besides, the real problem was that he only hit the nail every third time he swung. I should have taken it from him but the whole thing made me nervous, so as Cindy barked the others on, I skirted off around the corner.

Her car sat rusting on the side of the road. A light shone from the opaque glass of her bathroom window. Alex was there. Alex was real. Nothing had happened to her, none of my kidnapping or accident fears were true; she really had pushed me away from her. Wanting more, I walked closer, hearing my footsteps louder than my rubber soles could have been. Her door was flat, red. I laid my ear on its surface and it was cool also. Inside was movement, a television, further proof of her life in this world.

When I got back, it was done. The billboard's huge white back was a paper blanket strapped to the haphazard wooden frame. Natalie paced around it, adding tape to the random parts she could reach at its edges, everyone else stood back, sucking Kools. There was nothing left to do but eat our food, and then, with the rumpling of paper, even that was completed. Reggie, making a jump-shot of his balled paper towards a disused trash bin, said, 'I heard they're hiring over at Comcast Direct: customer service agents, ten dollars an hour.' He followed with, 'It might even be twelve,' and everyone nodded and raised eyebrows, hopeful.

'You sure this thing is gonna work?' Cindy asked, walking closer to our creation. Yes, it looked good. The tape should hold long enough for Alex to get a good look at it.

'If you fucked up with me, I'd want roses. That's what I'd want. Not them cheap ones you get at Wawa neither,' Cindy continued.

'She likes calla lilies.'

'Them shits is good too,' Clive offered, flinching when Cindy turned around.

They were ready to get moving before I was. It couldn't be avoided. Reggie got on one end and I on the other, and we struggled to lift our flag into the air. Clive was having trouble walking straight, so he was put in the middle and Cindy stood on the other side in case he or the structure started to fall. It was a tricky rising. Initially, I thought the frame would be the first to break, but once it was up and I felt the weight of the paper, heard the sound of it in tension, I thought it would surely rip before we could get it around the corner. Any strong gust of wind and either that would happen, or the five us would be carried away like hang-gliders. Walking in small steps, stopping to readjust grips when necessary, neither disaster happened. Tiptoeing in front of Alex's place, I thought that we would hold it in the street, but there was already a car behind me, honking. Reggie led us to the sidewalk across from her, and when I told him this was it, we were here, he brought his end closer to the apartment building wall and we leaned the rest of our structure there. In unison, 'Whews' and sore hands shook as we stepped away from it. Behind the image came a cry of complaint that we were ruining a tenant's view, to which Reggie helpfully yelled back, 'Pretend it's night.'

I stood around with the rest of them looking up at it, trying to figure out if it was going to fall, until I realized everyone was waiting for me to do this. So I walked to Alex's door and pushed the bell. The TV was on, I heard a commercial. Commercials ended, back to programming. I rang again, twice, then I started knocking, wanting to keep going till my fists hurt but knowing that might alienate her further. Stopped, feeling the impact on my knuckles subside, I heard no movement inside. Behind me my coworkers whispered; I could feel them looking at me. I waited for steps that wouldn't come. It wasn't until I walked away, resolved to find a pay phone and give her number yet another try, that I heard the creak of a hinge being pulled open. Alex stood, hands on hips. I prepared to explain, to apologize, but quickly she looked beyond me. She saw it. I knew this not only because of the focusing of the eyes, but also from the shock on the face that held them. I watched as she took in the spectacle of it, of odd Christopher and a group of strange negroes staring back at her, standing next to this displaced billboard image. And yes, by the narrowing of the eyes, the clearing of the throat, it was clear Alex was preparing to yell at me, to cast away my feeble attempt at a spell, but then came the savior of recognition, awkwardly muting her before a sound was made. Choking her by what this was, who must have done it, and what this act must say about where he had evolved to. Shutting her up long enough to crest with its climax. Fall with me. Drop into my baptismal. Look at his face, see the identity of that distinguished gentleman captured flat before you, and realize what that means about the nature of apology, growth and regret. That's right, look, my lady, and when you look, please see. See what sign towers before you. And when you see, please hear this also. That Alex I love you. That Alex, I love this place, too, no matter where I go in this life, I will never run away from either one of you.

'I see Saul gave you some work' were the first words she said to me, but when her voice cracked on the last syllable, I knew that I had her. I knew, that at some time in the future, I would tease her about the tears she was currently dropping and that she would punch my arm or roll her eyes in denial that this had ever happened.

'I got it. The job I'm supposed to have,' I said, stepping closer. Alex had no shoes on and her toes wiggled 'hi' to me through the holes in her socks. 'I want you to do it, too. It should last a few weeks, be a lot of work. It'll be great.' Alex nodded, looked back from the billboard to me again.

'And when it's over, what happens? What happens after you're done that?'

Chris Jones, stunningly prepared on this day, was so eager to give her the answer to the question that he nearly ripped her tickets while yanking them out of his pocket and slapping them into her hand. Alex knew what they were as soon as she saw the cardboard holder, but she opened and read them anyway.

'Roundtrip,' she said, nodding, inspecting them.

'That's right, lady. All there and paid for. Right there! You got to come with me.'

'What about yours?' she asked, motioning with her head to my still thick pocket.

'What about it?'

'You got roundtrip too?' Alex asked me. I looked back at her relaxed, hands at my sides, smiling lightly into her eyes. It was clear to both of us that I didn't. Alex sighed, but it was a sound neither of exasperation or exhaustion. I was her friend. I was who I was.

'That doesn't mean I won't be buying a ticket back again.' We both hung there for a moment, not saying anything, just knowing that.

When I pulled out the cash, everybody was happy. Nobody doesn't like getting paid, but for these folks it was something special. Despite the shoving, I still made sure to pay Natalie first, and by the time I had counted out her $200 the rest were in a perfect line behind her. Clive offered weak protests when Cindy demanded I give her guardianship of his money, so I ignored him and obeyed her. The only other words muttered were divisions of twenty as they re-counted their booty.

Behind us, a gust of a passing SEPTA bus sent the billboard flapping in large bass-filled waves that made us all prepare to be crushed. Reggie ran to the other side of the street. 'Yo Chris,' he yelled, 'what you want now?'

'I don't know. Take it down, maybe,' I offered, looking back to Alex to see if she still needed to see it some more. Alex was hugging herself, talking to Natalie in a way that said that they already knew each other from some other, distant context. Such a small town.

In moments, what was a dream became a ball of paper the size of a snowman's ass. Next to it sat bundles of barely used timbers with nails sticking out their ends. One vision discarded. Maybe the trashmen would take it when they came by. Maybe they wouldn't. The future was a hard thing to know. I walked back to Alex as soon as Natalie, with smiles and waves goodbye, walked away from her.

'Do you really like it?' I asked Alex when Clive, the last of the group to leave, had finally gotten his cigarette lit and turned the corner and it was just us standing there.

'I do,' Alex told me. Behind her door I could see the news on her television. It would be dinnertime soon, and I would cook something for us. If she let me, I would.

'What do you like about it?' I prodded. Let me know this. Let this be a hard thing I could hold on to in nights to come.

Alex looked down, turned around slowly and started walking back, stopping at her entrance. When she leaned on her door, the hinges in the back creaked and snapped loudly, but that didn't interrupt her concentration. It seemed more than a minute, her staring towards the ground, searching for what it was and the proper way to name it, before Alex finally raised her head again.

'I like that you did it' is what she told me.

Point

Knock-knocking on a tube through darkness, holding on so I don't fall, mainlining back into this land down the blue vein of the Victoria Line. Too fast. This train should slow, this trip should be given weight, its wheels aching as it pulled further against the improbability of my return. If my hands were big enough, I would reach out and capture every moment of rock and roar as we sped forward, every half-note of hollow echo, every lean of the car back or forth, just take the lot of it, squeeze it hard and give it form so I could cut it as thin as deli ham. Wrap a slice of that shit around every moment past this one. Wake up and with first bite know that each day could be this good. Chris Jones coming back to London, standing as tall as the curved tube ceiling would allow him.

Alex could bitch all she wanted, but I never said we'd be flying over together. She could wait the week I needed to feel my arrival, reacquaint myself with every inch I'd been barred from, do a posh crawl down Neale Street to find the packaging that would best present the product that I would be selling in my interviews in the days to come. I'd let the flat in Clapham for a month, enough time to enact my rituals and still offer Alex a few weeks for touristy persuals. I wasn't getting stuck in a queue for Parliament as the real city called.

Past one more '*Mind the gap*' and Stockwell was behind us. Soon we were slowing down again and this time would be the last stop. Immediately I seized my position in front of the doors, my nose perfectly aligned with the crack so that when they slid open, I stepped forth to Lambeth ground.

Escalator rise, rising. Me at the bottom, queuing to climb, looking on. It was worth telling Margaret I would meet her in Brixton, at the brasserie, as opposed to the sterility of Heathrow. This is how it was supposed to be. From the back of the tile valley, I watched as before me my heralds crowded in twos and glided upwards. I stepped onwards to moving stairs, not sure if it was elation or mechanics that raised me. Exits passed, I had two feet in this town once more.

Brixton! I flung out my arms, quickly poking the old guy on my right in his temple and having my left arm and suitcase swatted down by several passersby. Finding a safe place away from the traffic, hugging the urine-stained wall by the 7-Eleven, I looked up at that sky once more, my infinite duvet, as it drizzled back down on me. So polite it's misting; I didn't even have to squint my eyes as I kept walking on.

In the Iceland, tired people grabbed for one more frozen thing to go thunk at the bottom of their carts. Staring at pictures of airbrushed gourmet interpretations of the cardboard's contents, they imagined the meal soon to come, as well as the one that would always be sitting on ice, waiting to exist for them. They knew that the real version would be much duller in color, muted in curves, and be served on less attractive chinaware, but as they stood in long lines it was those pictures they looked down on. They were thankful they could afford such overpriced illusions. Outside the market's sliding doors, I walked slowly at irregular angles through the crowd of workers waiting to take buses further south than the tube line. They were so damn beautiful, so damn tired, necks elongated and to the side to see if the next red blur coming their way had their number in its eye. So damn fine because you knew the reason they were rushing home was that there was love somewhere waiting for them. Maybe love was just a bed or a dog or a list of responsibilities they would need decades of separation to romanticize, but they were still hustling towards it without question. Across the street, on the corner down from the bagel shop, were Brixton boys, stationary and proud of this. Leaning against the jaywalk fence with bomber jackets they had no business wearing in summer heat, sporting baseball hats touting professional teams for games for which they didn't even know the rules. Too cool to acknowledge the water falling down on them. It wasn't lost on me any more, the sense of familiarity, that of all the worlds within this city, I'd chosen the one that mirrored the place I'd been running from.

In front of the brasserie, there was no red Fiat to be seen, a quick glance inside revealed that Margaret was not yet present, even in that backroom where he used to sit and rant at me. Nothing back there but an old drunk laid out with his body on one chair and his feet on another, hat pulled over his sleeping face and trench pulled around him as if it were raining in here, too. I grabbed the remote control sitting on the table before moving far enough away to avoid conversation. After the barmaid took my order I clicked on the set hanging high in the corner.

That stink, that smell of whatever gelatin forms in carpets fed a daily diet of spilled beer, just like the one that used to ooze out of Café Society, back on Chelten, around the way. Like it all poured from one linked source. Like there was a certain amount you could drink, a certain darkness of shadow that you could pass through and end up at any other stank joint in the world. On the television, every unrecognized advertisement confirmed how long I'd been gone, and I studied them for whatever new trends had manifested, planning on doing the same thing that night in my rented room, preparing myself for the first interview tomorrow. I would get the job, I knew this. My portfolio was strong, and so it seemed was their interest, just in writing me a continent away. Still, there was the question of money, and more important, what position would they throw my way?

On the TV, a fifteen-second spot for Golden Crowns pulled my attention. Someone had pitched the idea of actually making a tiara compiled of cereal kernels, and that mess of a concept had made it all the way through production and onto the screen. An airbrushed, latex-coated crown sparkled thanks to video illustration; obviously brand recognition seemed more important to them now than making the product look edible. You need me, I nearly said aloud. I was just getting a flash of their rented ex–sports figure's smile when the box turned off suddenly. Snap, then dark, dead, and powerless. The remote, by my side just a moment before, had disappeared. I was looking underneath the table to find where when I saw the movement behind me. Not Margaret coming in the door, but the drunken corpse rising. Bent over in my chair, I could see his shoes and pant legs through my own, no doubt walking over in my direction to start a long and laborious conversation, one that he repeated on the hour with whoever sat in the room. This was England, homeland of social discomfort, so to avoid my own I pretended to finish tying my shoes, all the while fixing my sights on the bathroom I would soon be darting to. From there, after an appropriate pause, I would shoot back through, grab my pint and bag without stopping and take a seat at the bar, close to the exit door. When I heard him clearing his throat of whatever bacteria made its home there, my calves tensed, and I was almost up, when the sound of that voice hit me and I couldn't even manage standing any more.

'I told you you could get here without me.'

Ever feel you're falling, right there while you're sitting down? Like that sleep thing, when you jump awake, kick out your legs to fight the gravity you imagine. But you're not asleep, so there is no other consciousness to skip to, no place of escape, and the only thing that rises is the bile that climbs up your esophagus. That was my moment, right there, sunk back into the chair. The rest of the actions or opinions about this unreality that would appear later, in weeks and eventually years to follow, they would all be born of this grid, this measure of time that I was even sectioning off as it happened. So by the time I turned around and saw David, my David, no longer dead and standing there, that reality had already made its initial impact, had already passed on and left me with its complications as proof of its arrival. Standing there. Not a ghost because spirits don't smell like that, sweating alcohol and sucking Trebor's Extra Strong Mints on the side of their mouths. Ghosts don't get fatter with time, definitely not by a good two stone, or lose battles with male-pattern baldness so that they had less hair than when living. And most definitely, they sure didn't smile like that either. There is no gloating in the hereafter, that I was sure of. Not in heaven and definitely not in hell.

'You fucking bastard' was all I could offer, and even that little more than a whisper. Of all the thoughts causing traffic in my cortex, that was just the one that got through. David stared at me, watching the realization drip in as the blood in my face dripped out. Drop drop. After the block of time that it took for him to realize that I would definitely not be the one to do the talking, David, ever living, laid the pint in his hand on the table next to him and took a seat once more. Oh, this was his holiday. You could tell he hadn't had a day this good in a while.

'Nice one, right?' He laughs my way. 'You don't get a surprise like that every day, do you? That was too lovely! Too good! Originally, I'd had a mind to meet you in your hotel room. Had it all planned, see? You'd come in and I'd be laid right out there on the bleeding bed, all casual like! Brilliant, it would have been!' David yells, punching the air, nodding at me as if I'm in on this joke too, his arrogance waking me from my confusion. 'But then, when you *finally* called Margaret and said meet you here, I was just so excited. I mean, it was as if we were working together again. Just perfect! I've been here for three hours!'

'Oh, come on, please. You flatter me. I'm not a complete fool. You must have had your suspicions. Really, I don't believe you. Of course, I ran into your Fionna at Marks and Spencer two months past – I swear the little flit shat herself right there in the beverage aisle!' David laughed, biting his bottom lip, scrunching his nose and nodding each drop of truth in it back at me. My head throbbed with each motion. Even my eyes hurt; the room seemed unbearablly bright to me.

'Which are the lies,' I managed, forcing my breathing back under control to do so. Meaning: which parts of my past were constructed just for your deception, which monuments were real, and which made of putty and clay.

'Oh really, it's not all that, is it? After I nearly burned the house down on meself, it just offered a chance, didn't it? So I bribed the missus to go along with the . . .' He paused, enjoying himself. 'Appearances.'

'With what, my apartment?' I snapped. I wasn't even sure yet if I should be angry, but it was a good emotion and I was going with it.

'No. A guaranteed complete stay at a rehab clinic in Richmond. Lovely place. Enjoyed it even more the second time I checked in, three months later,' David said, toasting me, up in the air then into the mouth with a good gulp of the black stuff. The bastard is alive, and sitting right there across from me. What's more, David has always been alive. The only person that fact is new to is me. 'The flat was just to get you moving. For chrissakes man, I thought you'd *never* leave. Started worrying I might have to torch that bastard too. Margaret's there now still; she just had her number forwarded from the flat she was letting. She lets me visit, on weekends sometimes. Mornings.'

'Urgent?' I asked, almost fearing the answer.

'Still earning, mate. Still earning,' David said proudly. 'Bloody well insured, it was, wasn't it?' He winked at me over the lip of his glass ever so quickly. 'Did you like the obituary? Had to pull in a favor from a bloke who works the press for the *Journal*. Between that, the funeral, and keeping the mouth shut on bloody Raz, cost me a good bit of dosh in the end. But oh, the look of it.' With all the things I wanted to cry or scream at him, all I could do was nod back in disbelief. Head wagging. A matching sway for every thought that occurred to me. So many sentences, only the word 'why' linking them together. So that's the word I put to him. Not a plea or a demand, just one strong syllable for him to take from me, shape it like a 'U' and fill it up before giving it back. David stared at me through the distortion of the glass he was swallowing from. He looked like I'd just asked him the most obvious question in the world.

'Would you have ever left if I didn't?' David's voice was light, vulnerable, not arrogant but sorrowful, not for me but for himself, the one that necessitated abandonment. 'Would you ever have learned that you could?' he asked, rising from his chair as he did so, his arms outstretched, palms open, his face calmer than a newborn's while sleeping. The way he stood, the way that raincoat hung off him like a robe, so many folds it would take a lifetime to carve in marble; it reminded me of a picture I'd seen of a statue on a mountain in Brazil. David moved closer, and in the moment of his step I didn't know what I should be doing, whether to kiss him on his sweating forehead, grab that pudgy neck with two hands and take his life for daring to play with mine, or hug his ample waist in joy that something that had brought me pain was over. When the moment came that I touched him, placed my hands within his, my response was there waiting for me. A grip on each shoulder, I gave him the best Philly gesture I could manage, pulling David towards me as fast as I shot up my knee into that gut of his, politely missing his groin and forcing the bulk of my thrust into that gluttonous belly. I gave him a lift – upsy daisy, flying off his heels and even toes for a second as his weight rested on my thigh. Now there's a new look for that face's repertoire: astonishment. Didn't it look good on him too, along with that new vein bulging out of his forehead and the blood of pain bringing a glow to his cheeks. Flattering. David let out a burst of air; I felt it shoot up my chest and into my nose. Dropping him down to the floor again, I retook my seat casually and David, well, he just sort of fell into his. As he refilled his lungs in loud wheezes, I reached out for his drink, toasted him with it, then finished it off. All the while the fat bastard was actually smiling at me. Not just grinning either: the more David learned to breathe again, the bigger that gash on his face became, till it damn near reached both earlobes. Just joyful in his silent agony, the old cat hugging his waist as he got a good look at this man sitting in front of him. Me, I stared right back. Grinned along with him. Took care of my own drink before throwing down a tenner and walking out the door.

ACKNOWLEDGEMENTS

My greatest blessings are: my wife and world-Meera the Magnificent, the Johnson Family, Jaynes Family, Bowman Family, Freedman Family, Dwayne Wharton, Victor Durmot La Valle, Ric Pavez, Andrea Walls (of the Philadelphia Walls), Rob Seixas, Doug 'Boogie' Jones, Ted LaSalla, Beth Calabro, Owiso Odera, Loren Johnson, Ray Shell, Barbie Asante, Ric Wormwood, Gloria Loomis, Karen Rinaldi, Michael Cunningham, the Akers Family, Larry Wilkins, Stephen Butler. Dad-thanks for investing in me in so many ways. Marsha-you're cherished. O. Ben Karp-fully bonded. William and Elizabeth Johnson-thank you for the friendship. Carl Jaynes-thanks for letting me sleep on your floor so I could make this happen. Many thanks to the Thomas J. Watson Fellowship Foundation. Philly.

A NOTE ON THE AUTHOR

Mat Johnson was born and raised in Philadelphia. He was a recipient of the Thomas J. Watson Fellowship, and received his MFA from Columbia University. He now lives in Harlem, where he's working on and setting his second novel.